I0669020

ANNO DOMINA

Patrick S. Lafferty

For Bev & Clay

ACKNOWLEDGEMENTS

In addition to my parents, I raise a pint to everyone who had a hand in making this dream come true. To Bridget, Aidan and Conor, thank you for being so unbelievably supportive and enthusiastic during the writing process, but especially through the long slog of submissions. Thanks to Deb and Phil Harris at *All Things That Matter Press* for their vision and guidance. Thanks to Dan Lafferty, Murray Robinson, Brian McLinden, Cathy Lundeen, Katie Boyle Earle and the members of the Novel Group at the Milwaukee Writer's Workshop who helped me fine-tune my manuscript. And a special thanks to my niece, Rachael Lafferty, for a much needed kick in the ass.

Sláinte mhaith!

For Bev & Clay

ACKNOWLEDGEMENTS

In addition to my parents, I raise a pint to everyone who had a hand in making this dream come true. To Bridget, Aidan and Conor, thank you for being so unbelievably supportive and enthusiastic during the writing process, but especially through the long slog of submissions. Thanks to Deb and Phil Harris at *All Things That Matter Press* for their vision and guidance. Thanks to Dan Lafferty, Murray Robinson, Brian McLinden, Cathy Lundeen, Katie Boyle Earle and the members of the Novel Group at the Milwaukee Writer's Workshop who helped me fine-tune my manuscript. And a special thanks to my niece, Rachael Lafferty, for a much needed kick in the ass.

Sláinte mhaith!

CHAPTER 1

Judith Scarlet wore a bright white bathrobe over her comfy pajamas and a pair of brand new white slippers as she stepped out of her house and into the bright winter morning. In her right hand was a mug of coffee. It wasn't very good coffee, she thought, but it would help rouse her from her drowsy-headedness.

She walked slowly to the middle of her driveway and stopped. The air was typically cool and dry. The faint scent of sage kissed the air. She cupped her left hand and placed it above her brow to keep the sun from blinding her. She stared out into the middleclass neighborhood to see the hustle and bustle of children scrambling to catch a school bus as their adult counterparts got into their cars on their way to work. Her husband had done the same just a few minutes earlier.

At her feet lay the morning *Republic*; the reason she came outside in the first place. As one of the few remaining holdovers from a bygone era, she couldn't read the news on-screen without the visceral feel of the newsprint. Subsequently, she and those like her, helped keep the printed version from extinction.

Death It Is! read the headline. It ran from edge to edge, the letters as bold and as large as the typesetter could make them to fill every point of space within the live area. *Jury Hands Down Death Penalty,* read the subhead, smaller in size but still running from edge to edge, still bold and just as painful for her to read. Judith stood up, holding the paper in front of her as best she could with one hand, and wondered why the typesetters thought the exclamation point was necessary. She let the paper fold in on itself, tucked it under her arm and headed back inside.

Shortly after hearing the verdict on the 11:00 O'clock News the previous night, she had made out a somewhat lengthy "To Do" list for her morning and was now anxious to get done all the things she had written down.

But first, her coffee.

She sat at the small, round table in her kitchen and read the article that accompanied the entirely-too-large headline. When she finished, she was glad her name didn't appear in the text. She had been instrumental in securing the conviction for the prosecution. The article that had run the week before, when the jury came back with a guilty verdict, called her testimony the most damaging for the defense and the guilt consumed her. It consumed her still.

The article she read that morning gave more depth and detail to the individual jury members' sentencing recommendations and the judge's ruling than the court proceedings in which she had played such a major role. She was ashamed of what she had done: betrayed the woman she loved, loved like no one else, loved like nothing she had ever loved before. Her shame captured her soul and her soul asked no quarter. Her shame gave none in return.

Flipping casually through the paper, another headline grabbed her attention: *New Life for Dead Sea Scrolls*. The article explained how scientists had pieced together a few dozen comprehensive documents from more than 15,000 scroll fragments by applying facial recognition technology to their frayed edges, their graphology and other points of demarcation. It also reported that the documents were now in the process of being translated. Judith's interest in the article quickly waned, knowing deep in her heart that no matter how the pieces were assembled, the prophecies they proclaimed could not alter the inevitable; the woman she loved would die because of her.

She folded the paper and set it aside on the table.

She poured the dregs of her mug down the drain, adding just a little water to dilute what was left, before placing it gently into the sink. She'd get to the dishes after cleaning the house, Item #3 on her list, just below *Coffee* and *Read the Paper*. Judith meticulously ran down the rest of her item, ticking off the tasks as they were completed. After taking a quick shower, drying her hair and getting dressed, all that remained were the final two items.

She pulled a small notepad and pen from a drawer in the kitchen, the same notepad and pen used to generate the list the night before, and began writing. She had already decided what she was going to write, but the organization of all her thoughts into a single, cohesive narrative took a bit longer than she anticipated and it was nearly lunch by the time she had finished. She took the ten or so crumpled pieces of paper, her flawed, initial attempts to capture her thoughts, and threw them in the recycling bin, then returned to the living room to place a tick mark next to, *Write Note.*

Noises rumbled from her stomach and she contemplated eating lunch, but then thought better of it so as not to have to bother to once more clean the dishes. Besides, she thought, food would be counterproductive. Instead, Judith decided to fight through her pangs of hunger and get to the last item on the list, the one she'd never be able to place a tick mark next to upon completion.

The bathroom medicine cabinet was full, but not cluttered, a microcosm of her life. Judith reached in and withdrew a small orange bottle from the second shelf. She slowly unscrewed the child-proof cap, put the bottle under the faucet and filled it almost to the brim. The tiny capsules bobbed as her hands shook. She hoisted the bottle to her lips and began to drink the lumpy mixture, completely draining its contents. She shook out the droplets of water that clung to the sides of the small orange bottle, dried the inside with the corner of a hand towel, screwed the cap back on and placed the empty bottle back on the second shelf before shutting the mirrored cabinet door.

She looked at herself and blushed. She felt the sin of vanity welling inside of her and quickly turned away to prevent herself from crying. From the bathroom she made her way into the bedroom. She settled into the middle of the bed, perched on the slight bulge between the large divots she and her husband had created in the mattress. Crawling across the bed caused the plastic tarp she had laid across it, Item #9, to crinkle loudly. She had read once that the body voids itself upon death and, thinking of her husband, who would most likely find her when he returned home around six that evening, she thought it best to minimize the trauma by minimizing the mess.

Judith reached over and grabbed the two items on the nightstand she had set out earlier: a Bible and a rosary made of silver beads, a present from the woman she loved with her entirety, the woman she had betrayed. She placed the Bible on her heart with her left hand and, rapping the rosary around her right hand while pinching the first silver bead above the crucifix between her thumb and forefinger. With her right hand she made the sign of the cross.

"Bless me Father, for I have sinned," she prayed aloud. "It has been a week since I last confessed my sins and since that time I have done everything in my power to bring about the death of a person—me. I pray that in your mercy you take pity on my soul."

With that, she began to silently pray the rosary, notching one bead at a time. She pinched and prayed her way through thirty silver beads before slipping away.

CHAPTER 2

Damien, standing with his wife in the second row just off the center aisle, heard Father Enrique say under his breath, "Almighty God, cleanse my heart and my lips that I may worthily proclaim Your Gospel." Then, far more clearly as the priest spoke into the microphone, he heard, "The Lord be with you."

The congregation replied, "And with your spirit."

"A reading from the Holy Gospel according to Luke."

Damien traced a tiny cross on his forehead, his lips and then over his heart as he whispered to himself, "Christ be in my thoughts, on my lips and in my heart."

Father Enrique proceeded to read Luke 18, verses 1 through 8.

^{1} Then he told them a parable about the necessity for them to pray always without becoming weary. He said, ^{2} "There was a judge in a certain town who neither feared God nor respected any human being. ^{3} And a widow in that town used to come to him and say, 'Render a just decision for me against my adversary.' ^{4} For a long time the judge was unwilling, but eventually he thought, 'While it is true that I neither fear God nor respect any human being, ^{5} because this widow keeps bothering me I shall deliver a just decision for her lest she finally come and strike me.'" ^{6} The Lord said, "Pay attention to what the dishonest judge says. ^{7} Will not God then secure the rights of his chosen ones who call out to him day and night? Will he be slow to answer them? ^{8} I tell you, he will see to it that justice is done for them speedily. But when the Son of Man comes, will he find faith on earth?"

"This is the Gospel of the Lord."

Damien, along with the rest of the congregation, replied, "Praise to you, Lord Jesus Christ." He sat down and absentmindedly stared at the pulpit.

The first few sentences of Father Enrique's homily—a lighthearted comment that elicited a peal of polite laughter from those kind enough to give the priest their full attention—breezed by Damien unregistered. The priest's words fluttered through the incensed air only to become lost, windswept noise amid the swirling turbulence of his mind. Like the bulk of his morning, like the bulk of all his mornings recently, he was thinking about her. She occupied his every idle moment, especially the ten-or-so minutes he spent every Sunday morning ignoring the priest's homily. He couldn't help but gravitate to the singular fact that he held her life in his hands.

During his run at the governorship, he thought of her as merely an ideal, a means to an end, an issue to help him win the gubernatorial race. By the time the election rolled around, she was already convicted, relegating her to that of a mere distraction, a MacGuffin. She was that intrinsically unimportant, yet cauterizing rallying point, around which the people had amassed and clamored. Clamored for what, he could only guess. Peace? Salvation? Justice? As if they know what justice is, he thought piously to himself. Eventually, though, as with all remarkable things in its present time, the news cycle churned on. It took with it the polarizing editorials and the sometimes violent demonstrations that she once inspired until there was so little reporting of her, even on the eve of her death, few recalled her ever being newsworthy and even fewer now cared. Damien was one of those few and he *greatly* cared.

In the months since Damien Driver had become governor, Estephania Rodriguez had become more than just a woman on death row to him. She had changed him forever. Not in the clichéd way that a catastrophe makes one reappraise priorities and goals; that would come later. No, the way she had changed Damien was more subtle, less perceptible, like a glacial retreat that left the earth beneath it scarred and bleak, yet fertile and receptive to the inevitability of new life.

He sat on the hard, cherry stained pews of the cathedral, his once powerful hands clasped and resting in his lap, his stoic face belying the struggle raging behind it. He knew in his heart—though his mind could not yet admit such things—that she was no MacGuffin. She was intrinsically necessary. Vital. Yet, at noon the following day, she was going to be executed by the State of Arizona for her fallacious crimes and, regardless of the fact that she was charged, tried, convicted and sentenced during the previous administration, he would be blamed. Her blood would be on his hands.

It was an unbearable weight and an unbearable wait.

The bellwether announcing the end of his personal glacial retreat had come as three gentle knocks—as soft as sandaled footfalls—on the heavy, wooden door of his study.

"Come in," he said in a loud voice.

A slender gentleman in a suit entered the room as Damien stood to greet him. "Ah, Styles. Please, come in. Sit."

"Yes, sir, but just for a moment."

Styles crossed the room and moved to the antique leather wing-back chair while Damien took the woven, ergonomically designed swivel chair set behind the enormous desk.

"Just for a moment? Are you trying to brush me off?" Damien joked.

"No, sir. Not at all. It's just that I haven't spent much time with my family since I was given this assignment."

"So, you're not blowing me off, you're laying on a guilt trip?"

"No, sir. No, it's just—"

Governor Damien Driver brought his hands from his lap, tented his fingers and looked over them at his visitor. Damien was a relatively tall man, though not in the least bit imposing, especially not while sitting in his large chair. His face was strong and stern yet kindly, a significant asset in the world of politics in which he now belonged as well as in the legal community from where he came. His voice, too, was strong and stern, with a surprising lilt of gentility when the moment called for it. With Styles seated before him, he decided now was one of those moments.

"Relax, Styles. I'm kidding. I do want to thank you for coming on such short notice. Especially on a Sunday."

"No problem, sir. I put the finishing touches on this thing this morning and I'll be glad to finally put the ball in someone else's court." Then he added, "So to speak."

Damien leaned back in his chair, waiting. "So … what's the verdict?"

"The verdict, yes, very cleaver, sir," the man across the desk said flatly as he pulled the manila file folders from his briefcase. Styles rocked forward, not quite standing, using both hands to set the files down in front of the governor. And just as quickly, he rocked back into the soft leather again.

They sat silent for a moment, Damien fingering through the stack, scanning the various files, reports and other details assembled before him. It was a digital world, yes, it had been for decades. But the governor demanded this report be on paper. It made everything that much more real to his mind. It also provided peace of mind knowing it could be shredded or burned, if necessary, without the worry of leaving an imprint on one of the state's all-too-easily subpoenaed servers. He often told his aides and staffers, "Just because I'm paranoid doesn't mean someone's *not* out to get me."

He sunk back again into his chair, purposefully rested his elbows on the arms and tented his fingers. "You still haven't answered my question, Styles."

"The verdict?" Styles questioned. "The jury came back with a verdict of guilty nine months ago, sir."

The smile drained from Damien's face. "You know what I mean. What do you make of this ... la Hermana de Jesus."

"It's all there, sir. The top sheet is my executive summary. Everything else is support. The medical records, the files, the court transcripts, they've all been summarized and put in some semblance of order, or as close to order as can be expected."

Damien glared at Styles before he slowly untented his fingers, opened the top folder and removed a single sheet of paper with three relatively short paragraphs of copy. He slipped on his glasses and read, his expression remaining unchanged, as if he were reviewing a menu consisting entirely of gruel. He pulled his glasses off and stared sullenly at Styles.

"Yes, well, those are the bones of the matter, but where's the meat? Where's the substance? You don't offer anything in the way of a conclusion."

"You didn't hire me to speculate, sir," Styles said. "You hired me to investigate, and that's what I did. What you have there is the paper trail of one person's life. Her summation, if you will. I am neither capable of, nor willing, to stand in judgment of what she is or what she has done. Nor what the State has done in response to her, for that matter. To paraphrase Colonel Kurtz, 'I'm an errand boy sent by grocery clerks to collect a bill.'"

Damien regressed. "What the hell does that mean? Who's Colonel Kurtz?"

"It's from a movie, sir," Styles said as he grabbed his briefcase and stood, "and it means that I've done what was asked of me and now it's time for me to move on."

As Styles strode toward the door, Damien jumped out of his seat and shouted, "Styles!"

It was always Styles. Never Mr. Styles. Never in conjunction with a first name, whatever his first name might have been. Just Styles.

The anxious man, exceedingly overdressed, the governor thought, for an impromptu meeting on a Sunday afternoon at Heritage Manor, halted in the middle of the room and turned. There was no angry face staring back at Styles. Instead, he saw the governor's thinning, gray pate. The old man's body was slumped over the desk, his arms spread out and his palms flat against the polished walnut. When Damien lifted his head, Styles saw the unmistakably pained look of doubt and confusion on the face staring back at him.

Damien spoke softly, "You sat through the entire trial, the sentencing, all the various appeals, for Christ's sake. You must have some opinion."

Styles shifted his stance and stared at the intricate pattern on the rug. "Yes, sir, I have formed an opinion. And with all due respect, it's wholly my own. And even if I were of a mind to share with you that opinion, that's all it would be, an opinion. It would be based not on facts, but on the circumstances surrounding this entire affair as well as my beliefs and," he paused, "and my convictions of faith.

"I did as you asked, sir. As you paid me to do. As *they* paid me to do," he said pointing to the American flag standing in the corner of the room. "I spent the better part of a year investigating the most intimate details of this woman's life for you. I poured my heart and soul into that report. My heart and my soul!"

His eyes still cast down, Styles paused and regained his composure before continuing. "I know the State records the conversations that take place in this room, so I won't make any kind of statement which may come back to hurt me. But I will say this. If after reading the series of summaries I've written you still don't know what's in my heart and my mind, then God help me. God help us all."

Styles finally looked up and locked eyes with the governor. He shifted uneasily. "'You have to have men who are moral and at the same time who are able to utilize their primordial instincts to kill without feeling, without passion, without judgment. Without judgment. Because it's judgment that defeats us.'"

Styles looked away for just a moment, then back to the governor. "By the way, that was Kurtz again, sir." Then, he slipped out the door and closed it behind him.

The governor remained slumped over his desk, the pained expression of doubt and confusion still on his face. "Who the hell is Kurtz?" he whispered.

It wasn't until the soft cacophony of people rustling to stand penetrated Damien's distracted thoughts that he realized Father Enrique had finished his homily and the Profession Faith had begun. Damien stood and muttered the words he knew by rote, still haunted by the same thoughts that had germinated only a few years ago but had not until recently began to take root with any permanence: she just might be wholly innocent.

* * *

Immediately upon returning to the governor's mansion, Damien retired to his study, not even bothering to change out of his suit and tie. He sat at his desk staring at the neat stack of manila folders he'd read through what felt like a million times. It had been three weeks since Styles's visit, since the slender gentleman called the stack the paper trail of one person's life. *Her summation*. The phrase clanged against his skull. There her life's summation sat, parsed into chapters and summarized into easily digestible nuggets, stacked neatly atop his desk awaiting his review … for the one-millionth-and-first time.

He picked up the *Executive Summary* and, slipping on his glasses, read it again, aloud this time, hoping to hear in the words something he'd missed while reading them in silence the one million times before.

"Issue #1: An extensive background check and thorough review of the activities of the subject in question revealed no contradiction to the evidence or testimony presented during trial. Nor were there additional findings that could be purposed to legally invalidate the verdict of the jury.

"Issue #2: Anonymous sources within the offices of no less than the five of the seven Board of Pardons and Paroles members, all dutiful members in good standing of the GOP, portend a unified front against granting the convicted a stay of execution.

"Issue #3: All efforts to prove or disprove the subject's claims of deific origin were inconclusive. However, as these claims are based on an unquestioning belief that does not require evidence of truth or falsity, they cannot, therefore, be proved or disproved in terms of science or logic, only believed or disbelieved in terms of faith and thus inconclusive by their very nature."

Then, in the bottom left corner was a handwritten notation to which Damien smiled broadly as he read it aloud. "4 Q 5 1 0 dash 5 1 1." He had looked it up online the first time he saw it and it had told him everything. He felt no need to look it up again.

He set the single sheet of paper down on top of the stack, took off his glasses and slipped one of the earpieces between his teeth as he leaned back and swiveled in his chair. Facing the wall of windows, he noticed the sunlight was far less harsh than when he first came into the room, the light more ambient as the rays poured down from above instead of coming in through the windows at an angle. It was a subtle reminder that it was close to noon. Twenty-four hours remained before Estephania Rodriguez, la Hermana de Jesus, as she was dubbed by her followers, was to be executed by lethal injection, having been found guilty of the crime of treason by a jury of her peers.

Pangs of hunger mingled with pangs of distress rumbled from within him, prompting him to take a break from his seemingly interminable study of the folders' contents. In the refrigerator he found some salad greens on the verge of turning, miscellaneous vegetables and a loaf of hearty, multigrain bread. The greens, though wilted, were still fresh enough to snap when he tore at them with his hands as he prepared two bowls, side-by-side: one for him and one for his wife who was making herself scarce until after the execution, at Damien's request.

He pulled an avocado from the windowsill above the sink, sliced it in half with a large chef's knife and twisted one of the halves free from the seed. He placed the remaining half in the palm of his left hand and chopped at the bulging seed with his right, wedging the blade in the dense, fibrous material. The blade also managed to cleave a tiny wound at the very tip of his forefinger which was thoughtlessly placed in an exposed position above the rim of the avocado skin. Damien winced and moved immediately to the kitchen sink, cursing his stupidity. With water such a scarce resource, he filled a small mixing bowl halfway, set it on the counter and submerged his left hand. The cut was shallow, more annoying than painful. Thin ribbons of blood escaped from the slit as he squeezed the tip of his finger to cleanse the wound and the metaphorical significance became impossible for Damien to ignore. That thought forced a single, uncomfortable chuckle that hung in the air humorlessly as he continued washing the blood from his hands.

It was after one o'clock before Damien returned to his study, intent on reading every document on his desk one last time. However, the second he sat down, before he even had a chance to take the first folder off the pile, his All-COM, nestled into its case on his belt, vibrated.

"Hello?"

"Governor, it's Lilith." Her voice was even and toneless. "How are you?"

Lilith Samuel was the state's Republican Party chairperson. If asked, she would tell you she alone was responsible for Damien's current position as Governor of Arizona. She and Mike Hart, the executive at the state's Republican headquarters and a major politico rising star nationally, had pulled the strings and found the financial backing that won Damien the gubernatorial race during the special election following the tragic loss of both the incumbent and the incumbent's Lieutenant Governor in a plane crash.

Winning the election was the easy part. Getting the party's nomination nine months earlier had been the *real* challenge. In the wake of the Water Wars, where staying on point, mudslinging and the exploitation of the opposition's minor shortcomings were as important as spin control of one's own shortcomings, the actual election was a mere formality. Outside of California and New York, nearly every state was a red state. The country was just short of a theocracy. Some argued it had crossed that line years ago. Even the states that previously resided South of the Border, the S.O.B. states as they were called, had shifted far away from the social liberalism that dominated their political platforms when they first joined the Union. Now, only a decade later, even the S.O.B. states were voting conservative, a testimony to their strong Catholic presence.

"Truth be told, I've been better, Lilith."

"You've only been in office nine months and you're already complaining? Wait until the budget comes up for vote or when mid-term elections roll around."

Damien forced a chuckle. It was as humorless as his previous one.

Lilith continued, "I was wondering how things were moving on the Rodriguez thing. We've been getting a lot of calls from our major constituents. You're well aware of who they are. They have a vested interest in how this plays out. I thought for sure you'd have made a statement by now."

"I have to at least provide the appearance of due diligence."

"Of course, of course. I guess I'm just tired of fielding all these calls."

"That's the job you do, Lilith, so I can do my job."

"Absolutely. As long as we're all on the same page, here. I mean, just to let you know, this Rodriquez thing has moved beyond our state boundaries. I got a call Friday from the ELCA in Chicago and a couple this morning from staffers from two Ecclesiastical Provinces. I'm wearing diapers just in case I shit my pants when the fucking Pope calls. You know what I mean?"

"Look, my office sent out a public announcement on Friday, which the GOP approved, stating our intentions to let the process work. Hell, I think your office actually *wrote* the damn thing. And nothing has changed since then, Lilith, nothing. I'm not about to jump out there and say, 'The governor's office is not going to stay the execution,' just to make headlines and placate the anxious few within our constituency. It's too overt. You know that."

"Let's not be so hasty."

"Do me a favor, Lilith, will you? Relax. Play some golf, go on a hike, meditate. Do whatever it is you do on beautiful Sunday afternoons. But for the love of all things holy, relax."

"Relaxing really isn't my thing. And I think you might want to keep an open —"

"Good bye, Lilith."

"Governor!"

Damien could tell she was waiting to hear if he had disconnected. "Yes, Lilith?"

"I just want to make sure you're going to be there for dinner."

"I will be there at 5:30."

"Good. Maybe I'll have a chance to—"

"Good bye, Lilith," the governor said, this time cutting her off immediately and offering no opportunity for the conversation to continue.

Damien had been receiving calls like that, several each day as a matter of fact, since the moment he took office. The state's GOP headquarters was constantly calling to explain how the party's largest contributors would like matters handled. The Rodriquez matter, in particular. He knew what they wanted as well as anyone and it wore on him like windblown sand across stone. They had gently carved away the ideals he once held dear, the same ideals he had established as his platform during the campaign. That was when his life was his own. Since enlisting the help of Lilith Samuel and Michael Hart, he became something else entirely. He became the property of the GOP He slammed his fist on the desk.

As the anger passed, and it always did, he again reached for the stack and pulled the first file folder off. Neatly written on the tab was *Overview*. Damien vowed to read that one first; all of it. Then, mentally taking inventory of the stack's entirety, he read the folder tabs of the remaining folders from top to bottom: *Family, Childhood, College, The Peace Corps, Her Missing Years, Her Ministry, Her Following, Pre-Trial, The Trial, Appeals* and, finally, *Incarceration*. All but *Her Missing Years* and *Incarceration* were at least a quarter inch thick, while some, like *Her Ministry* and *The Trial*, were much thicker.

Damien set the *Overview* folder aside and grabbed the next folder in line, the one marked *Family*. He opened it and extracted a stapled, three-page document. It was a summary of the folder's documents. Styles did indeed put his heart and soul into the assignment, Damien thought. He placed the document back into folder and set the folder back on top of the pile. Then, he slid the entire stack to the upper left-hand portion of his desk, opened the *Overview* folder and began reading. He hoped to read more than half the stack one more time before heading out for dinner.

He breathed a sigh of frustration. The scheduled execution was hurling at him like a runaway train. He stood on the tracks of inescapability, trapped and immobile like an opossum in the glare of its headlight.

CHAPTER 3

He was in his car driving to the prison. An hour earlier, Father Joe was greeting his Christ King parishioners as they exited the nine o'clock mass. He shook hands and wished everyone a pleasant day as they complimented him on his homily, but his mind was elsewhere. This being the Twenty-Ninth Sunday in Ordinary Time and Cycle C of the liturgical calendar, Father Joe's homily was a reflection on Luke's parable of the corrupt judge and it weighed heavily on his mind. The entire week prior, his thoughts were stagnated by writer's block, filled with false starts and bleeding with redline corrections. His parishioners' compliments, he felt, were unjustified as he hadn't put much effort into the week's homily but he consciously eased himself into a feeling of contentment. He knew he was dreading his weekly visit to the correctional facility and that was the cause of his trepidation. It would more than likely be his last discussion with Estephania Rodriquez and, considering the final line of the liturgy, he was unsure how he was going to face her.

As he pulled into the back of the prison where the employees parked, he imagined the thousands of scenarios that might play out between the two of them. Questions she'd ask. Answers he'd fumble through, including the Church's stance on her claims. He was fully devoted to his life in Christ and the service to His Word, yet he couldn't understand how believing equally in this woman was a contradiction to his vows. The bishop had repeatedly explained to him this contradiction along with Father Joe's role in the legal and spiritual process; he was to stay out of the political maelstrom that had followed her but absolve her of her sins when she finally admitted them.

"But," he had argued with the Bishop, "if she is la Hermana de Jesus, what sins would she have committed? Would she not be without sin?"

"This is blasphemy," the Bishop would reply. "Even its consideration is to place a false god above Him."

"No. That's not true, Your Excellency. As she—"

"Please," he would interrupt, "Your Excellency is so … eighteenth century. It's Bishop DeMarco."

"Yes, of course. Bishop DeMarco, as she's explained, she will be sitting on the left hand of the Father, while Jesus sits to his right."

"She's obviously delusional. Did you know more mentally insane people believe they are Jesus Christ than any other persona?"

"But that's just the thing: she doesn't believe she's Jesus Christ."

"Obviously. She's a woman."

His mind would then cycle back. "But this is nothing like your traditional death row inmate. She's no rapist or murderer."

"No, she's a hydro-terrorist."

Father Joe would always press on. "She's a gift from God. A voice of reason in an unreasonable world."

"It concerns me, Joseph, that you find this world unreasonable. The laws she broke are not those of the Church, but of the state. Treason is a crime of conscience. We lobby against the death penalty even more vehemently now that abortion has been made illegal. But there is only so much impact we can make. It took us some fifty years to win the battle against the killing of the unborn. It might take just as long to abolish capital punishment or repeal the Twenty-Eighth Amendment and the slew of overzealous laws enacted in the wake of the Water Wars. For now, all we can do is help the incarcerated firmly resolve, with the help of His grace, to confess their sins, do penance, and amend their lives so they can enter the Kingdom."

"But, if she is la Hermana de Jesus, what sins would she confess? Would she not be without sin?"

"Again, it's blasphemy, Joseph."

It was the same circuitous discussion the two clergymen had had every Sunday since her arrival at P-ville, as the Perryville State Correctional Facility for Women was known. And every week, neither felt good about its lack of resolution upon their parting. The bishop felt Father Joe was losing his way, being led astray by a false prophet. Father Joe felt the bishop was speaking out of ignorance. If only the bishop could hear her speak, just once. If he sat with her in the visitor's room and discussed with her God's Word, his entire world would open up, just as it had for Father Joe the first time her voice touched his ears.

17

He swiped his security card and placed his thumb on the scanner and waited for the buzz and click of the locks to allow him entrance to the facility.

As a precaution, in response to the Muslim Riots of '24, he presided over the service separated from the general population from a room that overlooked the small auditorium style classroom. Only a scant few inmates were in attendance. Estephania was one of them, as always, listening intently to Father Joe's homily as it came to a close. He found it difficult to look at her as he spoke. He fidgeted like a six-year-old in church. The contradiction between his message and her situation made it unbearable. Yet, he persevered … for His sake.

"One of the hardest things to overcome is our perception of injustice. When we are persecuted or treated unfairly, our initial reaction is doubt in our Lord. How can we believe in a benevolent, loving Creator when bad things happen to us? This passage reminds us that when we face hard times, we shouldn't look at the injustices. Instead, we should look at the faithlessness of our persecutors and pray for them. Pray that God will bring justice. More importantly, pray that God will bring salvation to all who believe.

"If a corrupt judge can find it in his heart to take up the plight of the widow in Luke's gospel, then don't you think our uncorrupted Father will take up your plight and bring about justice for those he loves?"

He stole a glance at Estephania and saw that she was being interrupted by another inmate, a woman who, in his brief glimpse, he could only describe as cold and fiery, as if she were molten rock escaping a volcano on the floor of the Arctic Ocean.

He continued, "But when the Son of Man comes, will he find any faith on earth?' Pray, ladies, for yourselves and for those you believe have been unjust to you. That's the key that will unlock the gates of heaven."

Afterward, the prisoners passed by him in the visitor's room with as little passion as his parishioners had just a few hours prior. He dutifully went about his responsibilities as chaplain, listening to confessions and lewd comments in equal measure. He specifically requested to speak to Estephania last, hoping his uneasiness would subside by the time he came face-to-face with her. He never got the chance to find out. She had gone back to her cell, leaving only a message with a guard.

"She asked that you come tomorrow morning around eleven so you could pray together."

"Tell her I'll be here." He thought a moment and added, "One other thing. The woman who was sitting next to her during the service, who is she?"

"I wasn't paying attention. Do you remember her number? What she looked like?"

"I didn't see her number, but she was hard and rugged, black hair and dark complexioned, but not black or Latino."

"I don't remember any black-haired white women in here."

"Thank you," he said and slipped out of the room. He remained silent, deep in thought, from that moment until he arrived back at the rectory in Goodyear a few hours later.

* * *

He pulled his vibrating All-COM from its holster on his hip and spoke. "Hello?"

"Father Joe, how are you?"

"Bishop DeMarco. I'm surprised. And you?"

The bishop chuckled jovially. "I'm well. Why are you surprised?"

"It's Sunday afternoon. I'm usually calling you."

"Yes, well, I thought I'd save you the trouble, tomorrow being what it is. How did your visit with Miss Rodriquez go?"

"Unfortunately, she cancelled our visit today."

"That is unfortunate."

"She did request that I pray with her tomorrow morning before, the, um, well, the execution."

"Interesting. Interesting. I suppose there is no real eloquent euphemism for it, though. Anyway, Father Joe, what's your schedule look like this evening? I was wondering if you might not find some time to join me for dinner in the Pastoral Center."

"To be honest, Your Ex ..., ah, Bishop DeMarco, she kind of sprung this on me last minute. Obviously, I expected her to ask me, but I was hoping to use tonight to take care of some of the mundane administrative functions—"

19

"To be honest, Father Joe," the Bishop interrupted, "I'm sure those tasks can wait." There was an undeniable sternness in his voice that made Father Joe stir with discomfort knowing it wasn't a request, but a demand.

"Sure. I mean, yes. Absolutely! What time should I arrive?"

"It's about a half-hour's drive from Goodyear, correct?"

"Give or take."

"Do you think you could be here within the hour?"

Father Joe pulled his All-COM from his ear and read the time, 3:45. "I can be there by 5:00."

"Excellent. Oh, we'll be joined by the governor and some of his staff. Will that be a problem?"

"A problem? No, not at all."

"Excellent. I'll see you around 5:00, then."

Father Joe went about decompressing from his missionary work at the prison. He went into the rectory kitchen, poured himself a short glass of water and sat down at the kitchen table. That's when it set in. The bishop had invited to dinner the two individuals tasked with saving Estephania Rodriquez, body and soul: the governor and himself, respectively.

CHAPTER 4

Andrea and her sister, Petra, were in the back corner setting one of the two dozen linen-covered tables with meticulously folded napkins, glossy china, sparkling silverware and shimmering stemware. They weren't alone in their restaurant. Joining them at Fischer's Trattoria was the rest of the core group of individuals who helped Estephania Rodriguez spread her message of love and hope and tolerance throughout the greater metropolitan area. They called themselves her Adherentes.

At one table sat the Zeday twins, Jane and Joan, lawyers in their father's firm, along with Felipe Martinez, the former general manager of the local Latino TV station, and Nathaniel Crane, one of the city's indigent street people who called himself Nate the Great. At another table was Tom Jones, the creative director of the Idea Shop advertising firm. With him was Seamus McElroy, an IRS auditor. At the final table sat social worker Judy Antiesse, a writer named Matthew Pensiton and the pornography industry's most successful leading actress, Simone Amore. Had she not taken her life nine months earlier via an overdose of sleeping pills, Judith Scarlet would have most assuredly been in the restaurant, too.

In spite of their varied backgrounds, or perhaps because of it, they had become a tightly knit unit, sharing a devout belief in the teachings of la Herman de Jesus. Since her incarceration, they found themselves continuously assembling together and pondering what to do next, the same state in which they found themselves that particular Sunday afternoon. And without anyone saying a word, everyone knew what everyone else in the room was thinking, because it was what had always been on their minds since she was arrested. How could it have come to this? How had it all gotten away from them? How could their friend, a blessed proponent of peace, be accused, let alone convicted, of being a hydro-terrorist? It was a discussion seemingly held a hundred times and, just as probable, it would be held another hundred times without any finality.

That day, it was Nate the Great who first stood up and verbalized all their frustrations, though few could follow his meandering logic. "She gave it all. Bastards! Taking away everything. There will come a day."

It was Joan, one of the lawyers, wearing stylish business attire in stark contrast to Nate's thread-bare pants and shirt, who offered linearity as best she could to Nate's confusing rhetoric.

"It was all that paranoia at the beginning of the Water Wars," Joan had said. "We demanded action from our government to protect our water sources. Be careful what you wish for, right?"

"Our government?" Nate the Great had interrupted. "Ain't my fuckin' government! Ain't been anyone's government for a long time, now."

"I know, Nate," Joan continued. "It's just, I know I've said this a million times, but we were stupid. We asked our elected officials to legislate our fears away. And what happened? We let them bastardize our judicial system, putting in place laws that didn't just infringe upon our civil liberties, but totally trampled on them, all in the name of National Security."

On that particular Sunday, each of those present knew the answers as patently as the lawyers who had explained them over and over for months. But knowing the answers didn't make them any more palatable or any less ludicrous.

"She's being executed tomorrow," Simone said. "She, alone, is responsible for the life I am currently leading, one of meaning and substance. I don't know what I'm going to do without her presence in my life."

All those gathered made similar statements and wondered what lay ahead. A general murmur took over the small crowd, each table growing louder as those around it tried to be heard above their neighbors. The din was quickly silenced when Petra Fischer whistled and everyone turned their attention to her.

"Look, we've been sitting around for months now, griping about the same thing over and over again. 'Poor me. What's going to happen to me?' Well, I for one am sick of it."

"Hey," Jane, the older Zeday sister, objected. "We've been filing motions and working the system as best we could."

"Yes, yes, of course, we've all been doing whatever we can," Petra said, "but seriously, been doing the best we can for a year-and-a-half and it hasn't been enough. We've got one day left before they put to death the Daughter of God, la Hermana De Jesus, the *Sister of Jesus*! And here we are feeling sorry for ourselves. Worried about how this is going to impact *us*. What about her? What can we do for her, now."

The room was silent as they each internalized Petra's plea. No one dared speak. Instead they fidgeted in their seats and looked around waiting for someone else to lead the conversation or organize a plan, if there was to be one.

"What if we talk to the governor?" Tom finally offered.

"We've been trying to get an appointment for weeks" Joan said. "Months. We hold no political importance to him, why would he see us now?"

"We don't wait for an appointment," Felipe shouted, grabbing hold of the momentum. "We go and see him where he lives, the governor's residence, Heritage Mansion. It's public property. Our property. We simply go there and meet him face-to-face."

"I know how to get there," Nate the Great said and stood with his one hand in the air like a very large and unkempt second-grader.

"What if he's not there?" Andrea Fischer said.

"What if he is?" Felipe said in defiance. "It's better to go and find him not there than not go and sit here doing nothing."

This aroused them to no end as people were pushing past one another to get out the front door.

"Whoa, whoa, whoa," Petra yelled. "We can't just show up like an angry mob. Can we do something a bit more constructive? I mean, what are we going to do once we get there?"

"Okay," Tom Jones said. "Good point. How about an old fashioned sit-in? They used to do it all the time back in the 1960's. Why doesn't someone get some blankets, someone else go to the Big Box and get some flashlights, candles …"

"We'll pack up some of the food from the restaurant," Andrea added.

Tom then began assigning responsibilities to those who had gathered. "Everyone get what's on your list and we'll meet at Heritage Mansion at 5:00. Felipe, why don't you and I go together? Let's see if we can't get a news crew from your station down there … and I've got a friend at the paper."

"It's not my station anymore, Tom." Felipe corrected as they left the restaurant.

His statement was lost amidst the eager rumblings of the small crowd as they became excited, for the first time in a very long time, to have a purpose around which to rally.

CHAPTER 5

The day was warm and the scent of Yellow Trumpetbush blossoms, now falling from their stems, filled him with glee. Clay leaned back against the wooden slats of the park bench. He was dressed in jeans and a T-shirt. Both were dirty, as were his hands and face, from constant wear and exposure during the brisk days traversing the city and the long nights sleeping under various bridges. His black boots were worn and scuffed, but they still had a few months' worth of sole left.

Children flitted about the trees and shrubs and swings and teeter-totters while their parents paid very close attention to the disheveled man sitting on the bench. It was a prejudice of his unsightly appearance he had come to terms with many years ago.

It's a wonderful day to be alive, he thought.

He was glad he brought his heavy, navy blue, wool coat to place over the wooden slats; it acted as a comfortable buffer against the chipping paint and would allow him to sit for hours, if need be, with minimal discomfort. On that day, the need for comfort arose as his rendezvous was a little less than two hours late.

A huge, hulking man approached the bench and its lone patron from behind. He was dressed all in white from head to toe. His long and curly jet black hair rested on his shoulders. Unlike Clay, everything he wore was immaculate. His hands and face glowed with an almost unnatural healthiness. "Hello, Clay," the man in white said. "How are you?"

"I'm just fine," Clay replied, holding the palms of his hands over his ears. The timber of the man's voice grated on him. It always did. It was loud and garbled, something Clay had never quite gotten used to. Putting his hands over his ears didn't help, but it made Clay feel as though he was doing something to address the problem. "Is there any way you could talk more quietly?"

"I wish I could," the man in white said. He sat down next to Clay on the bench. "I was asked to find out if you understand what's going on?"

"Understand? We're at war, right?"

The man in white smiled. "That's right. The eternal battle of us against them."

"Yeah, but we're the good guys." Clay already knew the answer. It was an attempt at levity which passed by the man in white unheeded.

Instead, the man in white simply responded, "Absolutely, my good friend. Absolutely."

"So what's today's meeting about?" Clay asked, his hands still over his ears.

Clay had been meeting the man in white every Sunday for nearly a year. At first, Clay thought their meetings were random, never occurring in the same place or at the same time. But soon after their first few encounters, Clay knew there was no randomness. The man in white had sought him out and was preparing him for what was to come. As Clay understood it, he was to be part of something big and, for the most part, that it would be all but over by this same time the next day.

"I need you to do a few things for me," the man in white said.

"What things?"

"Simple things. Look in your jacket pocket."

Clay removed one hand from the side of his head and reached into his left coat pocket only to find it empty. He reached into the right pocket and pulled out an All-COM.

"You know how to use one of those?" the man asked.

Clay was sure the man in white already knew the answer. "I was an IT tech during the Water Wars. Trust me, I know how to use one of these."

"Tonight you're going to schedule an appointment at Heaven's Gate."

"The nightclub?" Clay exclaimed. "Old Town? No way, man! That place freaks me out."

The people in the park, who were once suspicious about the unkempt man on the bench, were now fully anxious, some even terrified. They scrambled about collecting their children and shuffling them into their vehicles. Their assumptions that the man on the bench was crazy were only validated by his unsettling outburst.

The man in white smiled widely. "I'm sorry, Clay, it has to be there. The symbolism is just too much to pass up. I'll call you with all the information you need and then you can forward it on to your contact."

"Is this thing clean?" Clay asked, wondering if the All-COM's PIC and GPS were disabled.

"Purposely not clean, but safe. At least for as long as you'll need it."

Then the man in white stretched wide and breathed in deeply, taking in the same floral aromas Clay had been admiring moments earlier. "It's a wonderful day to be alive, isn't it, Clay?"

"Actually," Clay smiled, "I was just thinking that very same thing when you showed up." He stared out at the vacant park. "It's gonna be over soon, right?"

The man in white looked down at Clay who wasn't paying any attention to him. "This is just the end of the beginning, Clay. There's a lot more to be done. But you don't have to worry about all that. You've been a good soldier, doing everything that's been asked of you." He placed his hand on Clay's shoulder. "We couldn't be more pleased with your faith in this mission, your support for the cause. You will be commended."

Clay continued to stare into the vastness of the park, seemingly oblivious to the man's kindly gesture. "I think I'll take a nap," Clay said.

He grabbed his coat, rolled it up and placed it at the end of the bench to use as a pillow. Clay rocked over on his side and closed his eyes as the man in white simply went away.

CHAPTER 6

Governor Damien Driver listened to the antique grandfather clock in the entryway announce the top of the hour. He had worked his way through a good portion of the stack of files and was now nearly at the end of the folder marked, *Her Ministry*. It was the thickest file of the bunch, nearly twice the size of the next thickest, *Her Trial*. From the first few files he read only the summary documents which ranged in length from a couple short paragraphs to the ten-pager that began the folder currently set before him. He breezed through those first few files in no time, barely glancing at the pages beneath the summaries.

Though he initially intended to read every word of every report, time would not allow it. The road to hell is paved with good intentions, he thought. He had already read them all once, some of them many times, and figured if he needed to come back later for something specific he could. What he was most interested in were the two thickest files. In the first he read a good portion of everything, skimming only the most dense and weighty material.

Aside from the reports and other documents in *Her Ministry* folder, there were disks of lectures and sermons recorded on one of her followers' All-COMs. They sat on his desk in their cases, watched once and replaced. He'd watch them again on Monday, time permitting, after he'd gone through everything on paper first and after he'd had a chance to once again discuss with his constituency exactly what they believed was his wisest course of action.

He knew what they wanted him to do. The *Executive Summary* Styles had created all but handcuffed him, forcing him to allow the execution to go on undeterred. Yet, after reading about her life up to and including her ministry, devoting years of her life as a Peace Corp volunteer to the war-ravaged area of India along the Pakistani border, there was no evidence that this woman had done anything illegal. It was as if the jury members disregarded the laws set before them and simply found her guilty because that was what they were supposed to do.

It sat awkwardly in the governor's mind and he couldn't help but feel he was aiding and abetting a felony, an accomplice to an assassination.

The fact that he would be joining his co-conspirators for dinner did not sit well with him, either. He knew that he'd have to make concessions once in office, but he had no idea that the values on which his platform was set would be eroded to next to nothing a mere nine months into his term.

His plan to reverse the tax credit for children was the first thing to go. He had made the argument quite eloquently, he was told by nearly everyone who heard him speak or read his 32 page positioning paper on the subject. But once the rubber met the road, it fell on deaf ears. He explained that as the world's population grew, the earth's ability to support it dwindled, particularly in light of the fact that more and more agricultural property was being designated for solar energy production rather than crop land to feed the hungry. Therefore, he proposed a zero-growth strategy. Initially he proposed no more tax deductibles for dependents. But then, he discovered the additional revenue of actually taxing any individual claiming more than one child as a dependent, or any household claiming more than two children. It was a double hit for those planning to have large families, though there was a grandfather clause for existing children and those born in the calendar year in which the law was enacted.

It was a novel idea quickly praised by the general population and the media as bi-partisan, forward-thinking, and not politics-as-usual. However, as soon as he took office it lost traction when his own conservative constituents pointed out Middle Eastern cultures were growing at a much faster pace than Western cultures. The state's ultra-conservative news outlets ran articles claiming it won't be long before "we're" a minority, explaining, "There is safety in numbers and if we are to survive, we will need to ensure we outnumber them." The logic was lost to the pervasive fear following the Water Wars and the idea shuffled to the very bottom of the GOP's *To Do List*, right below tightening gun control laws.

All these thoughts ran through the governor's mind in the brief few moments between the first and the fourth *bongs* from the clock. He wavered slightly, slipping the earpiece of his reading glasses between his teeth and debating whether he should take a shower before his dinner, or, finish reading the contents of the *Her Ministry* folder. He threw the glasses on the open files and rubbed his face with both hands. He was tired. Not just physically, but emotionally and, more than anything else, professionally.

In the folder open on his desk was a PHD, a small, portable external hard drive. Ignoring the previous thought to wait until tomorrow, he plugged it into the PHD port of his computer and watched, over and over, the nearly ten-minute clip that it contained. In the first half of the clip, a small woman delivered a moving speech to a group of people in the middle of one of the south side parks. In the years prior to his election, the parks had been all but taken over by the city's indigent Chicanos, particularly those on the south side. His Spanish was sub-par, but her speech, what little he could understand, was an impassioned plea for hope and patience. But, it was her facial expressions and body language that spoke even louder than the words, calming him, soothing him, even as he sat watching on his computer monitor nearly eighteen months removed from the actual moment. She explained to those surrounding her that those who suffered today will be rewarded with riches beyond measure. Those in need would want no more. Those who thirst would drink their fill. He watched and wondered how anyone who had seen this woman speak could refrain from tears.

And then, on the monitor, the police came.

The camera jostled as she was violently removed from her station in the park. Damien could see in the images that flashed on his monitor a mania in the officers' eyes, but the crowd, soothed by her words, her demeanor, her very presence, remained unfazed by the police's interference. He paused the clip as she was being forcibly shoved into the back of the police wagon. Her face remained a beacon of tranquility for everyone watching. He knew it. He could see it. He raised his hand to touch the pixilated image of her face.

"Dad?" came softly through the door followed by, "Are you in here?"

"Sweetheart, come in," Damien replied.

"Am I bothering you?"

"Not at all."

"'Cause if this is a bad time—"

"No, no. Come in. I've been in here all afternoon reading and was just looking for a diversion."

His daughter, Laura, a bright and bubbly woman, walked across the floor of his study to where her father now stood.

Damien kissed her on the cheek. "Have a seat."

"What're you reading?" Laura asked. "Is it about the Rodriquez execution?"

"Yes," he said curtly.

"God bless America, is that all you can talk about? I can't even talk to mom without that somehow finding its way into the conversation."

"I wish *I* didn't have to talk about it," Damien laughed.

"Is that the clip?"

He glanced at the monitor. "Yes. The full clip, not just the ten seconds everyone saw. The ten seconds—"

"Stop. I just said I don't want to talk about it. And thank God, this time tomorrow we can all get on with our lives."

"Fine. But it's up to you to find a suitable subject."

"Well, how about this? Julia's pregnant."

Damien was speechless. His daughter, Laura, had been with Julia Jimenez for almost ten years. It was the only real stumbling block to his candidacy within the ultra-conservative GOP. If not for the political support from Mike Hart and Lilith Samuel, he would have been dead in the water. But Mike believed in him. More precisely, he and his backers believed they could manipulate Damien, and they deflected the criticism with hyperbole, making Damien look like a saint for loving the freak-of-nature that was his lesbian daughter. It was another grain of sand blown across the surface of his principles.

"That's wonderful, sweetheart," Damien said as he embraced his daughter. "I didn't know you were even considering children."

"You're kidding, right? Mom's been hounding us for years for grandchildren."

"Yeah, but you two have always led such a cosmopolitan lifestyle, I thought you'd wait until you were past menopause before adopting a 10-year-old from some third-world country. I know how much you hate changing diapers."

"Stop it, dad. You're terrible."

"Have you told your mother yet? Who else knows?"

"Well, we decided since Julia's pregnant and not me, we should tell her mom first. So there's me and Julia, the pediatrician and Julia's mom. You make five."

"Where's Julia? Why didn't you bring her along to break the news?"

He knew the answer. They both did.

"She's not real comfortable—"

"Never mind that. She's always welcome here. As long as you both know that, screw the party piranhas. Maybe we can come by your place later this week to celebrate."

"Actually, I dropped by to see what you were doing for dinner tonight."

"Honey," he said, hearing his own condescension. "You know I can't tonight. I'm meeting some of the party leaders regarding the whole Rodriquez thing. Then I have these reports to read." He waved his hand at the top of his desk.

"Who's going to be there?" her tone turning instantly nasty. "The collars?"

"Among others, yes."

"Damn it, dad!"

"Sweetheart, please. You can't expect me to drop the most important issues in this state's recent history—"

"What ever happened to the division of church and state? And isn't treason a Federal crime? Why are you even involved?"

His tone turned soothing. "Don't you remember? Since water was deemed a state-licensed commodity, the rules and regs regarding its protection and distribution are considered state issues. For years the GOP has been trying to transition power, and therefore expenses, to state and local ..."

Damien stopped. Laura was sulking, paying little attention to the answer he'd been reciting since taking office. He took a deep breath, held her by the shoulders and looked deeply into her eyes. "Sweetheart, I've just been told the most wonderful news. My daughter is making me a grandfather. Can we please focus on that for the moment? Perhaps even for the next five or ten minutes?"

She fell into her father's chest and breathed a long loud sign of exacerbation. "You're right. I'll tell you what. If you want to ruin my day, let's talk politics."

"I neither want to ruin your day nor talk politics. I want to find your mother."

He squeezed her once more before leading her out of the room with his long arms draped over her shoulder. "Do you know what kind of trouble I'm in? I'd almost rather talk politics with you than have to hear from your mother how I somehow arranged to find out first."

CHAPTER 7

The first few minutes in the car were quiet. None of the members within the core group were particularly friendly. They attended to the needs of those to whom Estephania reached out during her ministry and then relied upon one another only for support when Estephania was first arrested. However, since her arrest, they'd come to appreciate one another for the personal dedication each had shown during the more recent, more trying times. Only now, with their Savior's execution a little more than a day away, did each of them realize he or she had little in common with any of the other Adherentes.

Tom and Felipe were fully aware that they had little in common. However, armed with this realization, Tom tried to make simple small talk nonetheless. "So, what's it like working in television?"

"You used to work in advertising, right?"

"Yeah. Still do."

"And you don't know what working in television is like?"

Tom didn't like the tone of voice that carried Felipe's words, so he responded with a cutting jab. "Yeah, well, it's been a fairly unsuccessful medium for most of our clients. We've been focusing our efforts on All-COM interludes."

"Interludes?" Felipe huffed. "People have been waiting for TV to die for decades. But it's a social medium, the only real social media left. You'll never get a family sitting around a handheld device. TV will always have a place."

"Interludes are targeted," Tom tried to one-up.

"So, you're entire client list is made up of companies …" Felipe stopped. The conversation was not going anywhere near where it needed to, so he refocused. "How about a plan for tonight? I'd much rather come up with some ideas about how to pitch this to the news department than argue the benefits of TV versus All-COM as a marketing message delivery vehicle."

"Pitch? Aren't you the General Manager? Can't you just tell them to cover it?"

"I told you, I don't work there anymore. When she called me into service, I gave up everything. Not just my job, but also my home, my fiancé, everything except this car and a few bucks to pay some bills." Felipe shot a look at Tom from across the car. "Didn't you?"

"I gave up all my worldly possessions, but I kept my job. She needed marketing support to get her message out to the masses. I would have thought you'd have helped her out with your TV connections."

"So, you admit TV still has a place in the marketing mix?"

Tom laughed out loud. "Yeah, I guess I walked right into that one."

Felipe picked up where he left off. "I would have helped out from the TV side, but by the time I was called, two of the network affiliates were already saturating the market with her every move."

"And where are they now?" Tom asked rhetorically.

Like all things new, there was a buzz about Estephania. The local coverage of her ministry was ubiquitous, as was the coverage of her trial. It made national news as well, but quickly died down once she was convicted and incarcerated. Even now, with her execution only a day away, there was still no coverage, as if her life was unimportant. The world had become apathetic to her message and her life.

"They were no different than the rest of her ministry. Even the most ardent believers, you know, the hardcore fanatics, even they packed up when both sides conspired to do her in. They ran and hid, too, to save their own hides," Felipe growled.

"But not you?" Tom asked.

"No, not me. From the very beginning, I was in it for the long haul. Trust me, I wasn't looking for a Savior. I had a great life, by secular standards. I wasn't looking for something to come along and fill a void or anything. I felt no need for penance or absolution. I was living my life by the golden rule and was happy as a pig in slop. Then, there I was, stopped to recharge my car, when I heard Her speaking to a group of people in a convenience store, of all places. There She was, this tiny little woman, the embodiment of God's grace, explaining what the Church had been trying to tell me for decades. 'Put your faith in Him. All the rest is distraction.'

"That very day I quit my job and dedicated my life to Her and never looked back." He thought about that first moment he heard her words and smiled. "How about you? Did you have an epiphany? Did a chorus of angels sing *Alleluia* when She spoke to you?"

Tom sat in the passenger seat and thought a moment. "I guess you wouldn't call it an epiphany. I was actually trying to pick Her up?"

"What? Like at a bar or something?"

Tom chuckled. "No, not a bar. We were both working a food line at one of the downtown shelters. I was doing community service for a DWI, She was doing, well, what She's been doing: helping save all of humankind. I asked Her out and She accepted. I had this really great dinner scam going with all my dates. A whirl-wind tour of the city's great undiscovered gems. Start at Miguel's, this tapas bar that's really a hot dog wagon over in Paradise Valley, burgers at the Neon Jungle and dessert at the Pinnacle Grill. It was a sure thing. Every time I hit those three places, I ended up nailing the lady I was with shortly after paying the bill at the Pinnacle."

Felipe was appalled. "You had relations with—"

"Please!" Tom interrupted. "We never even made it to Miguel's. She said She needed to stop at a hospice center on the way and we spent the whole night reading and playing cribbage with terminal patients. The next night we went into a flash house. Me, Mr. Whitecollar, sticking out like a sore thumb. I walked right into that dilapidated rats nest in the heart of the 'hood and brought three strung-out flash junkies out of there and placed them in a shelter that night. I swear they got clean just listening to Her talk. It was the single most fulfilling night of my life.

"There were no angels singing, but from that moment I knew I wanted to be with Her more than anything else in the world. I wanted to feel that sense of fulfillment, of self-worth, every moment of every day. And, until eighteen months ago, I did."

By the time Tom finished his story Felipe was pulling into the parking spot in front of the KPHE-TV studios.

"What do you want me to do when we get in there?" Tom asked.

"I don't know. Once both sides turned on her, pretty much everyone else did, too. Remember? People here are no different. In fact, the Mexicans, her own kind, they're even worse. They think of her as poison. It's going to be a tough sell getting anyone in there to cover a story like this."

36

"Are you kidding? She's the first woman to be executed by the state in nearly 25 years. And, the first *person* to be executed for treason under the new Water Security Laws."

Tom looked down at his shoes and forced a mean laugh. "Treason! What a load of crap."

"Treason, murder, it doesn't matter. Not now. This is different, Tom. Usually you have the right-to-lifers making noise or appeals being made by advocacy groups from around the world with a chip on their shoulders. Not here. Not with Her. It's like everyone wants Her dead, you know?" Felipe paused. "What am I talking about? Absolutely you know! I can see it in your eyes. You can feel the apathy for Her, the disdain for Her cause, just as well as I can. It's palpable. Showing a group of people protesting Her execution at the governor's mansion is like, I don't know, like, like showing a bunch of pedophiles picketing against the Salisbury steak on the elementary school menu. We'll be reviled. And, most importantly, it doesn't make for good ratings."

"So then what are we doing here?" Tom yelled, frustrated.

"To be honest," Felipe said, "I didn't know what else to do. You seemed to think coming here might do some good. So, here we are."

"Do you have any idea how we might be able to make this a success? My buddy at the paper's gonna want the same hook you feed your news director."

"Once again, he's not *my* news director. I haven't worked here in almost three years. And as for a hook, all I got are the points you already made: first woman in 25 years, first person for treason. They know all that. I just don't think they care."

"We'll figure something out" Tom assured Felipe. "Let's go."

Between the time they got out of the car and made it into the front doors of the station, Tom and Felipe had came up with several plausible hooks they could feed the news director. While plausible, they both agreed that none of their ideas seemed strong enough, not to persuade the news director to send a crew to Heritage Mansion. They walked in undeterred.

"Can I help you?" These words, husky and harsh as they came from the overweight receptionist's mouth, were spoken in Spanish. Tom stood unaware. Felipe replied.

"Is Dave Morales still the news director?"

"Yes. Do you want me to see if he's available?"

"Yes, please."

"And who are you?"

"Felipe Martinez. I used to be the station's general manager."

The receptionist spoke softly into her headset. Then, returning to Felipe, *"He'll be with you in a moment."*

"Gracias."

Tom walked over to Felipe and asked, "Would it be better if you two were alone. You know, 'cause I'm—"

"Gringo?" Felipe interrupted. "I don't think it's going to make a difference."

Tom walked off into the reception area with his hands clasped behind his back. Sections of the Sunday *El Planeta*, the city's Latino print news source, were strewn about the coffee table. Tom picked up the various sections and quickly scanned them hoping to find a photo, headline or some other recognizable mention of the impending execution of la Hermana de Jesus. He found none. It struck him as odd that in an era when sensationalism was more important than news, a story as derisive and polarizing as capital punishment was nowhere to be found.

Tom remembered the media coverage during her ministry as ubiquitous. Until her arrest, nearly every time she addressed more than a handful of people, someone would capture it on their All-COM and post it on some site somewhere. The coverage of her arrest was similarly overexposed, but as the ratings for her pre-trial proceedings dipped lower and lower, the media covered it less and less. The only bumps in ratings came when the guilty verdict was announced and the death sentence handed down nine months after her arrest. Since then, little coverage was available. It seemed everyone had become apathetic.

The realization that Felipe was right, that their cause was deemed unimportant by everyone around them, struck an uncomfortable chord within Tom and he threw the section of the paper he was holding down on the table in disgust. As if prompted, the station's news director came out a door and into the lobby. He immediately walked over to Tom and asked, "¿Pardon, está allí un problema?"

Before Tom could reply, Felipe answered the news director in Spanish, *"This is Tom Jones and I am Felipe Martinez. I believe your receptionist told you we were here."*

The news director leered at Tom disapprovingly and then looked back at Felipe. In Spanish, he said, *"Yes, Felipe Martinez. You left the station a few months after I came on board. I wasn't told you were accompanied,"* he continued, turning his condemning expression once again on Tom.

Felipe cleared his throat a bit to get the news director's attention before trying to lay the foundation for a more pleasant discussion, *"You worked in Santa Fe before coming here, if I'm not mistaken."*

The news director cautiously continued. *"Yes. I'm surprised you remembered."*

"Management Training 101: know your people," Felipe said jovially. Then, after a brief, yet thoroughly awkward silence, he continued. *"I was wondering, what kind of news day are you expecting this evening?"*

"Why, you got a lead for me?"

It was typical of the way news director thought, find the lead and go. If he were in Dave Morales's shoes, he would have done the exact same thing. Felipe continued in Spanish, *"I'm pretty sure there's going to be something going on at the governor's mansion tonight."*

"What do you mean 'something going on'?"

"A protest march."

"Protest?" The news director smiled widely. *"Against what?"*

"Against the execution of Estephania Rodriquez."

The smile dimmed. *"Oh, that's right,"* he said sizing up the man before him. *"You quit the job to follow that* pinche puta loco. *I forgot about that. Weren't you one of her Adherentes? You were!"*

The man paused and mulled something over in his head, looking at Felipe with the same disapproval Tom had initially received. *"So, she's finally getting the needle and you want me to send a unit to the governor's mansion to capture you and your Christian extremist buddies standing out front spewing the same bullshit you've been spewing for years. Yeah, well, I'll tell you what. If some anti-protesters come along and shoot you all dead, maybe, just maybe I'll get you on right after the weather. Until then, go to hell!"*

The news director turned to walk away and then turned back to deliver one final message, this time in English. "And while you're at

Heritage Mansion, be sure to tell the governor to keep up the good work."

With that, the man turned abruptly, pressed his thumb on the security pad next to the door he had come through, waited for the buzz and click, and disappeared inside.

Felipe felt the receptionist staring at him so he instinctively started to shuffle toward the entrance, motioning Tom to follow him.

"So," Tom said, "are you sure that wouldn't have gone better if I weren't here?"

"Well, I suppose it couldn't have gone much worse. But think about it. Do you think your friend at the paper will treat you any differently?"

"I don't know. My guy's a bit, umm, how should I put this? Nuts. You said it couldn't get worse. Well, we're going to put that to the test."

CHAPTER 8

Tom's meeting with his friend, the newspaper reporter, was similar to Felipe's meeting with his former colleague in only one respect, it was relatively short. Having seen the antagonistic behavior of Felipe's news director, Tom thought it best to meet his friend in a neutral location before explaining what they were doing. Tom had called the reporter at home and asked to meet him at the Saguaro Blossom. The Blossom was a brewpub centrally located two blocks from both the Capitol building and governor's mansion. It was also the noted hangout for the state's political talking heads and reporters who made the bureaucratic ineptitude of their state leaders their bread and butter.

When Tom and Felipe approached the restaurant a little after 5:00, they passed in front of the governor's mansion. They were surprised to find no traces of any of the other Adherentes.

"What do you think happened?" Felipe asked.

Tom only shrugged his shoulders as Felipe edged his car to the curb a block further south of Heritage Mansion: a short walk to the brewpub. When the two men got out of the car, they were instantly approached by two other men. Both were very large with deeply Mexican features. The larger of the two barked out, in a heavy accent, "Hey! What are you doing here?"

Tom turned around and gaped at the size of the man talking to him. "Aaaa, we're meeting a friend at the Blossom. Why?"

The man didn't answer. He didn't even grunt. He simply disengaged and nodded to his partner. Then they both walked back the way they had come.

"What was that about?" Felipe asked.

"Beats me. Maybe they're the governor's welcoming committee."

"And maybe that's why none of the others from the group are here."

"Maybe," Tom agreed, looking back at the two behemoths walking away from them.

Tom and Felipe entered the near-empty brewpub. It was a bright and cheery and smelled antiseptic, the direct inverse of the politicians who made up the bulk of its clientele. Tom walked immediately toward a booth in the back.

"You thirsty?" Tom asked.

Felipe said, "Sure," but then became quickly embarrassed when he realized the question was intended for the crazy-haired man in the booth.

"Yeah, I'll have an Agave Ale," the crazy-haired man said.

"Felipe," Tom said as he turned around. "Can you get two Agave Ales and whatever you want." Then he pulled his All-COM from his hip holster and pulled his money stick from the All-COM's casing. Handing the stick to Felipe, Tom added, "And why not get something to eat. Order a plate of nachos or something."

By the time Felipe came back and set the two beers and his small glass of iceless water on the table, Tom was already fully engaged with the crazy-haired man. But it wasn't just his hair that was crazy, Felipe noticed. The man sitting across the table had crazy eyes, sunk deep into his head as if he'd had surgery to jut his eyebrows out to block direct sunlight. His mannerisms, likewise, were exaggerated, wild and constant. The man was dressed warmly, wearing a grey parka, far heavier attire than was necessary for the weather outside.

Beer slopped onto the crusty, weathered hands of the crazy-haired man as he grabbed the glass and lifted it from the table. He didn't seem to notice. Felipe threw his napkin on the spill.

"Felipe," Tom started, "this is Luke Logan. He was just telling me a little bit about what's going on with the news media."

Felipe shook the man's wet hand and sat down. He reached into his pocket for a handkerchief, wiping his hands under the table and out of sight.

Luke nodded toward Felipe and whispered to Tom, more than loud enough for Felipe to hear, "You sure this guy's okay?"

"He's more straight laced and forthright than I am, which ain't saying much, but yeah, he's okay."

Then, flashing a crazy smile at Felipe, Luke said, "No offense."

Felipe waved a hand gesturing there was no offense taken and Luke began to speak. It came in quick bursts, like machine gun fire, terse and direct.

"It's like I was saying, I ain't never seen shit like this before, TJ. It's like a total communications embargo or something. I had a long piece with all the angles, just like you said, set to run in this morning's paper. But we got call after call from advertisers telling us if we ran any piece of any size about la Hermana de Jesus, they'd pull their advertising for the whole year."

"Everyone?" Tom asked.

"Not the national accounts. What the fuck do they care about some cult leader on death row down here? But all the big local accounts. Again, not just a couple, but all of them."

Luke took another sip from his glass. "And it's a cryin' shame, too, 'cause it was a damn good piece. Spent a couple weeks pulling stats and quotes and background."

"Every reporter I ever meet thinks any piece that gets cut is a Pulitzer Prize winner," Tom said with a laugh.

Luke smiled widely. "Touché. All the same, though, this was a good one! Damn editors are just a bunch of pussies scared they're going to get sued for hurting someone's feelings. I swear, if I see another piece come across the wire where some idiot gets awarded record punitive damages for some exposé piece that's on the money but hurtful and sad …. But, editor's, man, they just need to grow a pair, you know? Hell, they don't even have the fuckin' sack to grow 'em in!"

Luke and Tom laughed out loud, making it difficult to hear Felipe ask, "How did they know the paper was running the story?"

At the same time, Tom corrected Luke. "That would be 'they don't have a sack in which to grow 'em,'"

"What?" Luke asked, directing he crazy eyes on Felipe.

Tom started, "You're not supposed to end a sentence—"

"Not you, TJ," Luke said without taking his eyes off Felipe. "Gunga Din, here" he said, pointing to the glass of water.

It took a moment for Felipe to register that Luke was talking to him. When he looked into the crazy eyes, the expression on the face looking back didn't just allude to annoyance, it personified the word. "I'm sorry, are you talking to me?"

"You asked me how they knew I was running the story."

"Oh, yes. That is odd, isn't it?"

43

"For the editors to know what I'm writing? I fuckin' work for them."

"No, no, no," Felipe said apologetically. "I'm sorry, not the editors. The advertisers. How did the advertisers know you were running a story on Estephania Rodriguez?

No one said anything for a long while until Felipe could take it no longer.

"I mean, it's news, right? How does someone on the outside know content before it's printed?"

Luke's annoyed expression went blank, then angry. "Who are you, Bob Fuckin' Woodward?"

"He used to be in television news," Tom said, noting the palpable tension in Luke's overall disposition and trying to cut through it with some sort of salve.

"How the fuck should I know how they found out? All I know is my editor told me yesterday it was being pulled because of threats by all the big local advertisers."

"So, um, you, ah, never got a call?" Felipe asked, frightened of the fury he suddenly realized he might be unleashing.

Luke didn't answer.

"My point is, um, it could have been your editor who pulled the story and he, or she, as the case may be, just, you know, used the advertisers as an excuse."

Luke stared at Felipe for a moment and then whispered, "He wouldn't do that."

Trying desperately to make Luke's eyes focus elsewhere, Felipe gave his full endorsement to the idea. "Oh, well, then I'm sure it was the advertisers making noise. It used to happen at the station all the time. There was this one time—"

"He wouldn't fuckin' do that," Luke said more forcefully.

Felipe's hands trembled visibly as he lifted his water to take a sip. Then, as he was setting the glass down on the table, Luke slammed both fists down and growled through his teeth, low and slow, "That motherfucker!"

The shelf that was his brow jutted out even further than before, a crooked, undulating ridge of cantilevered muscles. His eyes were wide and his lids receded into his skull, leaving only the faintest remnants of lashes on top and bottom. His lips and cheeks were quivering as if he were speaking in tongues at a whisper's level. And, as the crazy-looking man across the table took several deep, audible breathes, his cheeks puffed out in rhythm as the air attempting to exhale was force back by his clenched teeth.

Felipe had never seen human rage expressed so poignantly. He was amazed he had the fortitude not to run out of the brewpub screaming like a frightened child.

"Easy there, Luke," Tom said as sedately as possible.

A tic on the left side of Luke's face began to flutter. Felipe thought the man now looked almost cartoonish in his rage and the slightest of smiles broke on his lips.

Low and guttural came, "Wipe that fucking smile off your face."

Felipe's fear instantly returned and he sat emotionless, expressionless.

Tom chimed in with another salve. "Okay, so, Luke, Rather than focusing on the seven uniquely unpleasant kinds of pain you plan to inflict upon your editor, let me just give you something else to think about. You remember the group of people who were Her followers? They called themselves the Adherentes? Well, Surprise! I was one of them. Still am one of them, I guess. Anyway, we were supposed to be meeting in front of the governor's mansion to form a protest, you know, to get him to stay the execution? Only when we drove past the place there was nobody out there. And these two huge goons came up to us and asked us what we were doing in the neighborhood."

"Huge goons," Felipe echoed for emphasis, sorry he did so when Luke turned in his direction.

Luke sat there seething, showing no signs of listening.

"As I was saying," Tom continued, "we were hoping maybe you could come along and maybe ask around and find out what the deal is."

The embodiment of wrath in Luke's entire disposition had subsided only slightly while Tom spoke. But when Luke finally did crack his stony façade, the reporter's voice was calm and decisive.

"The governor and a couple of his GOP cronies are eating with the bishop at the Diocesan Pastoral Center."

"How do you know that?" Felipe asked.

"I'm a reporter." Luke said, his voice calm, but his face still gnarled. "I make my living knowing things other people don't, and then writing them down."

"Hey, I have a question," Tom started, "In your article, the one that ...," he hesitated nervously, "um, you know, didn't run. Did you do any kind of research to support it?"

"There were some All-COM opinion polls I could draw from," Luke said softly. "Why?"

"I'm just curious about the relationship between demographics and the desire to see Her die."

"Why?" Luke repeated in the same flat tone he had a moment before.

"I'm getting weird vibes from the Latino population," Tom answered.

"Of course you are," Felipe said. "She's a disgrace to her people. That's not my opinion, of course, but theirs. When the U.S. absorbed Mexico and created the South of the Border States, you know as well as I do it was to reduce the size of its border and save money on border patrol."

"And to establish cheap labor to compete with China," Tom added.

"Yes, well," Felipe continued, "it took a lot of hard work and many years to overcome the bias and bigotry that existed all those years prior. Her people originally took Her teachings to heart, but then She started rocking the boat. Some of the things She said. And when She didn't stop Her ministry, even after the Catholic church and the state came down on Her, everyone in the community felt like She was setting those efforts back a couple decades. They felt like She was undoing all the good that had been done to that point. After she was arrested, they scattered like cockroaches and when the dust settled, She was the focus of everyone's anger from all sides."

Felipe paused as if to say more but didn't. Instead, he picked up his small glass of water and took a sip.

"Did you do any research that bares that out, Luke?" Tom said.

Suddenly, as if someone had uncoiled a spring, Luke eased back into the booth and brought the beer up to his lips. He took a long draught and calmly placed the beer down before he spoke. "Yeah, someone, not the *Republic*, sent out an All-COM interlude questionnaire. I think we got back something like 600 completed surveys. If the respondent was Latino,

46

they wanted her dead. Some crazy number like 94 percent. If they were Catholic, which, like, 112 percent of the Latino population is, it was really high, too. Even for the affluent white crowd. It was funny, the first question on the survey was: Are you for or against the death penalty? Even those against it said she deserved to die. Fucked up numbers all over the board."

"How about you?" Tom asked the crazy-haired man.

"How about me, what?"

"Do you want Her dead?"

"I don't give a rat's fuck whether she lives or dies."

"Are you for or against the death penalty?" Tom prodded.

Luke took a deep breath. "I think of the death penalty kind of like I think of the designated hitter in baseball. It is a completely ludicrous idea but the raging public debate it generates is intriguing. So I'm all for the death penalty, and the designated hitter, not as a concept in and of itself, but as a forum for social discussion."

"Interesting. Are you Catholic?"

Luke laughed. "Fuck no. I might be crazy but I ain't stupid. Look, I consider myself agnostic. I'm not so arrogant to think humankind is the epitome of all existence. What a depressing thought that would be. But I'm not stupid enough to be duped by organized religion. A bunch of guys in robes and scarves telling everyone else what to think, feel and be? Fuck that! Treat others the way you want to be treated and call it a day. When the time comes and I'm dead as a doornail, I'll take my chances on the other side knowing I gave at the office."

Luke finished his beer and started scooting out of the booth. "And speaking of the afterlife, I'm going to go have a little chat with my editor. Thanks for the beer, TJ."

"You bet," Tom said. "I'm thinking maybe we'll head over to Pastoral Center, see if our group is over there."

As Luke was walking out the door, he turned to the two men still in the booth. "Maybe I'll check in at the governor's mansion first just to see what the deal is there? Get the goons on record. Maybe get some ideas on how to torture my editor."

Just then, the bartender came with their nachos.

"Can you wrap those up?" Tom asked as he and Felipe were getting up to leave.

CHAPTER 9

The huge, oak doors to the Pastoral Center were at least three centuries old, a true salvage yard find; diamonds in the rough. The left panel depicted the birth of Christ, the right one His resurrection. Every time he entered the center, Father Joe covertly fingered the tool marks of the stigmata on the right door and quietly thanked Jesus for suffering on the cross to make his eternal salvation possible. Then he'd kiss his fingers and inhale the faint, piney scent of the safflower oil he knew the bishop demanded be used on any and all natural wood items in the Center.

He'd gotten half a step inside when he was graciously greeted by the bishop. "Father Joseph. Thank you so much for coming on such short notice."

Bishop DeMarco was not a particularly big man, standing about five feet and ten inches and weighing a svelte 170 pounds. He was, however, an imposing figure, filling up far more space than his frame possessed with an aura that could not be measured physically. His face was cut with hard, angular features offering little variance between expressions of happiness and sadness, making it difficult to know just what he was thinking. Father Joe always felt as if he were a schoolboy in the principal's office whenever they talked. Upon leaving the bishop's presence, Father Joe would consciously remind himself not to feel inferior, yet every time he returned, they took on the inevitable roles of student and principal in his mind.

Father Joe was, in fact, smaller than the bishop, though not by much, which probably enhanced his perceptions of condition. But even if Father Joe were an offensive lineman for a professional football team, dwarfing the bishop in height and girth, the mere manner in which the older clergyman carried himself would more than make up for the physical differences to reinstitute the feelings of lowliness Father Joe held while in the bishop's attendance.

"I'm sorry I'm late, Your Eminence."

"Bishop DeMarco, please."

"I'm sorry," Father Joe replied. "Your 'Father Joseph' must have thrown me off."

"It's quite all right. Please, come in and make yourself comfortable."

"Am I the first one here?"

"Actually, I wanted to spend a few moments with you alone, so I asked the other guests to arrive after 5:30. I hope you don't mind."

"Um, I guess not."

The bishop lead Father Joe to the center's large meeting room and asked him to sit.

"Would you like a glass of wine? The governor is quite fond of red wine, so I've taken the liberty to acquire a few bottles from a wonderful Italian vineyard."

"No wine for me, thank you, Bishop. Maybe with dinner. I will take a glass of cold water if it's not too much trouble."

"No trouble at all. I'll be right back." Then, noting that the priest had not sat down, the bishop added, "Please, sit. Relax." The bishop then disappeared through the swinging door that connected to the kitchen.

Father Joe stayed standing, purposely defying the bishop's attempts to get him to sit. He wandered around the room looking at the various paintings of the current pope, Pope Pius XV, as well as the previous seven diocesan bishops. He thought about going back to the front doors to study the craftsmanship of the panels when the bishop returned with two glasses; one filled with wine, the other with water.

"Come, Father Joe, join me over here in these chairs."

Father Joe walked over as the bishop placed the glasses on the small side table between the two very large upholstered chairs. Probably a donation from a parishioner, Father Joe thought. Only after the metaphorical principal eased into his chair did the nervous, defiant pupil do the same.

"So, your visit this afternoon didn't go according to plans."

Trying to put on a brave face, the younger, smaller man said, "Actually, everything about my visit went according to plan except that my last visitor cancelled Her appointment."

"Father Joe," the bishop said disappointedly. "Are we going to be coy all night? Your last appointment is what I was talking about."

Embarrassed, Father Joe nodded. "Yes, I know. But with the governor and his staff joining us, I thought I'd practice being coy."

"Come, now. I would have thought you'd consider the governor someone with whom you could speak openly, without reservations. After all, he has been very receptive to the concerns and desires of the Church. In fact, a good portion of the Republicans, and even some of the conservatives on the other side of the aisle, have asked our advice on a number of issues. We have to take advantage of these opportunities if we are to bring about a more just human condition."

"You, Your Eminence, are someone with whom I can speak openly and without reservations. And because of that, I can tell you I still believe in the antiquated concept of separation of Church and State. And not just within the letter of the law but within the spirit of the law as well. I'm well aware of the benefits afforded us by our financial contributions to the GOP. But the whole premise of being part of any political party's constituency seems contrary to the principles on which this country was founded."

"Joseph, I do not want to spend my time with you discussing at length the time and effort the United States Conference of Catholic Bishops has devoted to the very subject of which you speak. What I would like to discuss is your observations, knowledge, opinions and beliefs as they pertain to the woman being executed tomorrow.

"The governor has the power to stay the execution. As one of his major constituents, as you put it, I believe we must take advantage of this opportunity to bring about a more just human condition, as I put it, by pleading for the woman's clemency. With your obvious affinity toward her, however platonic, and the passion with which you speak of her work, I thought you might be able to provide a unique perspective on the subject to which the governor may not otherwise have access."

Confused, Father Joe asked, "You want me to convince the governor to stay the execution?"

"Of course. I believe it was the Great Communicator John Paul II who said the death penalty is both cruel and unnecessary. The U.S.C.C.B. has preached for years that the antidote to violence is not more violence. We encourage solutions to violent crime that reflect the dignity of the human person, urging the nation to abandon the use of capital punishment."

"But I thought you didn't believe in Her divinity."

51

"I don't. Personally, I believe she's as crazy as a loon, making the death penalty even more absurd in her case. But regardless of what I believe, she is a child of God, as are we all. And as such, we have a moral obligation to protect her life from those who have condemned her to death."

The bishop lifted his glass deliberately, swirled it and stuck his nose inside. Then he closed his eyes and took a long sip. Father Joe took the series of gestures to mean the bishop had said what he wanted to say and that all other rhetoric was superfluous.

The young priest sat in his chair and watched as the bishop set the glass down on the table.

"Now what?"

"I beg your pardon?" the bishop asked.

"Is there anything else we need to discuss before the governor arrives?"

"Since you bring it up, you didn't so much as flinch when I stated you had an obvious affinity for this Rodriquez woman. I find that a bit disconcerting."

"You also stated it was obviously platonic."

"Your relationship with this woman never concerned me from a physical standpoint, Joseph. But the term platonic isn't just about friendship, it also includes the spiritual. I don't think I've ever hidden my concerns regarding this portion of your relationship with a convicted, treasonous felon, a hydro-terrorist, a Christian extremist and cult leader."

"Convicted felon," Father Joe said through his teeth. "I think it was you who told me treason is a crime of conscience. And with the litany of Water Security Laws making it nearly impossible to defend the charges, once the bell is rung ..." He stopped suddenly and took a moment to collect himself. "Bishop, sir, I'm a pastor at a small parish in a small town that also happens to be the location of the state's maximum security prison for women. I enjoy 'the mission work', as I call it, providing spiritual guidance for the criminally wayward. But never in all my years of working, in that prison or elsewhere, have I come across a woman, or a man, for that matter, who so embodies God's grace and glory.

"She is not a Christian extremist but a Christian revisionist. She is not a cult leader but a captivating speaker with a dedicated following. And she is not a felon but a scapegoat."

"Yes, yes, so you've said."

"Please, your Eminence—"

"Bishop DeMarco," the bishop corrected, slowly and emphatically.

"Bishop DeMarco, please. Just listen to Her. Hear the words directly from Her mouth. Tomorrow morning, why don't you come with me to pray with Her?"

Bishop DeMarco smiled widely. "A bishop attending the execution of a cultist leader? My role as a dignitary of the Church brings with it certain responsibilities, both perceived and real. You know that. Even if I wanted to, which, believe me, I do not, it is not a precedent I can set, particularly for this woman who, by all accounts, has become a pariah in the Latino community, a growing population to whom we must at least appear to cater."

"Sir, the Pharisees condemned Jesus for eating with lepers and surrounding himself with tax collectors and prostitutes. The righteous questioned why He spent so much time with sinners. And the reason He did so was because they needed Him most."

The bishop leaned over slowly, lifted his glass and took another long sip. It provided him with the time he obviously needed to find a plausible excuse not to do what was being asked of him. However, before delivering it to Father Joe, a ruckus arose at the front doors. The governor and some of the state's GOP headquarters staff noisily entered.

Father Joe would not let the request go unanswered. As they both rose to greet the small, murmuring group entering the center, Father Joe leaned over and whispered into the bishop's ear, "Please, sir, pray with us tomorrow at 11:00. I beg you."

The bishop closed his eyes, slowly but perceptibly nodded his head in agreement and whispered, "No one can know I am there." Then he strode over to the murmuring group and, clasping the governor's hand in both of his own, he shook firmly.

CHAPTER 10

The guests were removing their jackets and milling about in the Pastoral Center's entrance when the bishop called out, "Governor, can I interest you in a glass of wine?"

"Ooooh, yes, please," he said walking further into the large room.

"How many glasses?" asked the porter.

A gentleman and one of the two ladies following the governor raised their hands while the porter tallied.

"Three, very good. And you ma'am?" the porter asked Lilith Samuel who hadn't raised her hand.

"A diet cola, please," she said.

The space had seemed cavernous to Father Joe when it was occupied by just the two clergymen, but when the small group filed into the space a low, perpetual din filled the air. Introductions were made and the volume of space seemed to mold around them and, like a down pillow, became much more comfortable.

Bishop DeMarco began the introductions. "Governor, I'd like you to meet Father Joseph Romano, pastor at Christ King parish in Goodyear. Father Joe has been the spiritual advisor of Ms. Rodriquez during her stay at P-Ville."

Father Joe shook the governor's hand and said, "Actually, I'm the chaplain for all the inmates. And for Ms. Rodriguez, all I've been doing is saying mass at the prison once a week and hearing Her confessions."

The bishop then reclaimed emcee responsibilities. "Semantics, Father, which I'm sure you'll address later." Then, leading him around the circle of guests, he continued, "And this is Michael Hart, executive director of the party."

"How do you do?" Father Joe said politely.

"Very well, Father, thank you," Mike said in response. "I look forward to your insights."

"And … I'm sorry," the bishop paused, "I don't believe I've met this fine lady."

Mike Hart took the hand-off. "Bishop DeMarco, Father Joseph—"

"Father Joe, please," the priest insisted.

Mike Hart complied, "Father Joe, then, this is Johara Melendez, the governor's liaison to the Latino community." Then, continuing around the room, Mike Hart said, "And while I'm sure the bishop knows Lilith Samuel, Father Joe, this is Lilith, the state Republican Party's chairperson and, my boss."

Father Joe shook her hand. The soft scent of her perfume masked something he couldn't quite place, a subtle smell he knew from his childhood, he thought, burnt hair, perhaps. And her face, withdrawn and dull, seemed familiar. She looked very much like someone he'd seen recently. Again, something he couldn't quite place.

As introductions concluded, the porter returned with a tray. On it were set three wine glasses, one opened and one unopened bottle of wine, a bottle of Diet Coke and a glass of ice. As he attempted to set the glass of ice on the table next to Lilith Samuel's chair, she asked, "Is the soda cold?"

"Yes ma'am," he replied.

"Then save the ice. I don't need the headlines."

Scandalous headlines of politicians abusing fresh water resources were common in the years following the Water Wars. The scarcity of potable water, particularly in the Southwest and the South of the Border states, made ice a luxury, one that an appointed official such as Lilith Samuel found easy to give up.

"I hardly think anything anyone says or does within the Pastoral Center will be offered up to the media," the bishop said, hoping for a chuckle from the crowd and getting only his own.

"Then let's just call it practicing sound resource conservation principles."

The porter filled the empty wine glasses, including the bishop's, and added the precious ice to Father Joe's water, without asking, before retreating into the kitchen.

"Father?" the governor asked Father Joe. "Is there a particular blessing you think might be appropriate for this gathering?"

"This gathering? Hmmm," he pondered. "I suppose you're looking for something more than the standard 'Hail Mary?'" the priest said meekly. He cleared his throat and closed his eyes. "Dear Lord," he started, "Guide us all here today through your grace. Grant us the

55

wisdom of your insight, to know your will, and provide us with the strength to carry it out if the path you lead us down is difficult. In this, and in all things, we pray in the name of the Lord ..." And a chorus finished the blessing, "Amen."

"Wisdom, insight and strength," the governor said. "Very appropriate, Father. Thank you."

"You're welcome," he replied, warmed by the sense of sincerity in the man's voice.

The governor sniffed and sipped wine. "Mmm, that's nice," he said. "Italian?"

"You have a very fine palate, governor," Bishop DeMarco replied.

The governor took a long, slow sip. "Mmm, I do like that very much. And it's my eyesight that is fine, not my palate. I saw the label."

A small rumble of laughter burst forth.

Then the governor asked, "And you, Father Joseph, do you not like wine?"

Startled at first, Father Joe quickly responded, "I'm not a wine coinsurer, governor. Not like you. Not like most, actually. Just a sip or two on Sundays as a specimen of the Blessed Sacrament. I mostly drink water. Vow of poverty helps keep overhead down."

"If you like a particular wine, that's all that matters," the governor said to the bashful priest. "I've had $20 bottles of wine that, for whatever reason, danced on my tongue, and $200 bottles that went down my throat without even a hint of body or flavor. But, this wine I like."

The governor waited to see if anyone else had any other small talk they'd like to get out of the way and, when no one came forth with a topic, the governor continued. "So, Father, let me get right to the point. Bishop DeMarco tells me you have a very special relationship with Estephania Rodriquez. I'd like to hear more about that."

Though he couldn't immediately place it, something felt odd about the way the governor said the name Estephania Rodriquez. He'd been hearing the name for a good long time, during her ministry and especially after her arrest. Since her incarceration, her name always sounded the same when Father Joe heard it; there was always a tone of abhorrence attached like the aftertaste left in ones mouth after vomiting. In a moment he was able to identify the oddity he heard in the governor's use of the name. It came out clean and fresh, as if Father Joe was hearing it for the first time. His immediate reaction was one of distrust. The governor obviously was playing his role of politician.

"A special relationship? I guess. As the prison chaplain, I think I play a very important role for all the women incarcerated at P-Ville. I was telling His Eminence, I mean, Bishop DeMarco, that I consider my work there a sort of missionary."

"And what do you make of this remarkable woman?"

"Remarkable?" Johara Melendez shouted. "She's a cult leader. A blaspheming Christian extremist who placed herself above her country and was sentenced to death for treason."

Damien sat with a whisper thin grin, staring at Johara. "While everything you said is true," he said plainly, "at least from a legal perspective, I use the word remarkable not in terms of being a positive or negative. I'm merely suggesting that in this day and age, when most Americans are so wrapped up in consumerism, instant gratification, the attainment of power and the monetary rewards it brings, I would think any Christian extremist, blaspheming or otherwise, treasonous or otherwise, would be out of the parameters of 'normal' and thus be worth discussion. That is, worth a remark or two. Hence, remarkable."

The Latino woman cowered in her seat as everyone's eyes passed over her. "Well, obviously she goes against the norms of society. And as such, would, yes, I guess, be deemed remarkable."

"Um-hmm," the governor continued. "I couldn't agree more. And you, Father. Do you believe she is worth a remark or two."

"Personally, sir," Father Joe said, feeling suddenly empowered by the governor's reprimand of his liaison, "I believe she is worth far more than just one or two remarks."

"Would you care to elaborate?" said the governor.

The power handed him by the governor washed away when all eyes were upon him and Father Joe was suddenly embarrassed by his beliefs of the divinity of his charge, la Hermana de Jesus. He didn't want to come right out and say what was on his mind. Instead, he thought he'd slowly work up to it, test the waters and build consensus before diving in over his head.

"Well, from the standpoint of treason, I believe this woman was falsely accused and prosecuted."

Johara jumped in again, "So, now you're a lawyer *and* a priest?"

"No, just a priest," Father Joe said immediately, "A priest who knows a thing or two about the justice system, and the human condition. I was a pre-med student at Notre Dame before I entered the seminary, studying to be a psychiatrist. But let me touch on the legal side for just a second. She was prosecuted under the guise of water security with relatively new laws designed to keep foreign companies from setting up operation here in the U.S. and exporting our potable water supplies. They were hastily put in place in a time of panic when our country's very survival was being threatened. And they were put in place without regard for how they might be utilized beyond those narrow applications. Even as we speak they're under review for their constitutionality. And I'm sure most of you here have come to realize, as I know I have, that the road to hell is paved with good intentions." Father Joe looked at the governor and saw a sinister smile stretch across his face. He continued. "So, too, has our legal system been paved with good intentions, yet sometimes, it leads us straight to places we'd rather not go."

"So, you think the law is to blame for this woman being in jail?" asked Mike Hart.

"No, I think we, the citizens of this country, are responsible for allowing our elected officials to do whatever they wanted to keep us safe when we can never be truly safe."

"How can you say that?" Mike Hart asked.

"Mr. Hart, there isn't enough bureaucratic red tape in all the world to protect you from someone who is willing to sacrifice his or her life to end yours. But this has nothing to do with Ms. Rodriquez. Let's just say for argument's sake that the newest constitutional amendment is just, that the Water Security Laws enacted to protect us are prudent, that the legal system as we know it works well, and this woman's case was another fine example of the process working properly. I don't believe any of that, but for argument's sake, let's say that all of that is true. That still doesn't mean la Hermana de Jesus isn't what She claims to be: the sister of Jesus and the Daughter of God. One does not preclude the other."

Silence filled the room. It was a meditative silence heard in mosques, temples, synagogues and churches during lulls in the ceremonial pomp and glory. It was a silence like that heard by parents of a newborn baby before it expels its first breath. It was the silence of the deaf and it lingered for just an instant before Father Joe filled the void.

"I assume that's why we're all here this evening. To determine Who this woman is and what to do with Her once we've made that determination?"

"I wouldn't put it quite like that," Mike Hart said.

"I would," said the governor as everyone looked to him. "That is exactly what I'd say we're doing here tonight. Does anyone think we're doing anything but that?"

Mike Hart tried to interject, "Sir, if I may—"

"No," the governor said. "Not now. I don't want to hear from you, Mike. I know where you stand. You're afraid if we stay the execution, we look soft on crime and lose points with our party core. You're also afraid that I'll lose the Latino community which, for reasons unbeknownst to me, wants her put down like a rabid dog that went crazy at a daycare center. Right now, in this room, I'm not thinking about the party. I'm not thinking about the All-COM blasts or Monday's six o'clock news. I'm thinking about the future, beyond re-election and all the crap I have to put up with from you and the GOP.

"In this room, tonight, I need to know: am I going to go down in history as the guy who killed the Daughter of God?"

"That's ridiculous, sir," Mike Hart said.

Johara Melendez agreed, "Totally ridiculous."

"Why?" the governor insisted. "Because you haven't seen her walk on water? Because you haven't seen her cure lepers or raise the dead?"

"Well, yes, among other things." Mike Hart replied. "I mean, at the beginning of her ministry she was doing a lot of good, but—"

The governor cut him off, "Do you know her parents' names?"

No one answered.

"Maria and José. Mary and Joseph. You want to take a guess what her mother's parents' names were?"

"Joachim and Anne?" Father Joe offered.

"Yes. Very good, Father. Only it's the Latino derivatives Joaquin and Anna."

Father Joe smiled and blushed. "The way you asked it, it seemed obvious." He looked at Lilith sitting idly in the corner and felt once again that he had seen her recently. He thought about the woman who sat next to Estephania during mass at the P-Ville prison, but quickly dismissed the notion. He moved past the brain lock and re-engaged with the conversation.

"Try this on for size," the governor said. "When Estephania was born, her mother's hymen remained intact. A baby's head," he said connecting both his thumbs and forefingers in a circle, "this big came out the birth canal and didn't tear the hymen. I read her medical records. The doctor annotated that he looked for another instance of this in all the medical databases but hers was the only recorded instance. The only one."

"There are thousands of medical anomalies unique to one individual patient," came plainly across the room. The group slowly turned to the new voice added to the discussion. It was Bishop DeMarco's.

"Perhaps, Bishop. But, what about all the other coincidences?"

"Sir," the bishop said in a voice that dripped with feigned patience. "I've been listening to this foolishness for long enough. Our faith and doctrine states we believe in Jesus Christ, His only begotten son."

"Okay, let's look at that," the governor said, setting his wine glass down on the table next to him and inching up to the edge of his chair with his elbows on his knees and hands out in front of him methodically gesturing. "This woman's divinity would not interfere with any of that doctrine. She would be God's only begotten daughter, leaving Jesus to stand alone as his only begotten son."

"And, Your Eminence," added Father Joe, "as I've mentioned before, she claims she will sit at the left hand of the Father."

The bishop, ignoring Father Joe, pleaded with the governor, "Governor—"

"No, hang on. Tell me where in the Old Testament it states unequivocally that the Messiah has to be an only child. Hell, there are well-respected theologians who claim the disciple James was Jesus' brother. Not a brother in the communion with God, but another son of Mary fathered by Joseph."

The bishop, almost indignant, said, "Mary was ever virgin, sir."

"Says who? A bunch of celibate cardinals huddled together in a golden palace in Rome some fourteen hundred years after the death of Christ? I don't even know what I had for breakfast this morning, so how could they possible know with any certainty that Mary was ever virgin? That even though she was a devout Jew by all accounts, she had no relations with her husband, as was and is required by Jewish law?"

"Sir, the Holy Father's unique and divine covenant with our Lord Almighty cannot be validated with facts and proof. It's one of the tenants of our faith."

"And that's what this comes down to, isn't it?" the governor said leaning back into his chair. He let the idea hang heavy in the air. Then he continued. "I was at mass this morning and when I heard the last line of the gospel, I nearly got sick. *When the Son of Man comes, will he find any faith on the earth?* What do you say, Bishop DeMarco? Is there any faith on the earth?"

"Absolutely," the bishop replied confidently.

"I'm not nearly as certain as you are."

A long silence took hold of the room and everyone sipped from his or her glass.

"I can't believe what I'm hearing," Johara Melendez finally shouted. "This woman *es pinche puta loco.*"

"Excuse me, ma'am," Father Joe said. "I've heard that phrase a lot from the Latino community. What's it mean?"

Johara, embarrassed, said, "There is no, um, direct translation for it really, sir."

"Come, now," the governor insisted. "Even I know the English equivalent."

Johara sipped from glass. Then looking the governor in the eyes, she said, "Crazy fucking cunt is about as close as you'll get. Pardon my language." Then, gathering steam once again, she said, "Everyone in *her* community, the chicanos and chicanas, says it, thinks it and believes it. How can anyone in this room even consider ...." Flustered, she trailed off and leaned back in her chair, her hands in fists and her arms crossed over her chest.

The governor shook his head. "One week the Jews were throwing palms down on the ground has He rode a donkey through the city streets and a couple days later they're screaming, 'Crucify Him! Crucify Him!'"

He paused again for effect.

"Look, I don't know if Estephania Rodriquez is the Daughter of God, *la Hermana de Jesus*. The point is no one *knows*. As the bishop pointed out, our faith cannot be validated with facts and proof. Faith is what we believe in the absence of such proof. And right now, I don't know what to believe. I'm here to collect information and then use it to base my decisions as the elected governor of this state. Doing otherwise would be neglecting my duties. Think about it. When Jesus was nailed to the cross, he was being sentenced as a criminal, a civil issue. The Romans had no idea he was the Christ, right? 'Those who ignore the mistakes of the past are destined to repeat them.' Mick Jagger wrote 'I was there when Pilate washed his hands to seal His fate.' I'd like to be far more informed about who this woman is before making any kind of decision that may be immortalized in prose and verse."

The porter entered the room and announced, "Ladies and gentlemen, if you would kindly make your way to the dining table, dinner will be ready in just a few minutes."

CHAPTER 11

"Gentlemen, good evening. My name is Luke Logan. I'm a reporter for the *Republic*. I was wondering if I could ask you a few questions."

"You can ask, but we don't have to answer," said the larger of the two men, his Mexican accent as thick as his neck.

"So noted. Now then, what are you doing outside the governor's mansion?"

"It's a free country, asshole," the smaller Latino titan said.

Then the larger one added, "We're exercising our right to assemble ...," He pulled back his jacket to reveal a pistol nestled in its holster, "and bear arms."

Luke peered into the man's jacket. "Very impressive."

As the huge man aggressively turned in obvious irritation and readjusted his jacket, Luke pulled out his All-COM and started dictating. "A Beretta M9. Semi-automatic, relatively light, 15-round magazine. And the safety was on. It's so very nice to see that the heavily armed are so conscientious about safety."

"You better keep walking, reporter, or you're going to feel a world of hurt."

"Well, let's see," he said with an edge, clicking his All-COM with a flair. "I have a recording of you threatening me with physical violence. Completely unprovoked, mind you." He pushed a few buttons on his All-COM and then said, "And, I just sent it to my voice mail, so destroying this thing does you no good. No, I think I'm going to exercise my right to assemble ... without bearing arms," he added, pulling his jacket open to reveal nothing.

"Last warning," the larger mountain of muscles said softly.

"Or what?"

A quick flash of yellow inside Luke's head faded instantly to black.

* * *

As the two Adherentes walked out of the Blossom, Tom pulled his All-COM from his hip and began scrolling through his directory looking for the listing for Petra or Andrea Fischer. He selected Petra, brought the device up to his ear and listened. The ringing went on uninterrupted until Petra's voice told Tom she was unavailable and to please leave a message.

"Petra, this is Tom. The governor's not at Heritage Mansion, he's at the Pastoral Center over on Monroe. Felipe and I are on our way over there right now. Call me back." He hung up and looked at the device's display screen, noting where the GPS in Petra's phone showed its location.

"She's not there, huh?" Felipe said through the mouthful of nachos he was eating as they walked toward the car.

Already on to the next call, Tom grabbed a chip and shoved it in his mouth. "She left her All-COM in the restaurant. I'm calling one of the Zeday's. I can never remember which is which," he said of the twins with a smile.

Ahead of him, a block away, were the two very large men who had greeted them earlier. Just as before, they approached the two pub patrons, the largest one speaking for them both.

"What are you doing here?"

"Leaving. What are you doing here?"

"Making sure you do just that."

"Hey," he spoke into his All-COM as he pulled it away to look at the display. He noted he was calling Joan, not Jane, and also saw that her GPS also showed her to be at the restaurant. "Joan, this is Tom. Why's everyone back at the restaurant? And why isn't anyone picking up? Call me."

Turning to the car at the curb, Tom was slipping his All-COM into its case when he noticed, across the street and a half way down the block, something odd on the ground. He recognized the grey parka covering the bundled mass and slowly, unconsciously started moving toward it, crossing the street without so much as a glance in either direction. Felipe set the nachos on the car's roof and followed. As they got closer, Tom broke into a run for a few strides and knelt beside Luke Logan, face down on the concrete sidewalk.

"Luke? Luke!"

"Is he with you?" came deep and thick from behind Felipe. It was the larger of the two Latino men who had followed them across the street.

"Kind of," Felipe said.

"You're going to have to get him out of here."

"What'd you do to him?" Tom shouted.

The big man simply replied, "Get him out of here or you can join him."

"We didn't do anything," Felipe whined.

"I'm not saying it again."

"Shit!" Tom muttered, shaking his head. "You guys are nuts. You know that? Felipe! Grab his legs."

Tom rolled his friend onto his back, sat him up and wrapped his arms around Luke's chest, grabbing hold of his own wrists securely. Felipe stepped between Luke's legs and, with an ankle in each hand, hoisted the heap of a man off the ground. They walked to the back of Felipe's car and set down Luke's legs. Felipe rummaged around his pockets for the keys and unlocked the doors.

As they struggled to get Luke into the back seat, Tom noted the two gargantuan men had remained across the street, watching. "Fuckin' animals!" he shouted across the top of the car. He shut the back door, opened the front door and slid into the passenger seat.

"What do we do now?" Felipe asked, still standing outside the car.

"You got a first aid kit?"

"Under the seat."

Tom reached below him and pulled out a small blue box with a big red cross on its white lid. Opening it, he said, "Start the car and go."

"Where? The hospital?"

"No, the Pastoral Center. But first, get the nachos off the roof."

Tom popped open the kit and pulled out a small yellow box, quickly shaking out one of the smelling salts and cracking it in half. As Felipe pulled away from the curb with the nachos in his lap, Tom reached back and waved the small paper-wrapped package under Luke's nose. A moment later, Luke sprang upright in the back seat, coughing and rubbing his eyes.

"What the ...?"

"Hey, Luke. It's me, TJ. You okay?"

Luke looked around, appearing more dazed than crazed. "Huh?"

"Do you know where you are?"

He took a look around and said, "It looks like I'm in the back seat of some piece of shit hydrogen import."

"Piece of shit?" Felipe yelled in his car's defense. "What do you drive?"

Tom simply waved his hand, silently asking Felipe to let it go.

Luke rubbed the back of his head and screamed, "Ahhhhh!" Then, pointing to the first aid kit, "Any aspirin in there?"

Tom turned and rifled through the small blue box and passed back a small paper packet. Luke tore it opened and popped the two pills into his mouth, chewing them like candy. "Anything to drink?"

Felipe grabbed a coffee mug from in between the seats and passed it back, "This is from this morning."

Luke grabbed it and tipped it back without hesitation.

"You weren't kidding, TJ, those fuckers were big. I think the little one jacked me." Then he chuckled, "Little one," as he rubbed back of his head.

"You want to go to the hospital," Felipe asked.

Still rubbing his head, Luke said, "And further tax our already overextended health care system? Not me, brother. I'd much rather go for a ride to the bishop's playpen. But if you'd like to make a stop at my editor's house, which is not even remotely on the way, I'm feeling particularly cranky at the moment," he added.

CHAPTER 12

Fischer's Trattoria was quiet as most of the Adherentes sat and contemplated what to do next. The very large men outside the governor's mansion were more than enough of a deterrent to send them on their way without so much as a single protest sign being waved. The white poster board and wooden handles remained untouched in the back of Petra's vehicle.

"Well, that was a big waste of time," Simone complained.

"It wasn't a total waste," Jane Zeday said. "At least now we know we're a bunch of pathetic losers who are afraid of our own shadows."

"I ain't afraid of my shadow," Nate the Great said. "Just big Mexicans with guns who threaten to kill me if I don't go away. Even on the street you learn pretty quick to listen to the big Mexicans."

"Okay, Nate, not our shadows. But what about the All-COMs?" Jane asked. "We know Tom's trying to get in touch with us and we're paralyzed with fear at the prospect of having to tell him we ran away. I'll say it again, we're a bunch of pathetic losers."

"Speak for yourself," Petra erupted.

"Yeah, well, you didn't mind me speaking for the whole group when I was filing all of those appeals, my firm slipping further and further in debt while you sat back and ran this restaurant as if you didn't have a care in the world."

Petra stood up and walked over to Jane. Then, she said, "Not a care in the world? Look at this place! Nate the Great has more money jingling in his pockets than I have right now. My husband's left me and taken the kids. No cares in the world, Jane? Is that what you think? We all sacrificed for Her. All of us! Don't think you're the only one hurting right now, because you're not. Every single one of us has a stake in this."

Simone stood and yelled, "C'mon, people! We all have a stake in this. Not you," she said pointing to Petra. Then pointing at Jane, "Not you. All of us. Everyone. And not just here, but everywhere. She is the Daughter of God. Every man, woman and child walking the face of this earth has a stake in this."

"So what are you going to do about it, Porn Queen?" Joan Zeday shouted.

"Well, I'm not going to start calling people names. That's first on the list. Second, just like all of you, I'm waiting. Waiting for something or someone to show me the way now that She's no longer here to do it. And I'm no leader."

"She was arrested almost a year and a half ago!" Jane yelled. "And all we've done is sit here week after week waiting, waiting, waiting. I'm sick of waiting."

"Then do something," Simone shot back.

Jane looked around and saw all eyes on her. She wanted to fight, to be strong, to come up with a plan. But she, like the rest of them, was lost without Her inspiration. "I wish I could," she finally said, "but I can't." She sat down and buried her face in her folded arms on the table in front of her.

Nate the Great looked around at the somber faces filling the room and whispered, "This sucks!"

Though it was but a whisper, everyone heard it.

CHAPTER 13

"Everyone's been served, your Eminence," the porter whispered into the bishop's ear.

The bishop nodded and stood. He asked everyone to hold hands as he offered an uninspired, traditional grace. When the bishop seated himself, Damien asked him, "Have you had any dealings with this woman? Have you done any investigative work into her divinity?"

The bishop glared at Father Joe as if the priest had had something to do with the governor's questions. The bishop looked down at his plate and answered, "Governor, the Church has no official opinion one way or the other. By looking into the matter we would lend a certain amount of instant credibility to her claims. Considering there are hundreds of such claims made every year, thousands actually, the Catholic Church has taken a 'wait and see' approach."

The governor didn't miss a beat. "Isn't that a bit like an ostrich burying its head in the sand? Wouldn't the Church be inclined to get in on the ground floor, so to speak?"

"Discretion is the better part of valor," Mike Hart said, "Wouldn't you say, Bishop DeMarco?"

The governor didn't even look at Mike, knowing all too well the man was simply trying to provide cover fire for the individual responsible for such a large portion of the party's annual budget.

"Is that true, Father Joe?" the governor asked.

Father Joe had, just moments before, placed a large piece of steak into his mouth and was not prepared to speak. He pulled his napkin from his lap and covered his mouth, chewing, embarrassed that everyone was staring at him and awaiting his comments.

"Father Joe cannot be expected to speak for the Church," the bishop offered.

"No offense, Bishop, but neither can you. You're a mid-level executive in a spiritual corporation. You toe the corporate line, stay on message, but in the end, you report to a cardinal who in turn reports to the Pope. He's the CEO and God's the Chairman of the Board. We, and I'm talking about all of us practicing Catholics, we're the employees, the shareholders and the end users all wrapped up in one. And what do we get for our investment of time, treasure and talent? The ultimate retirement plan."

Damien had come up with the corporate analogy on the drive from Heritage Manor to the Pastoral Center. He was secretly pleased with how he presented it. He was equally pleased that the bishop was visibly upset by it.

"From this corporate perspective," Damien continued, "I'd like to know what the general manager of a single storefront has to say about how the conglomerate is handling an issue with which he seems to be far more in touch."

Bishop DeMarco, incensed to have the Church compared to the Ever-Mart Corporation, took a moment to collect himself. He looked like he was about to say something, but then simply made a gesture indicating he had nothing to say and sipped his wine instead.

The governor turned to the priest. "Father?"

"I'm sorry," Father Joe said. "What was the question?"

"Do you think a wait and see approach is prudent in this particular situation?"

"Well, governor, the bishop is right. There are claims of divinity made all the time. To investigate all of them would be a major undertaking and a distraction of our spiritual duties. However," he said, looking sheepishly at the bishop, "in this particular instance, I have been personally involved for almost a year and I have struggled to understand the subtle nuances and the intricacies surrounding the Church's reluctance to investigate the matter more fully."

"So you believe she is divine?"

"Now, governor, I didn't say that," he said with a wry smile. "What I said was that I believe the Church should not, as you stated, take a wait and see approach or bury its head in the sand."

The governor persisted. "Do you believe she is what she claims. The Daughter of God? La Herman de Jesus?"

He collected his thoughts. "I believe Estephania Rodriquez is the most spiritually significant individual to walk this earth in a very long time, perhaps since Jesus ascended into heaven. If you had ever heard Her speak, you'd know exactly what I'm talking about," he said, trailing off in fond remembrance of his Sunday afternoon conversations with her. "Her understanding of the Gospels, Old Testament scripture, the entire bible. Her personification of love, God's love, unconditional and for all, all people and all things. The way She makes you feel just sitting with Her in total silence, knowing you are sitting with, with, well, with a most tranquil and loving being.

"I've sat in audience with the Holy Father in Rome when I was a novice. Just me and a few other seminarians. When he spoke, it was with the voice of a man, completely human. A holy man, no doubt, but a man of flesh and bones, nonetheless. When She speaks, it's as though She speaks with God's voice. Not God's message, God's voice, as if Her vocal cords were the harp of angels and Her breath the winds of heaven. It's so hard to explain. It's beyond anything I've ever experienced in my life."

Father Joe was startled after several seconds of blissful silence was broken by the bishop.

"Yes, Father Joe has been quite enamored with this Rodriquez woman for a while, now. But, governor, his story is not unique. All those with claims of Messianic divinity have a stream of followers who believe these claims, some with even more impressive pedigrees than our Father Joseph, here. And, once again, if we were to believe all of these, or even a small fraction of these, we'd be back to pagan worship, praying to a host of gods.

"The Church is founded on a somewhat difficult to articulate Holy Trinity: one God in three … the Father, the Son and the Holy Spirit. Someone once tried to explain it to me this way. You have a thought, someone thinking that thought and the act of thinking it. The three are all one—thinker, thinking and thought—in existence simultaneously yet distinctly different. That is what we believe and what we profess every Sunday.

"Now, governor," Bishop DeMarco continued, gaining steam, "I may not be the CEO of this spiritual corporation and it may just be me staying on message, but the fact is, I do not see the Holy Father initiating an investigation into this woman's divinity or the church veering in the least toward some holy quadrumvirate."

The governor smiled and looked at the bishop from the corners of his eyes. "Quadrumvirate? Did you have to look that up, Your Eminence?"

He didn't wait for an answer. "Before Jesus began his ministry, where was He?"

"What do you mean?"

"At twelve years old He's in the temple with the elders and then He shows up at the River Jordan to be baptized by John. Where was He all those years in between?"

"I'm sorry, I don't understand—" the bishop started.

"India, right? Most scholars say Jesus sojourned to India. It's where His radical teachings of love thy neighbor came from. Hinduism. Biblical doctrine was an eye for an eye, yet He's telling everyone 'No, turn the other cheek.' Isn't that one of the things the high priests and elders pointed to when they made the claims that He was a heretic?"

"Yes, well, it's never been fully agreed upon where he was."

"No. But there is a general sense that that's where He was, Your Eminence. Guess what Miss Rodriquez was doing before her ministry? She was in Raghunathpur, a decent-sized city in Purulia, India, digging wells and plowing fields for the Peace Corps. She was there for twelve years, from the moment she graduated high school until she started her ministry.

"How old was Jesus when he started His ministry? Thirty, right? And, according to most scholars, and the Gospel of John, if I'm not mistaken, He spent three years spreading The Word before dying on the cross. It took a year for the ministry of la Hermana de Jesus to get up a head of steam, and another nine months of solid preaching. And with the instantaneousness of information delivery these days, that was more than enough time to warrant a handful of TV news magazines and a few of the national news outlets to profile her and her ministry. Add on another fifteen months for her arrest, trial, appeals, whatever else, plus the fact that her ministry is still going—"

"Oh, please!" Johara Melendez shouted. "That ministry is all but dead. A few underground assemblies does not constitute—"

"Hey," the governor interrupted. "It may be small, but it does continue. Jesus had only twelve disciples and it didn't seem to hamper His following." Then he looked off for a moment. "Where was I? Oh yes, most scholars agree that the Gregorian calendar is off by three years, that Jesus was actually born in 3 B.C., not the year 0; something to do with when King Herod actually reigned over Judea. He was thirty when He started His ministry and died at thirty-three. Ms. Rodriquez was born in 1997, started her ministry in 2027 and is set to die tomorrow: October of 2030. Do the math."

The room fell silent. But only for a moment.

"You can't be serious, governor," Bishop DeMarco said in disgust. "The magical number 2000 rolls around and it's time for the second coming? That's ludicrous. It's no more significant than the Mayan's 2012 mumbo-jumbo."

Damien leaned forward with a seemingly insatiable thirst for knowledge. "Why?" And when no answer came immediately, he pressed, "What about absolution?"

"Jesus has already absolved us from sin," the bishop answered.

"I'm not talking about *original* sin, Your Eminence? Take a look back on the last two thousand years of human existence. Are you going to tell me there's no need for subsequent absolution? Even the Catholic Church—the Crusades, selling indulgences, the Grand Inquisition, the molestation scandals—*especially* the Catholic Church could do with a little spiritual cleansing, don't you think?"

The bishop dismissively said "Father Joe, would you please explain why a second resurrection is unnecessary?" and sipped his wine.

"Certainly, Your Eminence." Father Joe took a moment. "Okay, Jesus died for all our sins, not just original sin. You see, man, Adam actually, was made in the image of God and that image was perfect. When he ate the forbidden fruit of the tree he sinned and separated man from God. The punishment for sin was mortality: spiritual and physical death. We have no way to break the barriers of a physical death, but when Jesus died on the cross, sinless and perfect, by His choice, He absolved us of original sin and provided use with the opportunity to avert our spiritual death. Having died for us, He can forgive anyone's sins forever if they only chose to be forgiven. It is our personal choice, God's gift of free will, and He has left that decision to each of us. *For God so loved the world, that He gave His only begotten Son, that whoever believes in Him shall not perish, but have eternal life.* John 3:16

"So, any second resurrection would be superfluous. Like a second sunrise."

73

"Not according to the Dead Sea Scrolls," the governor offered. "The prophecy isn't complete. Has anyone been reading the translations of the Dead Sea Scroll fragments that have been coming out for the past few months? There are a handful of prophetic scrolls that identify this, right now, as the age of the resurrection of the second Messiah."

As the gathered faithful scoffed at Damien, he pulled his All-COM from his hip. "Hang on a second." He punched a few buttons and regained his momentum. "Here it is. 4Q 1021: 'And when the once fertile land ... becomes as arid as the dessert ... and tribes war for their thirst ... the second Messiah will bring His quenching water to all.'"

"A second Messiah comes after the Water Wars?" the bishop grumbled. "That's ridiculous!"

"Ridiculous," Johara echoed.

"Not at all," Father Joe interrupted. A look of contemplation and understanding crossed his face. "I don't know about the prophecy of the Water Wars, but Zechariah Chapter 4 talks about the two olive trees on either side of a golden lamp. The lamp is God, the Light of the world. Verses 12 through 14:

12 'And again I asked, 'What are the two olive tufts which freely pour out fresh oil through the two golden channels?'

13 'Do you not know what these are?' he said to me. 'No, my Lord,' I answered him.

14 He said, 'These are the two anointed who stand by the Lord of the whole earth.'"

Adrenaline coursed through Damien's body as he began to see a linear progression of the argument. He typed on his All-COM again and said, "And there are other passages in the Dead Sea Scrolls to suggest multiple Messiahs. 1QS 9.11: 'They shall be judged by the ancient precepts ... until the coming of ... the Messiahs of Aaron and Israel.'" Damien looked up. "It says Messiahs—plural." Then, punching a few more buttons, "And then 4Q 254 states 'the two [heirs] of oil of anointing ... observed the precepts of God ...' Two heirs. And 'the oils of anointing' ... nearly word-for-word with Father Joe's passage."

"Zechariah 4: 12-14," Father Joe beamed. "Well, the entire fourth chapter, actually."

Their combined efforts brought clarity to the governor's mind, a clarity missing for so many months due to his struggles. "Look, I may be grasping at straws here, but does anyone else think that all these coincidences add up to more than nothing? That they actually might add up to something?"

"No, you're not alone, Governor," Father Joe said before taking a sip of his water.

"What if," Damien offered, "the second coming isn't the *End of Days* with fire and brimstone and the four horsemen of the apocalypse but an end to the beginning Jesus began two thousand years ago and the beginning of something new, something wonderful. A second sunrise, warm and nurturing."

"We're missing the point, here," Johara Melendez said, unable to contain her annoyance. "You've all come back to the ridiculous and absurd notion that this woman is God, a new leaf on St. Patrick's clover. This woman isn't God. She's crazy. Just like the thousands of other nut jobs Bishop DeMarco says claim to be Jesus or the thousands of Christian evangelists who claim God spoke to them and told them to start a ministry in his name.

"This is no different, and it distresses me, governor, to hear you lend credence to these claims. This is not the kind of leadership the Latino community voted for." Her voice was layered with a hidden strength the governor hadn't heard from her before.

"With the removal of the border between the U.S. and Mexico," the governor said, "nearly half the state's population is Latino. I'm well aware of my responsibilities to that group. However, does the Latino community, does *anyone* want a governor who makes knee-jerk decisions based on emotions? Or are they looking for someone who makes decisions based on deep deliberations following the methodical collection of information?"

Johara's cheeks blushed through her heavy make-up.

"Ms. Melendez, I understand that your community's Catholic faith runs deep. So does mine. But it is the Bishop, here, who is responsible for decisions of faith. Not me. I am a civil servant whose responsibilities are secular. My religion and the religion of my constituents may very well play a part in my decisions, but they are not my focus. They are peripheral. Please keep that in mind as we move forward."

"Yes, sir," she said. "But sir, they call her ... *we* call her," she paused, embarrassed to say the words again in front of the bishop and Father Joe, *"pinche puta loco.* Has anyone considered the matter of her sanity?"

"If she's insane, she can't be put to death," Lilith, wholly quiet the entire debate, finally chimed.

"That will *not* sit well with the party core," Mike Hart said, shaking his head.

"At the moment, Mike," the governor said, his voice soft and even. "Screw the party core." Then he looked at Johara. "I have a few files on my desk to go through, including some court documents. Some of them specifically address her mental state. And tomorrow morning I'm meeting with the prison psychologist as well as the defense's and prosecutor's doctors who determined her fit to stand trial."

Johara sat back, apparently impressed with the governor's thoroughness.

"So, what now?" asked the governor.

"Pie," announced the bishop with a feigned smile. "Pumpkin or cherry?"

CHAPTER 14

The three men left the small, hydrogen import in the parking lot, walking briskly toward the front of the Diocesan Pastoral Center. In addition to rubbing the back of his head, Luke began squinting his crazy eyes and wriggling his scruffy jaw back and forth.

"Have you ever met the governor?" Felipe asked Luke.

"Couple times."

"How about the bishop?"

"Couple times."

"What do you think's going on in there?"

"Don't know."

The answers came so quick on the heels of the questions, Felipe wondered if Luke was even listening. "I thought you got paid to know things."

"I do."

"And you don't know what's going on in there?"

"No"

"You must get paid handsomely."

Luke stopped walking and the two others, noticing his absence, did the same and turned toward him. Luke walked up to Felipe, pointed his finger in his face and said, "Look, Gunga Din, I don't work the city beat, sitting in conference rooms and rummaging around City Hall for rumors. I write in-depth, investigative pieces: topical non-fiction more than news. My apologies for not having the meeting's agenda, but I've been working on other things."

"I see," Felipe said, recognizing he'd reached the limits of the conversation and Luke's patience.

As the three men continued, they turned the corner from the parking lot to the front of the center and were surprised to see two very large Latino men watching them approach the front door.

"Holy fuck! Are they cloning these guys or what?" Luke whispered.

"Can I help you?" the guard to the left of the entrance asked. His accent was thin and his annunciation precise.

Luke didn't hesitate. "Yeah, we're here to see the bishop."

"I'm sorry," said the large, eloquent man. "He's not available at the moment. Perhaps you can make an appointment at the office of the cathedral for some time later in the week."

"Did I say bishop? I meant the governor," Luke said, trying to slip between the two men. He was utterly unsuccessful.

"Sir, the bishop is having a private dinner at the moment. I can neither confirm nor deny who else is inside, but I *can* confirm that you are in serious jeopardy of being physically removed from the premises if you persist in trying to enter."

"Well," Luke scoffed, stepping back. "You're at least more pleasant about being an asshole than your buddies over at Heritage Mansion. You're not going to whack me on the head and knock me out, are you?"

"Not yet," the large, eloquent man said.

The two men stood silent, arms crossed, their bodies completely concealing the closed, hand-carved doors of the center everyone knew stood behind them.

Luke turned and walked away, muttering under his breath.

Tom and Felipe followed Luke beyond the front façade of the building toward the parking lot.

"So what do we do now?" Felipe asked before turning the corner.

When they finally reached the building's corner, the two men lagging behind found that Luke had burst into a sprint and was several yards away, turning the next corner toward the back of the Pastoral Center. They, too, sprinted to catch up and, when they came to the end of the wall and turned the corner, saw Luke standing on the back stoop fumbling with his notebook.

"What the hell are you doing?" Tom whispered through his panted breathing.

"I'm showing Gunga Din, here, why I get paid handsomely."

Luke stopped fumbling through his notebook and began pushing the keys of the keypad beside the building's rear door. A green light flashed and an audible click brought a long, toothy smile to his scruffy face. He grabbed the handle, pulled the door open and politely said, "After you, asshole."

* * *

78

Father Joe, seated facing the kitchen doors, saw them first. They were three men who looked nothing like the usually well-kept staff of the Pastoral Center. He wiped his mouth with his napkin and stared blankly at them as they strode into the room.

Bishop DeMarco, seeing Father Joe's attention elsewhere, turned and saw them. He exploded. "This is a private dinner!"

"So we heard," Luke replied. "I'm Luke Logan with the *Republic* and I was hoping the governor would tell me why he's dining with the bishop on the evening before Estephania Rodriquez is scheduled to be executed."

Johara Melendez stood and walked quickly to the front door.

Luke pointed in Melendez's direction and continued undeterred, "Governor? A quick reply before those gorillas out front come in here and tear my face off."

"This is private property," the bishop said. "You're not allowed in here."

"So, Bishop," Luke said smugly, "your official policy is that no one from the general public is allowed inside the Diocesan Pastoral Center?"

The bishop capitulated. "Well, of course that's not the policy of this ... it's just—"

Luke hammered again, "Governor?"

Mike Hart had positioned himself between the reporter and the governor. "The governor has no comment at this time."

Melendez came back into the room with the two giants in tow. The guards were circling around the three intruders when the governor finally spoke.

"Mr. Logan ..."

Mike Hart turned quickly around and, looking directly into the governor's eyes, said, "The governor has no comment at this time."

The governor smiled at Mike and then moved out of his seat toward the three party-crashers and their mountainous escorts.

"Mr. Logan," he said, "Would you care for some pie? The cherry pie is delicious."

The room fell silent. Tom and Felipe exchanged glances, as did the two guards, the two clerics, and Mike Hart and Johara Melendez. Lilith Samuel, remaining silent, smiled and sipped her cola.

"I haven't had a good cherry pie in quite a while," Luke said.

"You won't be disappointed," said the governor, motioning to the empty seats at the end of the large table. "Bishop, could you please find the porter and ask him to bring …," he looked at the two men on either side of Luke, "Three?"

Felipe and Tom nodded their heads, seemingly unaware they were doing so.

"Three pieces of cherry pie for Mr. Logan and his friends."

The bishop sat, paralyzed in disbelief.

Father Joe stood. "I'll see to it, sir. And I'll make sure the porter brings coffee."

"And a cold glass of milk," Luke shouted to the priest disappearing through the kitchen door. Then, he sat down where the governor had motioned, leaned heavily onto the table and added, "Nothing goes better with cherry pie than a cold glass of milk. Don't you think, Damien?"

The governor gave no reaction, he simply stayed standing and watched. The rest of the group retreated to their previous places, except the two large Mexican men who merely stepped back, ready to pounce should the need arise.

"Mr. Logan," the governor said, "I find your use of my first name somewhat disrespectful, particularly in light of the fact that I just invited you to join us for dessert."

Luke's face flushed. "Yes, well, I have issues with authority figures. My apologies, Governor Driver."

"Apology accepted. Now then, if I may reply to your previous inquiry, the reason I am dining with the bishop on the evening before Ms. Rodriguez is scheduled to be executed is because I was hungry."

The two men exchanged smiles. Neither appeared particularly happy.

Father Joe returned with two coffee pots in his hands. The porter followed behind.

Luke quickly acknowledged them and then just as quickly ignored them. "Did you discuss the impending execution of Estephania

Rodriquez while you and your esteemed colleagues sat down to what I'm certain was a scrumptious meal?"

"We discussed a great many things during the course of the evening."

"So, that's a yes?"

"No, it is not."

Luke looked at Tom and then Felipe and scoffed in an exaggerated expression of his frustration.

"Sir," Felipe said, standing up as he did so and causing Luke to do a double take. "I am one of Her followers, an Adherente, and all of us, well, not Mr. Logan here, but all of the Adherentes were going to march around the mansion tonight in protest, but two thugs were there to prevent such a thing from happening so we came here. We wanted to get some media coverage of our protest against the execution, but none of the stations would bother and it's just, this woman, if you ever met Her, you would instantly understand that She is, by all accounts, supremely divine."

"Pardon me, Señor ...?"

Felipe filled in the blank. "My name is Felipe Martinez."

"Pardon the interruption, Señor Martinez, but this particular subject falls under governmental policy. I am neither willing nor able to discuss with you, and especially not with your friend, Mr. Logan here, my stance on the situation." Turning to Mike Hart he added, "That's a fancy way of saying 'No comment.'" Then he turned to Felipe again. "You are more than welcome to stay here and eat some of the most delicious cherry pie you're ever going to taste, but, gentlemen, I must now leave you in the care of my gracious host, Bishop DeMarco."

The governor got up and as he walked toward the exit, his entourage scuttled about trying to keep up, muttering incoherently. The bishop walked hurriedly to shake the hand of each of his guests on their way out the massive front doors, speaking a few hushed final thoughts to Mike Hart. Then, the others gone and him standing alone in the middle of the Center's gathering area, the bishop announced, "Father Joseph, please see these kind people out when they finish their dessert." And with that, the bishop left them, disappearing through an interior door at the far end of the space.

Father Joe smiled awkwardly at the three men eating pie. His face wrinkled with surprise when he noticed Lilith Samuel from the governor's staff still seated at the table. Her perplexing familiarity brought a curious look to the priest's face. The other men saw the odd expression on and, in response, turned to the woman, offering her a cluster of awkward smiles.

Father Joe finally spoke. "I'm sorry, ma'am, was there anything else you needed?"

"No. Not really. I'm just a fly on the wall over here."

Luke shoved a large forkful of pie into his mouth and garbled, "Oh yeah? So what's your take on all of this, Miss ... Samuel? Is that correct?"

"It is." she replied. "Miss Lilith Samuel, Republican Party chairwoman for the state, but then you knew that, didn't you? And my take on all this is utter fascination."

Luke looked at Father Joe and then back to the woman. "Utter fascination, you say. What's so fascinating?"

"All of it," she replied. "The governor's thoroughness, Father Joe's struggles, the Bishop's obstinacy, your intrusion. All of it. Fascinating."

She took a slow sip of cola while the others sat dumbfounded.

Luke shoveled another piece of pie into his mouth and nodded his head as if he knew what the woman was talking about. He sipped his milk and wiped his mouth with his left hand which he then wiped on his pant leg.

"Father Joe, what's your role in all of this?"

Embarrassed, he hesitated, smiled and said, "I'm sorry, I'm here at the request of the bishop. I have no comment."

Luke turned to the woman at the end of the table. "What exactly is Father Joe struggling with?"

"They're his struggles," she said. Then holding up her hands, she added, "Fly on the wall."

"Father Joe?" Felipe asked. "Are you and the bishop trying to stop the execution?"

Father Joe cleared his throat. "The Catholic Church has always been opposed to capital punishment. I really have no other comment on the subject."

"Who are you?" asked Tom, wiping the residue of cherry filling from the corners of his mouth with a napkin.

"Me?" the priest asked. "I'm Father Joseph Romano."

"Not always," Luke said flatly.

"Excuse me?" Father Joe asked in reply.

"The Catholic Church. It hasn't always been opposed to capital punishment."

"Well, that's very true, Mister Logan. However, the past few centuries the Church's doctrine has been quite clear on the subject."

"So, what's your role in all this?" Tom fired back.

"I'm the chaplain at the P-Ville prison."

Felipe beamed, unable to contain his excitement. "Then you know! You know who She is. That She's the Daughter of God. La Hermana de Jesus."

The priest looked down into his lap. In Felipe's voice was the same excitement that comes from being in on a wonderful secret. He wished he could tell the excited Adherente 'yes,' let everyone know how he felt about her, but he knew his presence in that room was as a representative of the Catholic Church which took precedence over his love for her and for which all that she stood. He simply said, "I'm sorry, I have no comment."

"You're going to save Her, aren't you?" Felipe continued.

"Spiritually, if I can. If She's not already. As for stopping the execution, I have no authority and very little leverage. And, honestly, I have to return to my pastoral duties at Christ King in Goodyear. I don't want to be rude, but perhaps you could finish your coffee and be on your way. I believe the bishop and I have been as patient as can be expected considering the fashion in which you gentlemen arrived."

"Padre?" Felipe said, "Would it be possible for me to come with you? To Goodyear?"

"Excuse me?"

"I can see it in your face, Padre. You know. As surely as I do, you know. Please, let me come with you and we can talk. Talk about Her."

Again, he looked into his lap. Then he said, "I'm sorry, but ..."

"Me, too!"

All the men turned slowly to face the woman at the end of the table.

"I'd like to come as well," Lilith reaffirmed.

Father Joe stood up and sarcastically said, "Sure, why don't we all go."

Luke stood up. "Not me. I got an editor I need to beat the crap out of. But thanks for the offer." Then, as he made his way to the front entrance, the two large Latino men followed him. He said over his shoulder. "And thanks for the pie. Tell the bishop it was excellent."

Upon exiting the front doors, Luke's voice boomed. While the words were incomprehensible, his friendly tone, apparently aimed at the two large men accompanying him, was readily apparent and put a smile on Tom's face. Then, the door shut and instantly cut off all sound from the outside.

Tom spoke. "I know you weren't serious about all of us going with you, but even if you were, I can't. Felipe, you and I should get back to the restaurant. I'm sure everyone—"

"No," Felipe said, his timbre steady and resolute. "I need to be with Father Joe. The second I walked into this room I knew I was supposed to be here. I didn't know why, but now I do. I'm going with him. I have to."

"I'm going, too, Father," Lilith said. "Like Mister Martinez, here, there's a tiny voice telling me I have to go with you." An uncomfortable smile crept arose her face. "Call it an epiphany."

Father Joe knew Bishop DeMarco would never approve. To provide these two people with false hope that this woman deserved more than tertiary consideration outside the scope of anti-death penalty discussions was not his to give. Yet, looking into Felipe's eyes, the priest saw the yearning for something more and the same frustration he shared. They had the knowledge of what they knew and yet the inability to share it with anyone else.

Tom, trying to understand the dynamics of the group, took the opportunity of silence afforded him, stood and thanked the priest for his hospitality. Felipe threw him the keys to his car and, without another word, Tom left the three remaining guests to work things out amongst themselves.

Father Joe finally stood, smiling. "An epiphany, you say? Well, who am I to stand in the way of such an occasion? Grab your things. My car's out back."

As they headed out through the kitchen, Father Joe asked, "How do you plan on getting back here?"

"The Lord will provide, Padre," Felipe said solemnly with the slightest hint of a smirk.

CHAPTER 15

"This is fine, driver," Damien said plainly.

He had always made it a point to remember people's names and use them frequently to build familiarity. However, his drivers were being switched with such unusual regularity that he fell into the habit, a very bad habit by his estimations, of amalgamating all of his drivers into a single entity, dehumanized and referred to only by the service they provided.

The driver stopped and the governor exited the vehicle in a hurry. With everything he had read and heard throughout the day, his mind was consumed beyond distraction. Had he seen the two large Mexican men patrolling the streets in front of Heritage Mansion, his home, as he breezed past them he would not have known what to say. As it was, he strode past them in the waning twilight without cognition and without a word, as if they were figments of someone else's imagination.

He took the front stairs two at a time and lunged for the doorknob, which he did not turn fully, causing him to walk face-first into the door. His second attempt at entering his home was successful and, once inside, he allowed himself to feel silly and embarrassed, laughing a bit as he bent over, put his hands on his knees and rested his posterior against the door.

"What's so funny?"

He jerked his head up. His wife, Sophia, stood on the other side of the entryway and flipped on the hallway light.

He pushed himself off the door. "I was in such a hurry I nearly knocked myself unconscious trying to get through the door." He laughed as he spoke and she laughed with him.

"Too much wine?"

He looked at her quizzically. "How'd you know we had wine?"

"You always have wine. Bishop DeMarco always serves wine. What's not to know?"

Damien shrugged in recognition. He walked across the entryway and embraced his wife. Her hair smelled of honey and apricots. "To answer your question; wine, yes. Too much, no. I have a lot of reading to do tonight."

"Reading?" It sounded almost like a scolding to Damien's ears. "Your daughter is making us grandparents and you want to read? Damien—"

"Ah, ah, ah. No lecturing. We've been telling our children for years that we have to do what we have to do before we can do what we want to do. Tuesday night, after this has all settled down, we'll go over to Laura's place and celebrate properly. However, between now and then ..."

She broke the embrace and walked toward the hallway leading to the bedrooms. "Yes, yes. Blah, blah, blah. I get it." It was sarcastic, yet loving. She was telling him she understood and was poking fun at him all at the same time. It was her way and it was one of the many reasons she made such a wonderful politician's spouse. "Are you going to be up late?"

He thought about the stack of folders on his desk. "Probably. Don't wait up."

"Fine, I won't. But you stay away from the coffee."

He dismissed her parting shot with a soft wave of his hand but she had already turned to leave and never saw it.

Damien entered his study, flicked on the overhead light, walked around his desk and eased into his chair. He turned on his desk lamp and laughed to himself at his metaphorical need for more illumination.

The folders were just as he had left them, neatly stacked in two piles. To his left were the first six folders chronicling her life up to and including her ministry. To his right sat a slightly smaller pile consisting of the five folders he had not yet reviewed for the million-and-first time. Thoughts of Father Joe and the comments he had made ran through the governor's mind. He wanted to go directly to the last folder labeled *Incarceration* to see how Father Joe might fit in, but he resisted the urge and instead picked up the *Her Following* folder, set it down and opened it. Damien reached for his glasses case beside the folders to his left, pulled them out and slipped them on in a single, fluid motion.

God help me, this is going to be a long night, he thought to himself.

CHAPTER 16

Slate-colored storm clouds hung heavy in the evening sky. The light pollution emanating from the millions of residents who called the city behind them home reflected off the clouds and across the remote landscape which stretched out for miles in front of them. Even inside the car, the passengers could smell the approaching rain. Lilith sat in front, at Felipe's insistence, while Felipe, whose proper seat was in the back, wedged himself between the two front seats to better engage in the various conversations. The solar electric engine was inaudible above the low, droning hum of the road beneath the vehicle's tires which provided a steady white noise to occupy the few lulls in dialogue.

The initial social interaction between the three travelers was awkward and filled with distinct moments of trepidation and unspoken misgivings regarding the entire affair. However, just as they were able to navigate their way through the cluttered stop-and-go traffic of the city to eventually find a pleasant, comfortable driving rhythm on the highway, so, too, did their conversation eventually find a pleasant comfortableness.

"So, is he just being obstinate?" Lilith asked Father Joe of the bishop.

"I don't think so," Father Joe said.

"Or is he just spewing Catholic rhetoric?" Felipe asked.

"Catholic rhetoric, yes, but not in the negative way you're using the term rhetoric. He's absolutely sincere and he's unquestioningly devout to his calling. And because of that, he's unwavering in his acceptance of Church doctrine. I think …" He paused. "I think he's just being pragmatic. Or, better yet, dogmatic. He believes what he believes and until the hand of God comes down and either strikes him dead or enlightens him through some miracle of miracles, he can't even consider the possibility that—"

A thunderous noise filled the sedan's interior space as the car lunged forward and swerved back and forth across the highway. Father Joe instinctively pressed the accelerator to the floor and used every inch of paved roadway to regain control of his vehicle.

When he was fifteen and just learning to drive, Father Joe's father had stated over and over that if he were to panic on the road, panic with the accelerator, not the brake. It was tattooed onto his subconscious.

He eased up on the pedal and looked into his rearview mirror. He could barely make out a very large man behind the wheel of an enormous truck. Though not yet dark, the truck's high-beams made it difficult to discern any additional details save one: the man behind the wheel was dressed in white.

Father Joe began to pull over to the side of the road when Lilith began screaming. "Don't pull over! Are you insane? Keep driving! Keep driving!"

Father Joe, confused and pliable, pressed down again on the accelerator and remained in the rightmost lane.

"But we just had an accident," he pleaded.

"That was no accident!" Lilith replied.

The thunderous noise returned and echoed inside the car once more, this time layered with the sound of the back window's tempered glass spider-webbing into thousands of tiny pieces. Again, the car lunged forward and swerved. Father Joe hammered on the accelerator once more as he struggled to regain control. A handful of the glass nuggets popped free and rained down around Felipe, surrounding him in a puddle of light and dark green facets.

"And neither was that!" Lilith yelled.

"What's going on?" Felipe asked, his hands over his head.

"Don't let them pass us," Lilith barked out, looking beyond Felipe's head through the distorted rear window. "Go as fast as you can and don't let them pass us."

"I don't understand," Father Joe mumbled, pressing the accelerator harder, though it was already firmly pressed against the floor.

The vehicle behind them instantly lost ground to the priest's sedan but remained about one hundred feet behind them as the speedometer slowly rotated clockwise.

"Highway 101 is coming up, right?" Lilith shouted.

"I-I-I don't know." Father Joe said, seemingly petrified as his car screamed down the highway at nearly 100 miles per hour.

"There's a sign up ahead," Felipe said. "For 91st Avenue. One mile."

Lilith looked at Father Joe. His eyes were wide, his face pale and his hands gnarled into granite fists around the steering wheel. "Okay," she announced, "you're going to get off at this exit, drive straight through the intersection and get back on the on-ramp. No stopping."

"What about the cross traffic?" the frightened priest asked.

"No stopping!" she yelled. Both Lilith and Felipe stared out the cracked back window. Father Joe peeked as often as he could into the rearview mirror. All three anxiously watched the truck gradually getting closer and closer as their vehicles continued down the road.

"You're sure you want me to get off at the next exit?"

"Yes!" she screamed. "And everyone buckle up."

Instinctively, Father Joe put on his turn signal and carefully eased into the exit lane. A quick glance into the side mirror showed the large truck following after them in the exit lane with the large man dressed in white at the wheel.

Lilith watched everything with careful consideration. "Don't slow down."

As the exit ramp veered right, the road also sloped upward to meet the elevated cross street that bridged the highway. Father Joe could see traffic on 91st Avenue was flowing briskly in both directions, causing a cavernous pit in his stomach. However, as he approached the red light, he noticed in the fading twilight the light facing the travelers of 91st Street cycle to yellow. A quick couple turns of his head left and right eased Father Joe's fears as he saw all oncoming traffic come to a stop.

The light cycled red for the traffic on 91st Avenue and simultaneously green for those exiting the highway. With no one else waiting at the light, they crested the cross street as fast as Father Joe felt he could drive without being unsafe. Once on the down-slope of the 91st Avenue on-ramp, Lilith yelled, "Slam on the brakes and stop the car."

"You said—"

"Forget what I said. Slam on the brakes and brace yourselves. It's gonna get bumpy."

Father Joe pressed firmly on the brakes and wedged himself into the driver's seat by locking his elbows. Lilith hugged the seat as she stared intently out the back window, her vision distorted by the splintered glass. The forward tilt of the car, as it quickly decelerated, offered Lilith nothing

90

but a view of the tumultuous sky. The anti-lock brakes prevented the car from skidding and the car came to an abrupt halt, sending the pebbled glass cascading into the leg space of the back seat. Felipe, already in a fetal position with his arms wrapped around his thighs and his chin between his knees, whimpered in anticipation of the violent collision about to be felt.

The car sat idle on the exit ramp. Five second passed and nothing happened. Ten. Twenty. Lilith, still staring out the back window, watched the light cycle again. The cars under the dark, ominous sky moved along 91st Avenue, unaffected by their actions. And nothing crossed the street from the highway off-ramp.

Lilith was certain she saw the truck's headlights, bright and piercing, follow them into the exit lane. She would have sworn she saw them at the cross street just before Father Joe hit the brakes. She didn't see any tail lights driving off in either direction, though she couldn't say for sure since that's not where her attention was focused. For all she could tell, the enormous truck and its very large driver had seemingly disappeared.

Father Joe spoke first. "Is everyone alright?"

"I think so," Felipe said.

"Did you see the truck follow us off the highway?" Lilith asked both passengers.

"I did," they both replied.

"Then where the hell did it go?"

She stared blankly at them, only to have them stare blankly back at her.

"Let's at least get off the road," she said.

Father Joe slowly eased the car over to the shoulder of the on-ramp. The passengers in the front seat climbed out to inspect the vehicle. Felipe tried his door on the driver's side but it was pinched shut by the multiple creases in the car's doors from being rammed from behind. He waded through the glass in the rear seat to the other door and found it, too, would not open. He eventually climbed over the front seat and out Lilith's door, joining the others in the dusty swale beside the shoulder of the on-ramp. They stood, mouths agape, marveling at the damage sustained.

"Thank you, God," Father Joe whispered.

"For what?" Lilith shouted. "Almost getting us killed?"

"No. For watching over us and preventing that very thing from happening."

Father Joe took his All-COM from his belt and began dialing. "I'm calling the police. Perhaps you'd like to call a cab?"

Lilith, already engaged in a conversation with Mike Hart on her All-COM, turned from the others and walked back toward 91st Avenue, her off-hand firmly covering her off ear.

"What do you think the police can do?" Felipe asked.

"For starters, they can write up a report; for insurance purposes. This car belongs to the diocese. And maybe they can start looking for whoever did this."

Felipe took a few steps down the ramp toward the highway and watched the taillights of the cars continue westward. A large rain drop fell hard on his shoulder. He looked up at the dark clouds and caught another large drop in his left eye. He closed both his eyes, blessed himself with the sign of the cross and hurried back to the car as the rain drops became increasingly more frequent.

* * *

The storm only lasted thirty minutes but the volume of rain it dumped was vast. She had once heard someone refer to such a violent storm, one that quickly moves in, deposits its water and just as quickly moves out, as a "he rain." She also heard, in that same conversation, that the soft and tender all-day rain which gently soaks into the earth and nurtures new life was referred to as a "she rain."

She much preferred the "he rain."

A police car was already parked in front of Father Joe's crinkled vehicle. Yet, despite the pleading from Felipe and Father Joe, and even the police officers, Lilith stood on the corner of 91st Avenue and the westbound on-ramp, soaked to the bone from the subsiding downpour. She stared across the street at the headlights of the on-coming traffic as the cars and trucks continued on into the darkening night. The damp pavement glowed red and green and yellow in the aura of the reflected, diffused LED traffic lights. She stood and wondered if any of the drivers on the highway could see her standing there.

The pair of police officers had taken her statement already and had called for the tow truck. They now stood beside the vehicle and talked idly with Felipe and Father Joe.

Two sets of headlights veered off the highway, one after the other, and drove up the ramp toward her. A tow truck and a sedan idled across the street from where Lilith stood at the traffic light until it turned green. The tow truck rolled slowly across and lowered its passenger window.

"You all right, ma'am?"

Lilith looked into the truck. "I'm fine," she said. Then, pointing over her shoulder with her thumb, she continued, "They need you down there."

The truck rolled on.

The other vehicle at the light, the sedan, slowly rolled across the street and also stopped beside Lilith. She climbed inside.

"You're soaking wet!" Mike Hart said.

"Really? I hadn't noticed."

"You're getting the leather all wet."

Unconcerned, she demanded, "Who was it?"

"Who was what?"

"Who was it that tried to kill me?"

"What are you talking about?"

"Who was driving that truck? Was he one of ours?"

"Whoa, whoa, whoa, back up. We don't—"

"Don't give me that crap," she shouted, her face contorted in anger. "I need to know. Was it one of ours? The driver. He could have been one of those freakish *Montañas* Johara has stationed outside of the mansion. Stationed outside of everywhere, for fuck's sake."

Mike Hart stared at her from across the car. He saw through her eyes the wheels turning in her head and finally understood what she needed to hear. "No. Absolutely not. I would have known about it. Hell, you would have known about it."

She tilted her head, paused and looked down at the manufacturer's logo embossed on the floor mat. "A lone wolf, maybe? Going after the priest?"

Mike pondered this a moment. "Could be. But that's the beauty part about lone wolves, we have no authority and we can totally disassociate the party from their activities."

"Yeah, well I almost got 'activity-ed' all over the fucking road back there. If it was one of ours, we need to find out who it was. And I mean right now. Pull them all in. Find out who was driving that truck and who the target was. Me? The priest? The Adherente? Who?"

"The Adherente?" Mike questioned. "Why would anyone want him dead?"

"I don't know. That's what you're going to find out. He was dressed all in white, which scares the crap out of me. Makes me think it was …" She stopped and kept the rest of her thought to herself.

A long, uncomfortable pause sucked up all the air in the sedan and breathed it out onto the inside of the front windshield, fogging it up almost instantly.

"What if it wasn't one of ours?" Mike asked.

She looked straight into his eyes. "We'll cross that bridge when we get to it." Then, pointing to the windshield, she said, "Blast the AC. That should get rid of the fog."

She opened the door.

"Where are you going?"

Lilith gave him an awkward look. "To Goodyear."

"What? Why?"

"I have some things to do. Some very meddlesome things." She shut the door and approached the car being hoisted by the tow truck, joining all the men standing around it as they examined and contemplated the crumpled polycellulose panels of the car's rear end.

CHAPTER 17

Mike Hart's drive back into the city to GOP headquarters was a chaotic blur of LED headlights and raspy voices, having made dozens of terse, guarded conversations on his cars' enabled All-COM. He felt obligated to follow through on his boss's request sooner rather than later, calling all known liaisons to lone wolf operatives and handlers to find out exactly who the big man dressed in white was. Each call ended with one of two responses. "That doesn't sound like anyone I know, but I'll call around," or, "That could be any one of a dozen guys I know. I'll call around." Each response made the gnarled knots in Mike Hart's stomach tighten further.

He stepped into the garage elevator and ascended the four floors to the party offices. Johara Melendez was at her desk, having gone there immediately after leaving the Diocesan Pastoral Center. When Mike Hart passed her office, he waved courteously. She gave a quick nod acknowledging his presence, then went back to speaking quite loudly in Spanish into her All-COM. His office was just two doors down from Johara's, but the escaladed tones of her voice still pierced his closed door. When he finally noticed that she was no longer talking, he got up and went to the door. He aggressively pulled the door open as Johara was reaching for the same knob. They both jumped back in surprise, startled by the other's unexpected presence.

"Jesus H., Johara! You scared the shit out of me."

Johara chuckled. "That makes two of us."

Mike Hart took a moment to collect himself. "What are you doing here?"

"Working. Same as you. Did you need me for anything?"

As far as Mike Hart knew, Johara had neither an understanding of what a lone wolf was, nor its purpose. However, she had important connections throughout the Latino community, both legitimate and otherwise. The enormous men she recently employed as guards for the governor represented a straddling of those connections. He thought she might have some answers.

"Did you hear what happened to Lilith?"

"No. What?"

"She was in the car with that priest and that Adherente party-crasher from dinner heading back to Goodyear when they got rammed from behind on I-10."

"Are you serious?"

"As cancer."

"Is she okay?"

"She's fine. Pissed, but fine. Any thoughts on who might do something like that?"

"Run my boss off the road? No idea."

"No, no, no. The priest. Do you think any of your monstrous hombres, the *Montañas*, I think you called them, might be inclined to run the priest off the road since he's made it his personal goal to keep her from being executed tomorrow?"

"A priest? No way. Absolutely not."

Mike Hart looked at her questioningly.

"Look, some of those *gamberros* might be mean and ruthless, but they're reverent. They respect the cloth and the collar. Taking out a priest … that's an express ticket down, if you know what I mean. None of them would even think about something like that."

Without changing his expression, he asked, "What about the Adherentes?"

"What about them?"

"Would any of your *Montañas* consider taking out an Adherente?"

"Maybe," she said, not missing a beat. "But not if the collateral damage included a priest."

Mike Hart leaned back against his desk. He stared off in contemplation. His All-COM vibrated, startling him back into the moment. He pulled the device from its holster and looked at the display: Wolfe, Lonnie. He thought it must be a joke.

"Excuse me," he said to Johara. Then, turning to his All-COM, "Hello, this is Mike Hart."

"Um, yes, hello. Mr. Hart? I got a message you were looking for information about the … ah … traffic accident out on I-10."

Mike Hart stood up and ran around to his chair to sit down. Johara, seeing his excitement, leaned against the door jamb listening to Mike Hart's side of the conversation.

"A message? From who?"

"Look, the less I say over the phone the better, right?"

"Yes, of course. Is there somewhere we should meet?"

"I'm at a bar called Heaven's Gate right now."

Mike Hart closed his eyes and shook his head. Meeting a man calling himself Lonnie Wolfe at Heaven's Gate was almost more than he could stand. "Where is that?"

"Old Town."

Mike Hart leaned way back in his chair. He pulled the All-COM from his ear to check the time and then placed it back against his ear. "Fine. I'll see you around ten. How will I know—?"

"I'll find you, Mr. Hart."

The line went dead. He pressed end and then immediately connected to another number.

"Who was that?" Johara asked.

Mike Hart held up one finger.

"Larry. I need you to run a trace of the guy who just called me."

"Sure, Mike," came from the other end. "I'll call you as soon as I got something."

Mike pressed end and set his All-COM on his desk.

"Who called?"

"I'm not sure. He says he has some information about what happened to Lilith. I'm gonna go meet him in a couple hours."

"You need me to come with you? I could use a drink after that fiasco at the Diocesan Center. I mean, what is the governor doing?"

Mike Hart, looking intently at the women in the doorway, stood and placed his palms down on his desk. "The governor is doing exactly what he was elected to do. He's making decisions in the best interest of the people of this state. It's just that what you consider the people's best interest and what we consider the people's best interest aren't quite the same." He paused. Mike initially thought of asking her to join him, considering there was safety in numbers and discretion is the better part of valor, but since he was certain Johara was outside the loop on lone wolf activities, he decided it was best to go alone. "And, no."

"No what?"

"No, thanks. I think I'll see this guy solo."

"I can arrange to have one of those *Montañas* accompany you if you think there's going to be—"

"I'll be fine. Thanks for your concern, though."

CHAPTER 18

It was fully night in the barren outskirts and the air had become noticeably cooler. Lilith, wet from the rain, shivered in the back of the taxi. The cabbie was waiting for the tow truck, with its load secured, to pull away before he did the same.

"Where we headin', folks?" the cabbie asked.

The three of them looked questioningly at one another.

"Goodyear," Lilith finally said.

"Any place in particular?"

"Christ King church on Capitol and Lincoln," Father Joe offered.

"That's gonna run you maybe 50 bucks. You all right with that?"

"That's fine. Just get us there in one piece," Lilith replied.

With that, they all settled in for the ride. Despite the cabbie's attempts to spark discussions of varying relevance, the ride to Christ King's rectory was anxiously quite. The shock from and intensity of the night's events gave them pause, each of them taking inventory of their lives, in general, and the implications of the what had happened to them on the highway, in particular.

The two men stood on the sidewalk in front of the rectory, a small, two-story house which sat adjacent to the small brick church. Lilith remained in the back of the cab swiping her All-COM to pick up the $51.80 fare. She added a $10 tip and said, "I'm sorry to have to tell you this, but your wife is having an affair." Then she shuffled out of the vehicle and shut the door.

"What now?" she asked.

Father Joe, fumbling with his keys in front of the door, said, "Well, the rectory isn't really set up for women. And," he stuttered, "I'm still not exactly sure why you're even here. Why either of you are here. I mean—"

Felipe interrupted, "I need to be around someone who believes like I do."

"What about the other Adherentes?" Lilith asked. A smirk flashed across her face. "They don't believe?"

Felipe shrugged, walking in behind the priest who was busy turning on the lights. "Their hearts are in the right place, but I've listened to them bicker and complain since Her arrest and it gets pretty old pretty quick. When I heard Padre talking about Her at dinner I was immediately drawn to him, as if God told me this is where I'm supposed to be."

Standing in the modest foyer, Lilith looked curiously at Felipe. "Do you guys really hear God speak to you?"

The two men looked at one another and smiled.

"Let me see what we have in the way of guest bedding," the priest said and bolted into the darkness.

"I don't know about Father Joe, but for me, I think it's what other people call their instinct, their gut feeling. It's that little voice in the back of your head that tells you something is really, really right or something is really, really wrong. Sometimes, when I pray for guidance, I close my eyes and concentrate and that little voice guides me. Then, when I open my eyes, I know exactly what to do. It's always been there and *mi mama* always told me it was God speaking to me. And now I know she was right because when I first met Her, la Hermana de Jesus, the voice I had heard in my head all those years, it was Hers. Her voice has been guiding me throughout my life."

The priest's footfalls got louder as Lilith scoffed. "Hmm. Is that how it is for you, Father? Do you hear a voice and believe it to be God's?"

Father Joe, looking down in contemplation, came back into the hallway and stood with pillows and blankets. "That was beautifully described, um …." Father Joe smiled, embarrassed. "I'm sorry, I've forgotten your name."

"Felipe, Padre," he stated plainly.

Father Joe blushed and said to his guest, "I'm so sorry, Felipe." Then, turning back to Lilith, "And, as much as I'd like to claim that's how it is for me, I've never heard God. Not as a little voice in the back of my head or anything of the sort. No, for me, it's very different. It's as if God is all around me, like an ocean and I'm floating along with his every ebb and flow. And even though I feel like I know where I'm going and what I'm doing, the tack I take sailing through life, I'm merely pushed along by His gentle breezes and tidal waters."

Father Joe looked down again. "How's that for an analogy? I've never even been on a boat," he added. "But, I think the most important aspect of all this is that everyone finds God in his or her own way. And it doesn't matter what religion—Catholicism, Islam, Judaism, heck, even Wiccans and the agnostic—they all understand that there's something out there bigger than themselves."

"And Estephania Rodriquez, how does she fit in for you?" Lilith asked.

"To further the metaphor, she's the moon to His tidal waters." He smiled, pleased with his answer.

There was a pause in the discussion that Father Joe used to slip out of the hallway and into the room to the left, a converted living room that now served as an office. In the office was a couch, donated so many years ago it pre-dated Father Joe's appointment to Christ King parish.

"My apologies for the accommodations, Ms. Samuel."

"I sleep on the couch in my office all the time, Father. And this looks even more comfortable than that. I'll be just fine, thank you. And please, call me Lilith."

He nodded and pointed to the distant doorway. "There's a half bath, Lilith, just off the kitchen." Then turning to Felipe, "And for you there's a room upstairs."

Felipe was surprised. "Ms. Samuel should take the room, Father. I'll sleep on the couch—"

"No." Father Joe said quite sternly. "I'm sorry, but no."

"It's all right, Felipe," Lilith said. "I appreciate the chivalrous gesture, but I believe everyone will be more comfortable with me an entire flight of stairs away."

Father Joe again blushed. "The *appearance* of impropriety is as devastating as the impropriety itself."

"As a representative of the state's Republican party, I couldn't agree more."

Just then, her All-COM rang.

"Excuse me, please, gentlemen," Lilith said, walking into the kitchen. "Although, Felipe, I'd like to finish this discussion.

"Hello, this is Lilith Samuel."

He nodded but she missed it.

"If you'll follow me upstairs, Felipe." the priest offered.

* * *

101

After the priest had shown him where he was to sleep that night, Felipe, still restless from the events of the evening, climbed back down the stairs hoping to share his faith with the woman he'd just met a few hours earlier. He felt an immediate affinity for her that was difficult for him to explain. She was so reserved and contemplative at the Diocesan Center and yet so strong and forceful in the car after being rear-ended. He found the dichotomy mysterious and intriguing, drawing him in with the simple idea of finishing their discussion.

Father Joe had left the hallway light on and it spilled into the office area he had set up for his female guest.

"Lilith?" Felipe whispered.

Lilith walked in from the kitchen. She had a glass of water in her hand. "Yes."

"I'm still a little wound up from earlier. I was wondering if you'd like to take a walk with me outside."

Lilith winced, as if in pain. "I'm a bit hesitant to go outside considering someone was trying to run us off the road."

"You can't possibly think we're in danger here."

"Felipe, I have no idea if we're in danger. But I work for the GOP. That means I have lots of enemies." Lilith crossed the room and set her glass of water down on a stack of cardboard banker's boxes. "Besides, better safe than sorry has always been my policy." Then, she extended her hand and said, "Pull up a chair. What's on your mind?"

Felipe took the opening as an invitation to further explain his relationship with God in general and with Estephania Rodriguez, in particular. He took full advantage of the opportunity. Fifteen minutes into the discussion, Felipe realized he'd been talking nonstop, not once giving Lilith an opportunity to say a single word.

He stopped in mid-sentence. "I'm sorry. Here I am just yammering on and on. I guess having someone who hasn't heard it all before makes it all seem new and fresh in my mind."

"Oh, I've heard it all before, Felipe," she said, trying to make him feel at ease. "You think you're the only one looking for the next great leader who's going to save the world? I've seen it a million times in every election I've ever been a part of. People look to the president or their governor or mayor, hell, even their city councilperson, anyone who claims to want to make a difference. And the people want to believe so much that he's different or she's their savior. They think this is the one who's going to lead us out of all the bureaucratic sludge and slime. And you know what? They're always disappointed. Every time. I'm telling you. Every God damned time. You need to prepare yourself for the possibility that you're backing the wrong horse."

"Are you … are you talking about la Hermana de Jesus?"

"I'm talking in generalities, here. But, yeah, she wouldn't be the first false prophet. History's filled with—"

"I don't care what history's filled with," Felipe said. He was visibly angry. "You haven't heard Her speak."

"Actually, I have," Lilith said sheepishly. "A couple times."

"In person?" The idea of someone hearing Her and not believing She was the Daughter of God was completely foreign to him. "Not a broadcast on television or an interlude on the All-COM, but live and in person? Hearing Her words touch your soul?"

She nodded. "A couple times. But, there was no soul touching. All I saw was another bottom-feeder trying to get over on the public under the guise of religion."

Taken aback, Felipe couldn't make his mouth move.

"Bishop DeMarco was right, you know. There are more than a thousand individuals every year claiming to be the Christ. Of course, most of them are mentally unbalanced. And I'm here to tell you not one of them is the Christ."

Felipe stared into Lilith's eyes, his face sagging as if gravity had intensified ten-fold. "I thought you were a believer," he whined. "I thought you wanted to hear the Good News."

"Good news? I'm just trying to understand what you see in that crazy bitch."

"You can't say that!" he shouted. "She *is* the Anointed One."

"You can't be serious, Felipe. 'If anyone says to you then, 'Look, here is the Messiah!' or, 'There He is!' do not believe it. False messiahs and false prophets will arise, and they will perform signs and wonders so great as to deceive, if that were possible, even the elect. Behold, I have

103

told it to you beforehand. So if they say to you, 'He is in the desert,' do not go out there; if they say, 'He is in the inner rooms,' do not believe it.'"

"Matthew 24:23-27," Felipe mumbled.

"Damn-straight. And right from the horse's mouth, so to speak."

"You shouldn't be so flippant, Ms. Samuel."

"It's Ms. Samuel now? I counterpoint your point and we're no longer on a first name basis. Come on, Felipe. I'm merely telling you what you already know but are unwilling to accept."

"Oh yeah? And what's that?"

"She's no savior."

Felipe's shoulders slumped and he sat staring at the light cast across the floor of the room. The seed of doubt had germinated and was quickly taking root.

Lilith looked at his dejected face. "I'm sorry, Felipe. But she's going to die tomorrow and that'll be the end of it. You need to start thinking about what you're going to do with the rest of your life."

Felipe thought a moment and tried to respond with something strong and overwhelming, but all he could muster was a soft, "No."

Lilith, quite pleased with herself, said, "It's obvious I've upset you. Here you were looking to unwind and all I did was rile you up. Believe me when I tell you that wasn't my intention. Maybe now would be a good time for you to take that walk outside. Go get some crisp, clean, fresh air and look at things from a new perspective before settling in."

"You know what?" he said, angry and annoyed. "That's a great idea."

"I remember hearing once, 'Hope for the best but expect the worst.' That seems like pretty good advice from where I'm sitting."

"Begging your pardon, ma'am, but that sounds defeatist to me. If you don't mind, I believe I'll hope for the best and expect nothing less. Good night, Ms. Samuel. I'll try not to wake you when I come back in."

He walked out of the room without much purpose. It had been years since he felt so alone.

* * *

A deep, earthy aroma hung on the air like an invisible fog. The moon's aura refracted and reflected within the cloud cover to provide a

104

fluorescent-like illumination to the night, ghostly and pale. The stillness all around was broken by the hinges of the rectory's front door squeaking open, allowing a small Latino man to walk outside. He carefully and quietly shut the door behind him, descended the front stairs, looked up into the cloudy sky and inhaled deeply.

A man, dressed entirely in white, watched him from afar. He could see that the man who had joined him in the nakedness of the night was trying to clear his head. He couldn't decide whether the purpose of the deep breath was the physical act of taking a cleansing breath or the psychological desire to take the palpable, pleasant scent of the evaporating water deep into his senses. His not knowing "why" made the watching man uneasy and restless. Understanding human motivation was a quirky hobby of his but, more essentially, it drove his every action.

The Latino man stretched his arms a few times and headed down the street, past the man in white, and into the heavy night air. From his hiding place in the recesses of the adjacent church, the man in white stole through the soft moon shadows until he was standing behind one of the stout palm trees lining the property between the rectory and the church. The light from inside the building cast a warm glow out the side window and onto the small, meticulously landscaped yard.

He watched the woman inside pace in a relatively small area of the room while she talked on her All-COM. The sight of her brought forth the flames of repugnance and revulsion for what she stood for that burned inside him. He wished he could have killed her on the highway. And having survived, he wanted nothing more than to slip inside the house, silent and invisible, and slit her throat from ear to ear. However, he was told unequivocally not to kill her. She still had a part to play in the events that were to unfold. An essential role, though foul and unpleasant.

Rather than dwell on his brutal desires, he stood beneath the palm tree and waited, looking down the street in the same direction the small Latino man had disappeared. By his account, mere moments passed before a small figure drew near. As the distant figure got closer, the man in white moved again, this time to the far side of the rectory. He began walking toward the Latino man as if he were out for his evening constitutional. The two men were several feet apart, approaching one another in front of the church, when the man in white called out.

"Good evening," he said, stopping as he was about to pass by.

"Good evening," Felipe replied, a nervous tone in his voice. His eyes went wide as he looked at the enormous man.

"It's a beautiful night, isn't it?"

"Yes it is," Felipe said, a modest amount of his nervousness gone. "I love the smell of rain."

The man in white smiled, instantly feeling at ease to know why the Latino man had taken the deep breath when he first came outside. It was an itch scratched. "Do you know what the smell of rain reminds me of? Grass stains on a pair of denim jeans."

A look of awe gripped Felipe's face. "That is so weird."

In an instant, the man in white actually saw Felipe's stress and nervousness subside. Had Felipe not been a believer, the man in white might have eviscerated him and left his splayed corpse on the sidewalk for the nocturnal animals to feast.

"What's weird?" the man in white asked with a nonchalant smile.

"That's exactly what I tell people the smell of rain reminds me of. Everyone thinks I'm insane when I say that."

"You're not insane. You are absolutely right. About rain. About Her. About everything."

Felipe's quick progression from fear to relief to awe was now followed by confusion.

"Well," the man in white continued, "I have to get going. Good night." He walked on past the church and down the road just as Felipe had done some time earlier. Felipe stood and watched the man in white, his large frame taking a long time to disappear into the night.

He instantly felt the walk had done him some good.

CHAPTER 19

Mike Hart drove to Old Town, the heart of the city's regentrified industrial district. What had been row upon row of bleak and worn buildings vacated or abandoned by corporations that shuttered their factories and relocated them to the S.O.B. states was now the vibrant, artsy district filled with clubs, cafes and high-end antique shops. Mike Hart had little time and less inclination to visit that part of town on his own, but he was surprised to see that it was still relatively active late on a Sunday night.

On the way, Mike Hart's assistant, Larry, called him with a handful of details regarding the registered owner of the All-COM that had called him nearly an hour earlier. Lonnie Wolfe was the owner of a small masonry business. He was a consistent financial contributor to the GOP's general elections fund, but had never attended a single rally, dinner or fund raiser as far as Larry could tell. He completed two tours in the Army during the Water Wars, was a current reservist and had no criminal record. Larry sent the party's most recent photo of Lonnie Wolfe to Mike Hart's All-COM. Upon seeing the man, Mike Hart thought he looked safe.

He found a parking spot just a few blocks from Heaven's Gate, a seemingly small, cement block building wedged between two much larger corner buildings, each with heavy, vertical, steel beams running up the entire height of its exterior to the roof. From the opposite side of the street and looking up, you immediately understood how the club got its name.

Inside, the club was bright and colorful. Mike Hart was certain it was the polar opposite of the décor prior to its renovation. There were only a few patrons, but the place appeared deceptively vibrant. He scanned the faces of those seated at the café tables that lined the dance floor which was sunken two steps down from the rest of the floor space. A lone figure sat on stage and played a classical composition, Mozart, he guessed incorrectly, on his accordion.

Not surprised that he didn't recognize any of the faces in the club, Mike Hart walked over to the bar and sat on a sleek, slender barstool. The bartender came over immediately.

"A Sprite, please," Mike said.

In the mirror behind the bar, he watched a man in a watch cap and wrapped in a worn Navy pea coat approach. As the bartender delivered his drink, the man leaned in and whispered in Mike's ear, "Outside. Two minutes." Mike turned and watched the man quickly walk away toward the door and glance from side to side, making himself look even more conspicuous, he thought, than had he set himself on fire.

He threw a five dollar bill on the bar, grabbed his glass and chugged half its contents in one quick gulp. Then he cleaned the corners of his mouth with his fingers. Another minute passed and he finished his drink. He nonchalantly got up out of his seat and walked toward the exit slowly, taking in the classical music bellowing from the accordion.

The temperature outside seemed to have dropped ten degrees during his short stay in Heaven's Gate. A rapid pan to his left revealed the man in the pea coat across the street blowing into his hands to keep them warm. Mike Hart checked traffic and walked purposely toward the man.

"How's it going?"

"Walk with me," Clay said, wrapping the pea coat tight to his chest.

They walked away from Heaven's Gate, crossing a side street before the man in the lead settled into the cold metal bench in a bus shelter. Mike put on an air of confidence and sat down, too.

"You work for the gop right?" Clay asked, pronouncing *G-O-P* as if it were a three-letter-word instead of initials.

"The GOP, Yeah."

"You know who I am?"

"No I don't."

It was a lie. At least Mike thought it was a lie. Even though the man on the bench didn't look anything like the photo Larry had sent, Mike was fairly certain that he was sitting next to Lonnie Wolfe. The only thing that gave Mike the courage to sit next to the man in the first place was the fact that Lonnie Wolfe had never done jail time.

"Do you know who Lonnie Wolfe is?"

The question scared Mike to his core. "Should I?"

"I think he was one of your lone wolves."

"You're not Wolfe?" His voice betrayed him.

A laugh escaped from within the pea coat. "Nah. But that's pretty clever, don't you think? Lonnie Wolfe: lone wolf."

Trying to regain some composure, and relieve some anxiety, Mike laughed, too. "Yeah, well, I work mostly with the party core. I don't have much contact with, well, with people outside the core."

"The fringe? The extremists? The Lonnie Wolfe's of the world."

"Sure. I guess."

Clay took a long look at Mike from head to toe. "I was told I needed to contact someone at the gop."

"Who?"

"You."

"No," Mike said, frustrated. "Who told you to contact me?"

"Michael."

"Who's Michael?"

"Um, I really don't know him that well. But that doesn't matter—"

"This Michael, was he responsible for the accident?"

"Responsible for it? No."

"What about you?"

"What about me?"

Mike instantly seized with frustration, but tried to slowly work through the communication roadblock. "How do you play into all this?"

"I'm just a servant of God."

And with that sentence, the hope and confidence Mike brought with him to Heaven's Gate were nowhere to be seen in his disposition. They had wafted away past the bright city lights into the cloudy night sky.

"You said you had some information about the accident out on I-10."

"Do you believe in hell, Mr. Hart?"

"I'm not sure," he replied, his voice shaky and weak.

"You're not sure?" the man quipped. "You either do or you don't, there is no middle ground."

Mike Hart felt his heart racing. Trying to placate his informant, he said what he thought the man wanted to hear, "You're right. There is no middle ground. Yes, I do believe in hell. I guess I just get so wrapped up in my own world and go about my business without paying much attention to the grand scheme of things that heaven and hell kind of get lost."

"The grand scheme of things is all I pay attention to." The man's voice was flat and soft. "Out there," he said, nodding west, the direction where the accident occurred, "That was about the grand scheme of things. It was about heaven and hell."

Unable to restrain himself, Mike asked the only question looping through his mind, "Were you driving the truck?"

The man's eye barely peeked out from between the watch cap and the collar of his coat. "So there it is. You came out here not knowing if I was the one who tried to kill your boss, yet here you sit next to me on a city street bench. That's brave of you. If I lunged at you would you fight back or run away? What's your head telling you? Am I a killer?"

"I have no idea if you're a killer," Mike said without skipping a beat. "All I know is that you claim to have information that I'm looking for. I just hope it's not worth killing for."

The man's eyes opened wide. "Or dying for."

The man let that last line linger for effect.

"Let me tell you a few things, Mr. Hart. Make no bones about it, I am a killer. But no, I didn't have anything to do with what happened to your boss and those two true believers."

"What do you know about it?"

The man paused and looked at his hands clasped on his lap. "I asked you before if you believed in hell. Everyone believes in heaven, Mr. Hart, that there's an eternal resting place for the righteous. And everyone believes they are righteous. But hell? No one wants to believe in eternal damnation. Yet, with heaven comes hell. And with heaven and hell come God and the devil, Lucifer, the fallen angel. With God comes angels and with the devil comes demons."

He paused and looked at Mike Hart. Mike was paying attention as a means to an end, not at all concerned with the words or the meaning of the sentences, but absorbing just enough to appear engaged.

"There are demons among us, Mr. Hart." He looked back at his hands. "They don't have red skin and horns and wings. They look just like you and me, but they distract us, like you said, from the grand scheme of things. Televangelists, newspaper editors, teachers, lawyers

110

...," then, casting his eyes again at Mike, he said with a sneer, "... politicians. There are demons everywhere. Everywhere!"

Mike Hart stood up, no longer nervous and no longer feigning interest, but angry. "Demons," he said, heavy with sarcasm. It came out of his mouth all wrong but he didn't care. "My boss was almost killed because some whack job thought there were demons in the car? That's why I'm here?"

For the first time, Mike looked at the man on the bench. Really looked at him. His face was pale and expressionless. His eyes were, too. The stubble around his face softened any hard features he may have once had. It suddenly struck Mike that his tirade didn't elicit a response of any kind from the man, which only enraged him further.

"Look," his voice boomed, "Do you know who was responsible for the accident out on I-10? Who was driving the truck?"

"Those are two different questions."

"What?"

"The man driving the truck was not responsible."

"Look, um. What is your name?"

"I'm Clay."

"Clay?" Mike Hart said as if he couldn't believe anyone could bare such a name.

"Yes, Clay. You can make me into whatever you want."

Mike almost laughed out loud at the ridiculousness of the man's statement. Instead, he paced in the small space of the shelter. "Fine, Clay. Who was driving the truck?"

"Michael was driving the truck."

Mike thought a moment. "Is Michael a lone wolf?"

"No, not in the sense I think you're speaking of. The man driving the truck works for Him?"

"Him? Him who?"

"Him," Clay said, pointing up into the cloudy sky.

"You got to be fucking kidding me!"

"No sir, I am not. Michael's been planning this for quite a while, now. He gave me this All-COM today around lunch specifically so I could contact you. To get you inside Heaven's Gate."

"Why me? Why there?"

"He never said."

Mike paced more frenetically. "Demons. Gods. Heaven's Gate? What's next? The president is the anti-Christ?"

"He never said anything about the president," Clay said plainly. "And it's God. Singular."

Mike began to walk away but turned, walked back to the man and leaned in to whisper in his ear. "Do me a favor you psycho fuck. Lose my number. I don't ever want to hear from you again. You understand me?"

"Yes. Except—"

"Except what?"

"I was told to give you a message, Mr. Hart."

He began to leave once more but turned again, this time speaking to the man from where he stopped. "Fine. What's the message."

Clay, sitting in the bus shelter, said just loud enough for Mike Hart to hear him, "There's two things. The first thing you should probably write down."

"Just give me the fucking message!"

"4-Q-5-1-0-dash-5-1-1."

Mike Hart's face went blank trying to process the seemingly random gibberish flowing from the man's mouth. "What the fuck is that? The combination to Satan's locker?"

"No. But you really should write it down."

He pulled out his All-COM. "Run through that one more time."

"4-Q-5-1-0-dash-5-1-1."

Mike transcribed it. When he hit save, he asked, "And the second thing?

Clay looked at Mike Hart with sad eyes. "He's gonna kill your boss."

Clay said it so matter-of-factly, Mike's fear pierced his anger and appeared on his face instantly. "What? Why?"

"Heaven and hell, Mr. Hart. She's one of them."

"One of what?"

"Them. You know, not us. She's playing for the other team. I think she'd already be dead if not for the fact that she has something important to do tomorrow. Plus, those other two guys were in the car with her. He likes those two a lot. He wouldn't harm them."

112

Then, just as he had tried to do several times before, Mike turned and stomped away. He was annoyed, and, for anyone watching, he put on a performance that truly showed his full annoyance. He pressed a few buttons and brought his All-COM hastily up to the side of his head in an effort to continue his performance. However, all he managed to do was hurt his ear.

Clay sat in the bus shelter, alone, picking at the dirt under his nails. A few moments later, a crazy-looking man in a gray parka sat next to him. Any on-lookers could have easily mistaken them for brothers.

"My name's Luke Logan," the newcomer said. "I'm a reporter for the *Republic*. I was wondering if I could ask you a few questions about the conversation you just had with that man."

CHAPTER 20

Chicken drills. That's what he and his frat brothers called it, the way people's heads pecked away at the keyboard or a book in front of them as they fought off the temptations of sleep just before consciousness snapped their heads back upright. He'd been doing chicken drills for a few minutes, trying to will himself to stay awake and finish reading the stack of seemingly endless files. The last chicken drill nearly gave him whiplash.

He pulled off his glasses and threw them onto the desk. They made a very loud *thud* when they landed. It took a moment, but Damien realized it wasn't his glasses that had made the thud, but something somewhere else in the house. He got up and went to the door, peering out into the hall. There was darkness all around. He could almost feel the night itself as if it were weighing upon him, heavy and relentless. The light from his study spilled out across the floor and ceiling and met on the other side of the hallway. His shadow cast only a vaguely human shape.

"Sophia?" he called out. "Is that you?"

There was no response.

Damien stood in the door jamb, waiting. His Psych 101 class came rushing back to him, his subconscious choosing to freeze rather than engage either his fight or flight reactions. His mind—in its heightened state, filled with adrenaline and extra oxygen from rapid, shallow breathing—was now picking up what had typically passed by unperceived: the house's ever-present draft breezing across the follicles of his neck and arms; the soft wind rustling the leaves outside; the sweet aroma of cactus buds wafting in the air; and, in his peripheral vision, a tiny wisp of hazy mist moving through the hallway, disappearing when he finally turned his head to look directly at it.

Turning back toward the hallway that led to the bedrooms he called out again. "Sophia?" Backed by the adrenaline, it was louder this time, and shakier. But again, there was no response.

Damien stood in the door jamb. To what end he was unsure, but he stood there nonetheless for thirty more seconds. He scanned the darkened corridors for something misplaced or incongruent, but nothing stood out. His mind, trying to place the *thud* he had heard remained baffled, though still utterly alert. Off in the furthest reaches of his senses he heard through the deafening silence the screech of an owl. It was a nearly inaudible scratching at the thin night air, more of a feeling than a sound, but it was there and he perceived its presence. Then, just as soft and nearly imperceptible was the low bellow of a trumpet chasing away the sound of the screeching owl. Damien heard only a few notes before it disappeared completely. He couldn't be sure, but he thought it sounded like *Amazing Grace*.

Just then the grandfather clock in the hallway came to life, its inner workings clicking and clacking in preparation of its tolling. Then it chimed through its four four-note quarter parts to announce the top of the hour before striking its deep, resonant gong ten times.

Damien rolled his head around his neck in an effort to relax. Then, taking one last look down the hallway in the direction which the hazy mist had disappeared, he joked under his breath, "Must have been a ghost."

Damien retreated back to his desk, looking over his shoulder as he went to ensure that whatever he had heard would not sneak up on him. Looking down at the desk, disappointment seeped into him. He hadn't gotten through the entire stack of folders yet. He willed himself to re-read the document that caused the chicken drills, hopeful to find something somewhere that might help him understand more fully how to do what was inevitably needed. Then, he read the document that followed it, and the one after that, and the one after that until he had read every document in the *Pre-Trial* folder.

He placed his glasses in their case, tidied the stacks of folders on his desk and glanced at his watch once more. It was almost ten-thirty. He was tired.

"A little more than thirteen hours," he said aloud. "Or, maybe more than an eternity."

He turned off the light on his desk and walked through the dark hallways to his bedroom.

CHAPTER 21

Bishop DeMarco was typically a light sleeper. The various subtle noises in and around the rectory that the other priests were able to tune out or transform into white noise caused him to stir frequently. He had recently begun the habit of getting up in the darkness, walking through the hallways to the kitchen and pouring himself a glass of milk. There was one cup in the jumbled assemblage of cups and glasses residing in the cupboard that the bishop used almost exclusively on the nights he drank his milk. It was a small, blue plastic cup with a worn silkscreen print of Spider-Man swinging into action. His initial affinity for that particular cup arose, he supposed, from his fond memories of Saturday morning cartoons and of *The Amazing Spider-Man*. However, there were long nights when he wouldn't gulp down a swig of milk and head right back to bed. Rather, he'd sit in the dark, slowly sip his milk and pray. On those occasions, the words of Ben Parker, the uncle of Spiderman's alter-ego, Peter Parker, would creep into his mind: *With great power comes great responsibility*. Whenever he thought of that line he marveled at the ability of humankind to capture and disseminate God's message in such unexpected ways.

Like most Sundays on which he had had a conversation with Father Joe about his affinity for the incarcerated cult leader Estephania Rodriquez, Bishop DeMarco went to bed concerned. And like most nights he went to bed concerned, he awoke from a disturbing dream. Upon waking *that* night, he was unable to remember any details of the dream, only that Father Joe and his fourth grade Sunday school teacher, Señora Ruiz, were both in it.

He looked at the clock on the nightstand. It read 3:07. He decided tonight would be a milk night, though he hadn't decided if it would be a gulp-and-dash or a sit-and-sip.

The terrazzo floors in the rectory halls were getting colder as fall approached and the bishop wished he had taken the time to put on his slippers. He winced at the harsh light of the refrigerator when he got the milk out, wondering if it wouldn't be better to replace the bulb with something dimmer. The bishop sat at the large table and sipped his milk, thinking about his rancorous conversations with Father Joe and the others regarding the Rodriquez woman.

Looking up from his glass, he saw in the hallway a single, slender figure dressed in a loose-fitting nightshirt approaching him. At first he thought it was one of the parish priests, but as the figure moved closer it became clear the bishop had no idea who it was.

"Yoo-hoo, Your Grace," came in choral harmony, soft and gentle to the bishop's ears.

"Good evening," was all the bishop could think to say.

"Can't sleep, huh? No sheep to count?"

He nodded, speechless, staring into the stranger's bright, glowing eyes.

"It's no wonder you can't sleep," the stranger said, taking a seat across the table from the bishop. "These, here, are tough times. I think your young parishioners would say, 'It's daft!' And it is. All around us, things are all screwy. It must be very difficult for people to rest easy when they're blind to the changes happening, let alone the meaning of these changes. I mean, 'Yikes!' Right? And yet, here we are, right smack dab in the middle of all this change, and you're still clinging to the past like a rich man to the brass ring unwilling to change with the changes. I mean, c'mon, that's the 'what was.' You gotta get with the 'what is!' Know what I'm saying?"

The bishop continued to stare, dumbfounded.

"Manuel DeMarco, son of Jose and Serena DeMarco, do you know who I am?"

Bishop DeMarco shook his head.

"Think hard, Manny, my man. I have come to deliver a message of great joy. A wonderful message for all eternity." The stranger looked deep into the bishop's eyes. "Anything? C'mon, take a wild guess."

The bishop whispered, "Michael?"

"No," the stranger angrily dismissed. "Michael's a fighter. A do-gooder and a smiter of the malevolent. I'm ever merciful and wholly mighty. Try again."

"Rafael?" the bishop offered, with no conviction whatsoever.

"Oh, for crying out loud! Are you even trying?"

"Gabriel?"

"A ring-a-ding-ding, Manny! I think Señora Ruiz would be a little bit disappointed you didn't get it on the first shot. And by the way, you'll be happy to know she passed through the pearly gates when her time in the corporal world ended and is enjoying eternal bliss as we speak." The stranger seemed quite pleased with delivering that bit of news. "Oooo-doggie, it's been a long time since I last delivered tidings of great joy and gladness. Actually, I've been trying to get the word out about this for the last thirty-some-odd years, but it's almost impossible to get people to listen, let alone believe. Everyone wants an All-COM interlude to tell them what to do, think, feel. If you ask me, the thing's nothing but a distraction. And then there's everyone's need for irrefutable proof. Tangible evidence, you know? I mean, science and technology are surely gifts from God, don't get me wrong. Where would you be without them, right? But their residuals … Holy harps! Let me just say they leave something to be desired."

Gabriel trailed off in thought for a moment before snapping back. "No matter. Here I am with tidings of great joy and gladness and I'm rambling on and on. Whaddaya say we get right to it, huh? Manny, you are going to love this. It would totally knock your socks off if you were wearing any. Are you listening?"

The bishop nodded.

The entity before him slowly clasped its hands together on the table, leaned over them and whispered, "Estephania Rodriquez really is the Daughter of God."

Gabriel sat back, smiled a Cheshire smile at the bishop and waited for a reaction.

The bishop sat, expressionless and unmoving. Then, he got up from the table and started walking away back to his room.

"I know," Gabriel said, trailing the bishop down the hall. "Pretty incredible, huh? Do you know how hard it is for me to keep from blasting my trumpet from every mountaintop and shouting out with all the choirs of angels, 'The second Messiah has finally come! Rejoice and be glad!'"

Bishop DeMarco staggered and pawed his way, hand over hand, down the hallway trying to get away from the stranger. His legs melted beneath him as he tried to run, yet he still pawed at the walls, dragging himself along the corridor, a corridor suddenly lined with trellises of blood-red roses blooming in full splendor.

"Now, here's something to think about." The stranger paused for effect. "You were chosen. That's right, chosen. From the nine billion men, women and children roaming this great world, you and a couple dozen others were hand-picked to hear the Good News. I say hand-picked, but that's really just an expression since He doesn't really have any hands to speak of. But back to the point. You were chosen, Manny. Isn't that awesome?"

The bishop's pawing found a doorknob which he turned and, with some effort, pushed open to reveal a vaguely familiar room. He quickly shut the door behind him and turned to face it. Staring at the door, he staggered backwards, away from it, deeper into the room. The stranger, undeterred by the obstacle, continued to follow him. The bishop retreated step-by-step until something caught him just above his calves and he fell back into a seated position on a bed, the sheets of which bore the same silk screened image of Spider-Man found on his cup.

"Look, no one's asking you to *do* anything," Gabriel consoled. "I mean, it's not like you're being asked to lead a nation of people through the desert for forty years or allow people to throw stones at you until you bleed out from all the internal hemorrhaging, or, even give up your precious red wines from Italy. All you're being asked to do is listen and believe. That's it."

Gabriel's hands helped the bishop shift his weight, lowering his head onto the downy pillow. Bishop DeMarco closed his eyes and heard one last choral whisper: "Listen and believe."

He suddenly awoke. His pajamas were damp with sweat as was his pillow. He looked at the clock on the nightstand. It read 3:07. He sat up and rubbed his eyes trying to keep the details of his dream fresh, trying desperately to move them from the fogginess of his short-term memory to the more stable architecture of his long-term memory. He stood and walked to the door and then suddenly stopped.

Slippers, he thought. *The floors are so cold this time of year.*

Bishop DeMarco walked down the hallway, his slippers clipping and clopping as he shuffled along. He went into the cupboard to find his Spider-Man cup but found it absent from its usual resting place. Though the room was dark, there was enough light streaming in from the windows to search the countertops, the table and all the other horizontal surfaces in the room. When he didn't find the cup, he was surprised at how disappointed he was. He shrugged it off, grabbed one of the other small plastic cups in the cupboard, a green one, and went to the refrigerator. The harsh light made him wince, an unwelcome detail he remembered from his dream. When his eyes adjusted, he looked into the refrigerator and saw, on the shelf next to the milk jug, his Spider-Man cup three-quarters-full of milk. The bishop stood in front of the wide-open fridge door staring, his mouth agape.

"Are you all right?"

Bishop DeMarco nearly collapsed with fright at the intruding voice. He staggered back, groping for anything to grasp, until he reached the table which lurched with a low growl. The green plastic cup he clutched in his hand fell to the floor, bouncing and rolling into the corner, clattering as it did.

"Oh my," the other man chuckled as he lunged to help steady the bishop. "I didn't mean to startle you."

The bishop steadied himself and stood up straight. "I'm fine, Enrique," he said to the cathedral rector. Then, with a chuckle he added, "You scared me half to death."

They stood silent in the stark refrigerator light smiling at one another. Father Enrique reached into the fridge, pulled out the Spider-Man cup and closed the door. "Here, Manuel, drink your milk."

Bishop DeMarco took the cup and looked at it curiously.

Father Enrique spoke. "I've noticed that whenever you speak to Father Joe from the P-Ville prison this little cup ends up on the kitchen table the next morning. I thought I'd save you a step so I poured your milk before I went to bed."

The bishop edged around the table and sat in his usual chair clutching the cup with both hands.

"Are you sure you're okay?" Father Enrique asked.

"To be honest? No, I'm not sure. I had the most unusual dream, Enrique. Most unusual." He sipped his milk despite his shaking hands. "I think this whole Estephania Rodriquez business is starting to get to me."

"A nightmare?"

The bishop looked into the younger priest's eyes and then looked away shaking his head. He sat and stared, thinking of the dream. "I dreamt I'd woken up, came here for my milk and, after some witty banter, the Angel Gabriel told me that this Rodriquez woman was indeed the Daughter of God and that I should listen and believe."

Father Enrique smiled broadly. "*The* Gabriel? The exalted Messenger of God, Gabriel?"

The bishop nodded slightly. "Yeah."

"What'd he look like?"

"What?"

"What did he look like? White gown? Wings? Halo?"

Bishop DeMarco found the question entirely irrelevant. "I don't know." It came out clipped, harsh and filled with annoyance. Seeing the instant hurt it brought to his colleague's face, he apologized. "I'm sorry, Enrique. It's just, I don't really remember her appearance."

"Her appearance? The Angel Gabriel was a woman?"

"I think it was a woman," the bishop said, trying to remember as many details as he could. "It was hard to tell what gender it was. Hermaphroditic, I guess. Is that the right word? Regardless of whether it was a he or a she, that voice. My God, that voice and the way she spoke." He trailed off and sipped his milk.

After a few moments, Father Enrique asked, "What about them?"

The bishop was lost in thought. "I'm sorry, what?"

Father Enrique reached across the table and gently embraced his friend's hand. "You said there was something about her voice and the way she spoke."

"Yes," the bishop laughed, "The way she spoke." He stopped for an even bigger laugh. "Like a game show host. Good heavens, Enrique. If that's how they speak in heaven, then God help us all." He laughed once more before his face turned somber. "But her voice." Again he trailed off and sipped his milk. However, this time he didn't need to be prodded to continue. "You know how in Scripture they speak of the choir of angels? The nine choirs of angels? I remember my Sunday school teacher, Señora. Ruiz, she made us memorize the hierarchy of the nine choirs." Bishop DeMarco drifted once more.

Father Enrique picked up the thought. "Seraphim, Cherubim, Thrones, Dominions, Virtues, Powers, Archangels, Principalities and then just plain old Angels."

"Yes," the bishop mumbled.

"My Sunday school teacher was Señora. Martinez" Father Enrique said. "Now that was one tough little lady."

The bishop smiled appropriately.

"A choir of angels, Enrique. In my dream, Gabriel spoke as a choir of angels, a true choir, every word spoken in four-part harmony, like a baseball stadium filled with sopranos, altos, tenors and basses all speaking as one. I remember thinking in my dream it was the most beautiful thing I'd ever heard."

The two men sat in the dark, silent for a moment.

Then, Father Enrique stood up. "I'm not sure I can be much help to you, Manuel. Certainly not at three in the morning." Father Enrique walked over to the glass the bishop had dropped, bent over and picked it up. "My throat's a bit scratchy, so I just came to get some water." He reached into the freezer and pulled out a few cubes from the tray. As they *clunked* when they hit the plastic bottom, Bishop DeMarco thought of the political scandal ice might cause if the parishioners of the archdiocese discovered his friend's predilections.

"If you need someone to talk to in the morning, Monday's are usually slow around here."

"Thank you, Enrique," the bishop whispered.

Father Enrique poured some water from the gallon jug in the refrigerator and left the bishop sitting in his chair. The bishop sat confused and alone, holding his Spider-Man cup and staring off into the relative darkness of the kitchen.

Listen and believe, the bishop thought.

CHAPTER 22

The Trial folder Styles had prepared sat open on Damien's desk. It had been open for quite some time. Though he'd read the court transcripts several times since they were released to the public, noting, as Styles had in his *Executive Summary*, no incongruities, lapses of due process or malicious manipulations of the legal system which would invalidate the verdict of the jury, he wanted to read Styles' take on the matter once again. According to Styles, by every standard recognized, she'd been given a fair trial. Damien had feared as much. Hoped as much.

The bulk of the prosecution's case was statements made by Estephania Rodriquez offering to deliver state-sequestered natural resources to any persons requesting them, regardless of whether they were U.S. citizens or foreign nationals. These statements were read into evidence and played over and over on a large-screen All-COM in the courtroom. The statements and videos were validated by a number of witnesses, most notably Judith Scarlet, one of Rodriguez's own devout followers. Estephania Rodriquez, herself, admitted, under oath, that everything the prosecution had presented was true, leaving her lawyers all but helpless in her defense.

Damien picked up Styles' *Summary* of his *The Trial* folder and read it again, unconsciously nodding his head in agreement with what was written.

The Water Security Laws are flawed: severely so. Even those who were responsible for their initial creation recognize their shortcomings and are in the process of amending them. However, it must be kept in mind that when they were enacted, time was in even shorter supply than potable water and the fear of drought, which had already ravaged most of Africa and Asia and made even the European and South American nations weary and distrustful of one another, won out over prudence.

Pertaining to the trial of Estephania Rodriguez ...

a) The laws as they stand are clear:

i) No water which falls or flows through the boundaries of the United States shall be made available to anyone other than the citizenry of the United States. (Canadian and Guatemalan exceptions notwithstanding).

ii) Any individual aiding or attempting to aid non-U.S. citizens in the collection and/or distribution of state-sequestered potable water will be tried by the state in which the offense occurred as a hydro-terrorist.

iii) Any individual convicted of being a hydro-terrorist shall be sentenced to no less than 25 years in prison and, if the crime deemed particularly egregious, in accordance with state statues, may be sentenced to death.

b) The prosecution effectively presented its case and, according to the jury's verdict, proved beyond a reasonable doubt that the defendant is a hydro-terrorist as defined by the Water Security Laws.

c) The judge, well within his authority to do so, sentenced the defendant to death.

Damien pulled his glasses from his face and threw them across his desk. He looked at the short stack of folders sitting to his right and, just as the night before, was disappointed he hadn't gotten further. He rubbed his face wearily with his hands, reapplied his glasses and reached for Styles' *Appeals* folder.

* * *

It was just getting light outside. Sophia had slept well but presumed her husband had not. She busied herself around the kitchen building a savory breakfast tray with which she was going to surprise him. On the tray were a toasted bagel with cream cheese and pepperoni slices from his favorite Italian deli, a cup of diced prickly pear cactus dollopped with a few spoonfuls of sweetened condensed milk and coffee served in the mug she bought the day before with "World's Greatest Grandpa" printed on the side.

Damien sat at his desk, still in his pajamas and without a robe or slippers, engrossed by the contents of the folder spread out before him.

"Who's hungry?" she cheerfully asked walking into the study with her hard work in her hands.

Damien pulled off his glasses and slipped one of the earpieces into his mouth. "Damn!" he said.

Concern gripped her face and she stopped in the middle of the room. "What?"

"I wish I were still in bed," he laughed. "I can't remember the last time I had breakfast in bed."

Sophia relaxed and placed the tray on the only part of the desk not covered by papers. Damien closed the folder in front of him, placed it on the stack to his right and then slid the two stacks of folders further out of the way to make space for the tray.

"Set 'er down right here, sweetheart."

She did and then turned and leaned against the desk looking down at him.

"This is really nice," he said. "Thank you."

"I just thought with everything you've got going on the rest of the day that you should at least have a few pleasant minutes to start your morning."

He reached around her and hugged her, his face firmly pressed against her stomach and the top of his head nestling between her breasts. She, in turn, wrapped his head in her arms and stroked his hair a few times before he disengaged from her.

"Is that pepperoni from Gianetti's?"

"Absolutely. And look at your coffee."

He read the mug and beamed. It was an easy win for her, but in the weeks leading up to that day, the wins, easy or otherwise, were hard to come by.

"I love it," he said. And with that he attacked the meticulously prepared meal.

She moved from beside him to one of the chairs on the opposite side of the desk and watched. It pleased her a great deal to see him enjoy her simple gesture.

"Is it going to be over today?" she asked.

He looked up and, with a smear of cream cheese on the right corner of his mouth, said, "Honestly, I don't know. There doesn't seem to be any legal grounds to stay the execution and the constituency—the Latinos and the right wing conservatives alike—they all want her dead. The only ones who don't are—"

"The Church," she said with disdain.

"Yes, the Church, and a small handful of stragglers."

"So, she dies and it's all over."

"Unless …," he stopped and looked up from his meal, hoping she wouldn't engage any further but knowing all too well she would.

"Unless what?"

He cringed at the question. He took his napkin from his lap, wiped his face, getting all of the cream cheese she suspected he didn't even know was there, and took a deep breath. "Unless she's, you know, she's, um, what she says she is. The Daughter of God." He couldn't even look her in the eye while saying it.

She sat up and leaned forward in her chair. "You don't believe that, do you?"

"That's the problem. It shouldn't make any difference what I believe. My ultra-conservative constituency believes my daughter is going to hell because she shares her bed with another woman, but they elected me their governor because they think I'm well-suited for the job. Or, at least my affiliated party is well-suited to help me do the job. Remember the weeks leading up to the special election?"

"Oh, God! How could I forget?"

"This woman's trial was the swing issue. The only reason I was elected was because our party came down hard on the side of capital punishment. 'If she is found guilty she gets the needle.' We actually used those words, Sophia. Hart and Samuel didn't even ask me my opinion, they just sent out the written release because they knew it would get me into office."

"She's the psychotic leader of a religious cult. She was found guilty of being a hydro-terrorist. This shouldn't be that hard, Damien. You might not like the idea of the death penalty, but it's not up to you. It's law."

He shook his head and laughed. "This woman, yes, was found guilty, but only because of the arcane laws we put in place as a knee-jerk

126

reaction to the exportation of our drinking water. I read the entire transcript of the trial a dozen times and there's no basis for a guilty verdict."

"Then the judge would have set aside the verdict. But she didn't."

"Maybe she was swayed by public sentiment."

"Maybe. But you don't know that. All you know is what you've read. If what you believe shouldn't make any difference, then why are you still torn?"

He didn't want to answer. He knew what was in his heart and at any other time on any other day he would have told her exactly what that was. But he couldn't. He was ashamed to admit it to himself, let alone say it aloud for anyone else to hear or infer or judge.

"You were a pretty good lawyer, once, Damien," Sophia said. "How many men and women did you believe in your heart of hearts to be innocent only to find out they lied to you? Dozens? Hundreds? You left the Public Defender's office for that exact reason, remember? How many truly were innocent?"

"But that was ages ago. And this is different."

"How is this different?"

He shrugged and fidgeted in his chair. "It just is."

She rolled her eyes. "What are you, in kindergarten? That's not an answer."

"Okay, how about this? Everyone thinks she's crazy. The Latino community calls her *pinche puta loco*."

"What's that mean?"

He savored the meaning in his head, laughing internally knowing that to externalize it would bring a blush to his wife's face. He simply said, "They think she's crazy." Then he added, "Five minutes ago even you said she's psychotic. If that's true, she's insane, which means the state can't execute her."

"That's hyperbole and you know it. I think *you're* psycho, yet you're more than capable of running this state. No one's going to impeach you on the basis of my personal opinions."

They both smiled. Yet with her reply came the realization that the discussion had reached its end point. Or more specifically, he had reached his limit of discussing the matter any further. He'd talked himself sick, over and over, arguing both sides, for the past nine months. He was tired and he wanted it to end. All of it.

"Sophia, I love you with all my heart, but you're going to have to leave now. I still have a tremendous amount of work to do before heading over to the capital building for my nine o'clock. I thank you for this delicious breakfast. I thank you for your gracious efforts to make this part of my day special. But you have to go."

Her face remained stoic, but her eyes betrayed her concern. She stood up and walked out. She would be there for him when he needed her.

Damien finished his breakfast. Then, he continued reading his files.

CHAPTER 23

Father Joe awoke. He sat up, rubbed his eyes and stretched and scratched various parts of his body in an effort to awaken himself more fully. It didn't work as well as he'd hoped. He heard the soft hum of a car passing by outside as he staggered toward the bathroom. A lengthy stop in front of the toilet was followed by a short stop in front of the mirror over the sink to look at how the years had altered his features.

Rarely did anyone take a shower on consecutive days since the stringent conservation policies were enacted following the Water Wars, but since it had rained the night before and the cistern would most assuredly be well stocked, Father Joe afforded himself this small luxury in an effort to more fully prepare him to face what lay ahead.

No sooner had he undressed and slipped into the shower than a knock came.

"Father Joe?" It was Lilith's voice. "I realize these are close quarters and all, but the door to the bathroom downstairs somehow got locked and I am about to wet myself."

"Are you sure it's locked?"

"I jiggled the knob for a good couple minutes."

He thought about the impropriety he had warned them all of the previous night and weighed it against the need for being hospitable. "Um, yes, fine. I guess if it can't be helped."

He heard the door swing open and close, followed by the sound of clothes ruffling together and finally a low, steady hiss from where he knew the toilet was. "You know, this whole celibacy thing is really overblown. I mean, why shouldn't priests marry? Then there'd be no reason to worry about the perception of me even being here."

Father Joe stood under the shower spray no longer scrubbing himself with the soap, but looking up in thoughtful contemplation at the hexagonal tile pattern on the ceiling. "Are you looking for an answer or are you making idle small talk?" he asked.

"I suppose a little of both."

"I guess the short answer for celibacy is that as priests we're married to the church and we can't serve two spouses."

"Is that what they teach in the seminary?"

"No, that would be the long answer: the teachings of St. Paul, Leo IX and Gregory VII, various other popes throughout the ages, Vatican II."

"Is Vatican II still relevant? That was in the 1960's, right?"

"1962, actually. The Second Vatican Council wrote that they were confident in the Spirit that celibacy is, was and always will be a divine gift. 'And the more that perfect continence is considered by many people to be impossible in the world of today, so much the more humbly and perseveringly in union with the Church ought priests demand the grace of fidelity, which is never denied to those who ask.'"

"But what about human nature? What about procreation and the continuance of the species? What about desire?"

The word 'desire' echoed in his mind and a sense of arousal shuddered through him. He tried to focus on something else. "In Corinthians, Paul wrote, 'For he who is without a wife is solicitous for the things that belong to the Lord, how he may please God. But he that is with a wife, is solicitous for the things of this world, how he may please his wife; and he is divided.'"

His attempt to distract his mind failed. The physical manifestation of sexual desire had taken hold of his body. His blood flowed and he became erect.

"That's Paul," he heard from the other side of the curtain. "What about you? Surely there are times when you long for human contact. It, too, is a divine gift, isn't it?"

He closed his eyes. His left hand rubbed soap across his chest while his right hand moved down and, with the tips of his fingers, he gently swirled and caressed his penis head.

"Clerical celibacy is not a Church doctrine," he explained without a hint of emotion. "It's a discipline, one that we, diocesan priests, take very seriously."

The hand that held the soap drifted downward and with both hands he lathered his shaft and began giving it long, delightful strokes: three in a row, then a fourth, then more.

His voice got fainter. "The pope could decide tomorrow to allow priests to marry. Permit the pleasures of the flesh offered those bound in the blessed sacrament of marriage."

His mind produced swirling images of various women from his parish, naked, bent over on their knees, their arms wrapped around their hindquarters and pulling open their vaginal lips, begging him to enter. And in his mind he did, over and over, his hands forcibly pulling at their hips, penetrating them deeply, their faces pushed, with each forceful thrust, harder and harder against the marble top of the church altar.

He stopped. On the precipice of climaxing, Father Joe stopped and opened his eyes.

The warm water made rivulets down his body. He felt them run down his arms to his hands where they dropped into the tiny pool surrounding the tub drain. He released the hold he had on himself, ashamed. The bar of soap, slightly misshapen from his tightening grip around it, he placed in the slotted dish that sat on a shelf in the shower corner. He tucked his head fully under the shower spray and, with both hands, rubbed his face, slowly at first, but then more vigorously, as if trying to wash the images of his naked parishioners from his mind.

He edged to the front of the shower and pulled back the shower curtain. Aside from the fixtures and the steam, the room was empty. She had left.

When? he thought. What does she know? What could she hear?

He closed the curtain and turned around, his back to the showerhead. He looked down to see that he was flaccid. He thought a moment, turned around again and sat in the tub, letting the cleansing water flow over his entire body. He turned off the water, sat in the tub and prayed for forgiveness.

* * *

Father Joe eased down the stairs and walked into the kitchen. Both Felipe and Lilith were at the table, helping themselves to bowls of cereal. Father Joe looked at the two of them just for a moment and then busied himself with his own breakfast.

"Lilith," Father Joe said and then cleared his throat.

"How was your shower?" she asked before he could continue. A certain playful edge accompanied her words.

He blushed, ashamed. "Fine, thank you."

"You were in there a while," she said smiling. Her eyes flashed to Felipe, seemingly looking for a reaction, but none came as he was not paying attention to her.

"Yes, well, I spent some time praying."

"Is that what the kids are calling it these days? *Praying* in the shower?"

She stared at him. When he showed no signs of retort, she asked, "Why today?"

"Why what today?"

"Why pray today?"

"I have a lot on my mind," he said, thinking of Estephania Rodriguez. A Cheshire grin crept across her face. "Oh, I'm sure," she laughed. "I'm sure you had an awful lot on your mind while you were in the shower. And I suppose your hands were full, too, while you were in there."

Some of the self-respect he thought he regained through prayer left him then. He pressed on. "While I was praying I thought a little more about your question of clerical celibacy."

"Um-hum," she mumbled with a mouthful of cereal.

"Well, aside from the spiritual reasons I mentioned earlier, there's also a practical side. The average salary of a diocesan priest is miniscule. Believe me, I know. And living in a rectory, owned by the archdiocese as part of the church, is basically free room and board. Married priests, especially those with families, would most likely live in a private residence, which our current salaries could never support. Add to that higher insurance premiums for families and it just doesn't make economic sense."

She held her spoon a few inches above the bowl as milk dripped from its bottom. Then, with contempt oozing from every word, she said, "I'll grant you that church-think has come a long way since the Dark Ages, but for you to even entertain the idea that the priest within a married couple is obligated to support his family is absolutely ridiculous. There was a whole movement where women burned their bras to show their contempt for that kind of thinking." She went back to crunching her cereal. "Hell," she said, spitting some milk, "Even *my* organization's ultraconservatives aren't *that* narrow-minded."

132

Felipe threw his spoon into his bowl. "Father Joe, just ignore her. She is a mean and hateful woman. She has no business being here."

"But I do!" Lilith said. "I'm going to watch that bitch beg me to save her."

Felipe and Father Joe exchanged glances of disbelief.

"You know what, Ms. Samuel?" Father Joe said. "I'm going to have to ask you to leave. At dinner last night you seemed so quiet and contemplative and respectful. But this? This wickedness and impiety is unacceptable. I'm sorry, but you have to go."

She shoveled another mouthful of cereal into her mouth.

"Now, please, Ms. Samuel." It was as forceful as the mild-mannered priest could get.

She looked up at her host. Then at Felipe. "You can't be serious."

They both looked at her sternly.

"What happened to Christian kindness?"

"You get what you give," Felipe replied.

"Ah, that's good ol' fashion Old Testament justice, there, Felipe. Christians are all about turning the other cheek. And this Estephania woman you two think is all holy and whatnot, she was preaching all that crap about, 'When someone steals from you, give to them what they take and more.' Where's the compassion she asks of you?"

"What you took from me," Felipe said, "was my conviction of Her divinity. But since we talked last night, I've found I'm so overflowing with it that you can have your fill, along with my pity."

"Your pity?"

"Yes, my pity. Because you'll never believe like I do."

"When you know what I know, you don't have to believe," she sneered. Then, she stood and walked out of the kitchen toward the front door. She pushed the door open so it slammed against the side of the house.

"Felipe, Father," Lilith smirked, looking back through the doorway, "you are small men with small ideas about a small world." Then, pointing at them, she said, "I'll see you two later."

She reached for her All-COM and walked beyond the frame of the door and out of their sight.

Felipe went back to eating his cereal while Father Joe went into the office to gather up the sheets on the couch. He untucked one end from the cushions and wrapped the sheets into a tight ball around his arm. He stripped the pillow case from the pillow and stuffed the sheets inside, tucking the bare pillow under his arm.

"Felipe," he called out. "The parish's office manager is likely to be coming in soon. I see no reason to tell anyone that foul woman was ever here. Do you?"

"What foul woman, Father?"

"Miss Samuel, of course."

Felipe laughed. "Yes, I know. I was going along with your request to—"

"Ah," he interrupted, finally understanding the small joke. "I get it. I'm a bit slow without my morning coffee."

Father Joe hurried upstairs to throw the sheets in his hamper and the pillow back into in the linen closet in the hallway. Then, just as quickly, he hurried back down the stairs and walked back into the kitchen. A sudden pall fell upon them both as Father Joe set a mug of hot coffee before his guest. They sipped in silent solace.

"Today is going to be sad day, Padre."

"We don't know that for sure. Who knows, it might be the happiest day of our lives."

"Well, if I'm going to thank God for small favors, whatever the outcome, it will be far more tolerable and pleasant without that woman around."

"Amen."

* * *

He kept out of the sunlight, close to the church, conforming to the soft curves of its shadows. While others found shadows cold and dark, he found them warm and inviting, particularly the shadows cast by a church, a silhouette of the Community of God. And from the shadows he watched as she left the rectory. Hidden within the shadows, he followed her, wanting more and more, with every step he took, to spare the world of her wretchedness.

134

He relished the thought that her time was soon, and when it did come, the man in white would be the one to send her back to hell.

CHAPTER 24

Bishop DeMarco was the concelebrant at the Monday morning Mass alongside Father Enrique at Saints Simon & Jude Cathedral. Throughout the ceremony his mind was led astray by the dream he had the previous night. Rarely did he ever remember his dreams staying so wholly in his mind. Typically, he'd remember bits and pieces of dreams, moments and themes, perhaps, but never entire sequences. Nothing like this. He could recite, if asked, every word the Angel Gabriel spoke. He could expound upon, again, if asked, the most insignificant detail. He could describe the phosphorescent glow of her skin, the pale, dead grayness of her irises, the flowing edges of her billowy garment. The one item upon which he focused with severe skepticism was her lack of a halo.

Everyone knows that angels have halos, he reminded himself.

"The Mass has ended. Let us go in peace to love and serve the Lord," Father Enrique concluded.

"Thanks be to God," the two dozen or so attendees replied in chorus.

While the parishioners filed out to get to their vehicles, the two priests crossed the chancel, in front of the altar, and headed to the south door leading to the sacristy. As they removed their cassocks, albs, vestments and stoles and hung them in the closet, Father Enrique struck up a conversation.

"So Manuel, did you have any other dreams last night? Any other divine guidance?"

"Are you making fun of me, Enrique?"

"Not at all. Not at all. I'm just curious. It's not every day that someone tells you the Messenger of God spoke to them in a dream."

The bishop did not reply.

"You seemed … agitated last night. Unresolved. Have you found solace?"

"Solace?" he laughed. "No. I think solace is in short supply these days."

Father Enrique furrowed his brow. "What an odd thing to say. We live in troubled times, sure, but tell me a time when there were no troubles. And throughout time, hasn't Christ been our solace? Is, was and shall be, world without end?"

"Amen," Bishop DeMarco replied. He thanked his friend for his words of encouragement by smiling and placing his hand on his friend's shoulder. "I think I might sit in one of the pews and pray a while. You know, see if I can't find me some of that solace," he said like an old bluesman.

The two of them laughed.

"Oh, I almost forgot," the bishop said, grabbing his All-COM from the countertop and clipping it onto his belt. "Just to add fuel to the fire, I promised Father Joe that I'd pray with him and the Rodriguez woman before, you know, her execution. So I won't be joining you for lunch."

"Well, I suppose there's something to be said about getting closer to an answer through proximity. If you need me," he said, pointing to the All-COM, "let me know."

Bishop DeMarco exited the sacristy and aimlessly walked the aisles while adoring the cathedral's stained glass windows. They were not depictions of Gospel passages or memorials to the Church's martyrs and saints, but beautiful abstract mosaics made from large blocks of stained glass randomly fitted together and cemented into place. He stopped in front of each window frame, staring, struggling to find a common theme within the randomness. He counted the number of pieces in each to see if they all matched. They didn't. Many were predominately blue, but after counting the number of blue pieces in consecutive frames and finding their totals differed significantly, he attributed their dominance to a glut of supplies. No matter how he tried, he could not find any commonality between frames other than the overall aesthetics of being similarly random. It ate at him mercilessly and for the first time since being appointed bishop, he decided he didn't like the cathedral's windows.

He shuffled up the aisle again, staring up. From underfoot he felt something odd and heard a soft scrape, like a tool on stone. He lifted his foot to reveal a weathered penny. It was heads. He bent down to pick it up and recited in his head, *Find a penny, pick it up and all the day you'll have good luck.* Then, he scrutinized the penny as he did the windows. At least *it* had order: the profile of Honest Abe; LIBERTY, 1997; IN GOD WE TRUST.

He tried to rub some of the accumulated grime off of it to no avail. It was old and it was going to stay old no matter how much he rubbed it.

1997? he thought. *That's a penny that's seen its fair share of things.*

He slipped the penny into his pocket and walked out of the cathedral.

* * *

Governor Driver had finished reading all of the files Styles had placed on his desk well before heading to his office in the Capitol Building. He was more than an hour into his nine o'clock meeting, having heard all three doctors argue over the minutia of Estephania's sanity. They all agreed that she met all the criteria to stand trial as a mentally fit defendant, that she understood what was happening and why it was happening, that she was aware of her actions and that her actions had consequences and that she could aid in her own defense. However, beyond those specific items, they could not agree. Not on her mental condition. Not on how she should be treated, or even *if* she should be treated. They couldn't agree on how much she weighed had she been standing in front of them on the world's most accurate scale. And none of them were capable of using lay terms, throwing around acronyms and abbreviations as if the governor had not just read but memorized and understood the *Complete Medical Encyclopedia*. He was even more confused now, by their jargon and incessant bickering, than he had been before they showed up.

Abruptly, Damien said, "Gentlemen, you can go now."

They all stopped their yammering and looked at him, perplexed.

"I've heard enough. I wanted to know if this woman was mentally competent to stand trial to which you are all in agreement. Therefore, I thank you for your time. You may leave."

"But she's still in a very delicate condition," said one.

"She would be a tremendous addition to my study on Dissociative Identity Disorder," said another.

"She's not D.I.D., you buffoon," said the third.

"Gentlemen!" the governor shouted above the din, standing as he did so. Then, more gently, "I am no longer asking you to leave but rather telling you. Thank you."

The three doctors grumbled their arguments to one another as they shuffled out of his office. They shut the door behind them and the governor collapsed into his sturdy leather chair. He folded his arms on his desk and buried his head in them, wondering how it was possible for the medical profession to produce a higher percentage of idiots, morons and dolts than the legal profession.

The All-COM on his desk beeped. "Sir," his administrative assistant called, "The bishop's on line four."

The governor didn't move his head. "Thank you, Dave," he said, his voice muffled.

"Sir, are you going to take it?" Dave asked.

The governor lifted his head and answered, "Yes, Dave. Thank you."

He grabbed the All-COM and pushed line four. "Hello?"

"Damien, this is Bishop DeMarco. Am I interrupting anything?"

"Not at all, Bishop," he said leaning way back in his chair and rolling his eyes. "What can I do for you?"

"Are you going to the prison for the execution?"

"I hadn't planned on it," he lied.

A long silence followed and the governor felt obligated to explain further.

"I don't think I should get into the habit of visiting inmates just before the state puts them to death. Favoritism and bias and such."

More silence.

The bishop finally said, "Is there any way I can persuade you to join me there?"

"Join you? You're going out there? I thought—"

"Yes, I'm going. Father Joe laid on some of that good old fashion Catholic guilt on me last night so I promised him I'd pray with him and the Rodriguez woman. But after last night and this morning, I'm pretty sure I'd be going out there anyway."

"Really? What happened?"

"Well, I guess I had an epiphany."

The governor chuckled until he didn't hear the bishop chuckling along with him.

139

"An epiphany," the bishop continued, "in the truest sense. A revelation of divinity. I'd love to tell you all about it. It should take all of about 30 minutes to get out there."

The governor had already resigned himself to the idea of attending the execution. He was unsure how he would explain it to his constituency, but he was certain there would be backlash. Being invited by the party's largest contributor provided a legitimate excuse, but he didn't want to seem eager.

"I can't just up and leave, Bishop DeMarco. I have appointments."

"Cancel them!"

"Bishop," the governor said, readying himself for a long-winded explanation as to why he couldn't attend the execution of Estephania Rodriquez. He never delivered his response.

"Governor, last night you were looking for a reason, *anything* to stay the execution."

"Last night I was fact finding, doing my due diligence. Nothing more."

"Oh, bullshit!" the bishop yelled.

The governor paused. "I'm sorry, did you just say 'bullshit'?"

"Yes, I did. Bullshit! And you are full of it."

The governor rubbed the palms of his hands against his closed eyes causing bright lights to flash inside his head. "Wow. A bishop in the Catholic Church just told me I was full of shit. My day's just getting better and better.

"Please, governor," the bishop pleaded.

Damien rubbed his eyes again. "I can't believe I'm doing this," he sighed, feigning annoyance. "Give me a couple minutes to … move some things around. I'll be in front of the cathedral in fifteen minutes."

CHAPTER 25

Both passengers in the back of the taxi had expected there to be a near riot as those "for" and those "against" faced off in their bitter struggle to be heard above the other. It was a scene that played out so routinely at every state sanctioned execution. However, as they passed in front of the prison, only a handful of supporters and even fewer protesters stood before the main gate with signs aligning them with their causes: *You Can't Kill God* and *¡Dios Es Eterno!* faced off against *Death Is Not Enough* and *¡Mate la Pinche Puta Loco!* There was no shouting, no real crowd to speak of and no media. Both their hearts sank.

"I would have thought that there'd be a much larger crowd out here," Felipe said, angry that none of the other Adherentes had bothered to make the trip to P-Ville.

"Love and hate might be at opposite ends of the emotional scale," Father Joe explained, "but without emotion you have apathy. Didn't you say you and your friend ran into this at the TV station last night? No one cares."

"I guess I was just hoping that the station was the exception and not the rule."

Their taxi pulled around the side and into the prison's employee parking lot. Father Joe swiped his All-COM to pay for the fair and the two men exited the cab. There was a quick glance between the two men before Father Joe swiped his security card and placed his thumb on the print scanner. The employee door buzzed and clicked and opened. As soon as the two men walked through the door an intense, beeping alarm and bright, flashing lights swirled around them. The two guards stationed at the end of the narrow hallway dropped to one knee and drew their weapons.

"Put your hands where I can see them," shouted the guard on the left.

Terrified, Father Joe and Felipe threw their hands straight up. The two guards got up from their stance and advanced slowly toward them.

A panicked daze overwhelmed both Father Joe and Felipe. With their hands in the air they crouched down, backing into the corner, cowering.

In Father Joe's hands were a Bible and his security card. Felipe's hands were empty.

"I'm allowed to be here," Father Joe said defensively, showing his security card.

The guard on the same side of the hallway as the priest, the one who initially shouted at them, grabbed Father Joe and pulled him away from Felipe. "Quiet, Father," the guard said.

The other guard grabbed Felipe's right wrist with his left hand and roughly pulled Felipe forward, his momentum carrying him to the ground. The guard wrapped the Latino man's arm around his body, placed his knee into the small of Felipe's back, holstered his weapon and cuffed Felipe's wrists together in a single flash of motion.

"He's with me," Father Joe pleaded, though he was certain no one had heard him.

The two guards each reached under Felipe's armpits and dragged him into a doorway at the end of the hallway, right by the entrance the two visitors had just come through. Father Joe followed them in and watched as Felipe was pulled to his feet by the two guards and forced to stand facing the wall.

"He's with me," Father Joe said again, this time with some power.

"Only one person is authorized to enter at a time," one of the guards said while the other traced Felipe's entire body and appendages with his hands. "The bio-filter alarm counted two."

"Yes, two," was all the priest could muster. "I didn't even know there was a filter."

"¿Habla ingles?" the guard touching Felipe asked.

"Yes," he answered.

"I'm going to reach into your pockets. Is there anything in there that I should be made aware of: weapons, needles, flash vials, anything like that?"

"No. I carry a wallet and a set of keys."

"Really, gentlemen," Father Joe insisted. "Is this necessary?"

"Father," the other guard said, "the only reason you're not in cuffs right now is because you have a security card. Now, I don't know if this guy is your Mexican *gemelo* or some head case trying to help one of his *cuadrillato* escape. The fact is, I don't have the luxury to care. You're allowed to be here. He's not."

The other guard pulled out a set of keys and a wallet from Felipe's pockets.

"Can't we just go around to the visitor's entrance?"

"You should have thought about that before you set off the bio-filter."

"We're here for the … I mean, we're going to pray with Estephania Rodriguez."

"That cult leader?" they both shouted and laughed.

Father Joe ignored their laughs. "Now that you've searched him, can we go?"

"He's not going anywhere, Father. Not for a while. Not until we check him out. And unless he's family, the only place he's going is back out the door he just came in."

"Can I speak with him, please?"

The guard shrugged.

"Felipe, I'm sorry. I guess I didn't think this all the way through."

"No, no. It's not your fault. I'm the one who didn't think it through. You go, Padre. Be with Her. Tell Her I'm here. And tell Her that I love Her."

The guards made vulgar comments insinuating the only thing she really loves is of a sexual nature which the two other men in the room found disgraceful.

Father Joe stood up and walked over to the two guards. "Gentlemen," he said, inspecting their security cards. "Last night I had dinner with the governor." He scribbled something in his Bible. "Needless to say I have his ear. Please treat my friend well."

One of the guards walked over and stood toe-to-toe with the priest, bullying him with his imposing presence. "Is that a threat?"

"Absolutely not," the priest replied defiantly. He was pleased with how it came out. "It's a simple request. Treat him well and the governor will be told of your hospitality."

Walking back to Felipe, his hand rested gently on the man's shoulder. "As soon as I attend to Her needs, I'll see what I can do for you." He walked out of the room and down the hall, wondering how in the world he could possibly attend to Her needs.

143

* * *

The two men sat in the back of the governor's luxurious car provided by the people. It was one of the few perks the governor actually enjoyed.

The bishop did most of the talking, ceaselessly, on the way to the prison, telling the governor about his dream in animated detail.

The governor listened intently, trying hopelessly to understand how any of this provided a loophole he could use to keep Estephania Rodriquez from being executed. As the words flowed from the bishop's mouth, the governor was further filled with dread at the inevitability of his actions.

"Bishop, I am so happy for you. Sincerely. Unfortunately, I wasn't visited by the Messenger of God. My soul hasn't been touched by her teachings like Father Joe and her Adherentes. And even if it were, I'm not sure how it changes anything."

"You must stay her execution."

"On what grounds?"

"On the grounds that she is not the Daughter of God, la Hermana de Jesus or whatever else she calls herself. She's obviously delusional, insane. Therefore, under State law, it would be cruel and unusual to execute a mentally unfit criminal."

"Wait a second, you just said in your dream—"

"I was clicking around the internet this morning and read several theories about dreams. The most compelling was that dreams are your subconscious mind cleaning up the neural network of the debris and useless information it had obtained throughout the day. Random synaptic firings during R.E.M. sleep to release the stress of information overload.

"Considering our dinner last night, the debris regarding this whole Rodriguez affair would be quite extensive, wouldn't you say?"

"Possibly."

"And then there's Pope John XXIII who said, 'Consult not your fears but your hopes and your dreams. Think not about your frustrations, but about your unfulfilled potential. Concern yourself not with what you tried and failed in, but with what it is still possible for you to do.'

"That's when it hit me," the bishop continued. "I know what I can do, governor. I can persuade you to let this woman live."

The two men sat in contemplative silence for a moment.

The bishop pressed on. "Dreams are just that, Governor, dreams. They're not reality. They're random thoughts your subconscious mind fires off during sleep. And did I tell you about the penny?"

The governor shook his head.

"I was looking up at the stained glass windows in the cathedral. They don't depict anything, they're abstract. Anyway, I'm looking up at them paying no attention to where I was going and I stepped on a penny. I bend down to pick it up and it was heads. Good luck, right? I study it a bit and see it was minted in the year 1997, the same year that you said Estephania Rodriguez was born. And then I see it, the inscription on all U.S. currency: *In God We Trust.* Is there a more elegant reminder of the Almighty's omnipotence?"

The governor looked confused. "That didn't reaffirm that your dream was a message from God?"

"In *God* we trust, Governor. Not the human mind. True divinity is not a dream."

"So, by your reasoning, Joseph should have ignored his dream and divorced Mary. The magi should have gone back to Herod and told him where to find the Christ child. Daniel. Zechariah. Hell, the *Hail Mary* comes from the words of an angel in Mary's dream."

"Yes, true. But I am no Daniel or Joseph."

"Joseph was a carpenter!" the governor shouted. "He was no one special until his wife had a baby. Why do you have to be special to hear God's word?"

"My vocation makes me special, Governor," the bishop said, indignant. "I have heard God's word my entire adult life."

"Proving my point," the governor interrupted.

The bishop went on undeterred. "And, it is through my vocation that I have determined that I had a dream, a plain old ordinary dream. In *God* we trust, governor. Not dreams."

Still confused, now at the bishop's logic, he said, "Wow. That makes no sense to me at all. But, be that as it may, I can't stay the execution. My actions have to be within the realm of civil law and the secular and nothing I've read or heard, by you, by the doctors, by Father Joe last night provides me with the authority—"

"Authority!" the bishop shouted. "You're the governor! That's all the authority you need. You can stay her execution because you believe it to be just. With great power comes great responsibility and with the power you wield, to allow this woman to be executed would be irresponsible. Criminal, perhaps."

"No." The governor said it plainly and simply.

A blank stare controlled the bishop's face.

"Look, I'm a public servant, elected by the people to do a job."

"Some things transcend what the people want."

"While that might be true—"

"We are one nation under God," the bishop said loudly. "We are obligated to obey His will."

"And who's to say what His will is? You? Have you now superseded the Pope with the dogma of infallibility? Ex Cathedra?" He crossed his hands and watched the muted landscape pass by. The terrain appeared paler to his eyes, painted with dull pastels, as if the rain had washed away the saturated colors. The sky, too, was sapped of its vibrancy, a soft bluish-gray fabric clinging to the stratosphere.

Still looking out the window, he said, "Bishop, I feel for you. For the last three weeks … no, since I took office, I've been holding meetings and reading documents and consulting tea leaves, anything to help me get my arms around this whole issue and I keep coming back to the same thing over and over again. Without something more, I cannot grant this woman clemency. It would be nice if Miss Rodriguez could live a long and happy life, preaching to the throngs of needy people her message of peace and forgiveness, providing a salve for all our ills, but I can't."

The governor sighed and then went on. "Let me give you a hypothetical. Just for a moment, consider that Jesus was just some guy, Not the Messiah, not the Lamb of God, just another Jew killed by the Romans. Now, think of all the good that has been done in Jesus' name based on this singular mistaken belief. Schools and hospitals tending to social needs. Missions and non-profit organizations helping the sick, the poor and the war-ravaged. Hell, the founding of this country was based on Christian dogma. Hypothetically speaking, love they neighbor is a crock, the philosophical ramblings of some schmoe.

"Yet, all that good, based solely on the *belief* that Jesus was the Son of God, has merit. Don't you see? It doesn't make a difference if He is the Son of God or not."

"I'm sorry, Governor, I don't see how this—"

"It doesn't matter if she is the Daughter of God. Even if I wanted to stay the execution, I can't. Not now. My hands are tied. We'll let the history books determine whether or not what I did was right."

The bishop, dejected, looked out his window. A long pause came between the two of them. The droning hum of tires against the road had become almost cacophonic, drawing his attention inward. "So why are you here?" the bishop finally asked.

The question caught the governor off guard. "What?"

"If there's nothing you can do, then why did you agree to come with me to P-Ville?"

"Because the party's largest financial supporter asked me to come."

"I believe," the bishop said calmly, "that I'm already on record as saying 'bullshit.'"

The governor laughed. "Yes, Bishop, I believe you are. However, I've never heard her speak. Have you?"

"No."

"I pray fairly regularly, Bishop DeMarco. And if she is the Daughter of God, I think I'd like to talk to God and get an immediate response."

The bishop thought a moment. "You do realize you've just lost the support of your party's largest financial supporter come re-election?"

"Some things transcend what the people want, Your Eminence."

* * *

It was a bright autumn day, though cooler than usual. The downpour from the previous night was a distant memory, evaporated into thin air leaving only small cuts of erosion in the tiny sand dunes lining the street's gutters. Lilith Samuel was walking from the rectory to the prison. It's only a couple of miles, she thought. Why not get some exercise?

147

The first fifteen minutes into her trek were uneasy. She could sense someone following her, she always could. It was a hypersensitivity she had attained as a by-product of the uneasiness she instilled in others. However, after a while, her uneasiness subsided. Had her stalker wanted to do her harm, she thought, there were ample opportunities among the deserted, sometimes desolate streets and none of them were seized.

As she made her way she concentrated on the task before her, the one she was ultimately sent to complete, how she was going to go about doing what needed to be done. It played over and over in her head, the questions she'd be asked, the answers she'd give, the lies she'd tell. The imaginary conversations splintered and veered into discussions so unlikely so as to ensure she knew how to handle anything thrown her way.

Upon arriving at the prison, she stood with the protestors outside the building, continuously playing over various scenarios in her mind. A glint of light from the parking lot caught her eye and she watched as a muscular man, the driver of the long black sedan, help his two passengers get out from the back seat. She watched the three men slowly approach the building and listened as the meager crowd became more vocal as they got closer. None of the three paid much attention to the protestors. However, the muscular man reacted swiftly when Lilith approached his two charges, placing himself between her and them, his right hand buried beneath his blazer.

"Governor!" Lilith cried out.

The governor turned and looked over the driver's shoulder. "Lilith? What are you doing here?"

The muscular man had eased his stance even before the governor spoke, having recognized the woman in the crowd. To him she said, "Excuse me," and she curtly moved around him. To the governor, she said, "After you left last night, I thought I'd come out here and see firsthand what all the hullabaloo is all about. Mind if I join you?"

"Please, please," he replied. "I'm sure the bishop won't mind."

The bishop's face stated otherwise. "Of course, Ms. Samuel," was all he said.

CHAPTER 26

It was mid-morning and the office was all abuzz. The Young Republicans streaming through the various cubicles that cluttered the interior space of the state's party headquarters all noted the excitement and commented relentlessly about how stimulating things were. Most were starry-eyed volunteers from the university, poli-sci majors, presumably, either trying to pad their résumé with practical work experience or trying to make the world a better place through the legislative might of the party. Mike Hart couldn't stand any of them. Their parents, on the other hand, Mike Hart loved all of them. That was his job, or, at least a significant part of his job.

Having all but ignored the events from the previous night, Mike had gotten an early start on the day, one that would include, among other things, the final act regarding the State vs. Estephania Rodriguez. It was in regard to this particular part of his day that a knock rapped at his door.

"Mr. Hart?" said the young and pretty volunteer about whom Mike actually cared enough to remember her name.

"Yes, Loni."

"It's Lori," she said. "There's a really weird guy up front who wants to talk to you."

"No."

"He's a reporter."

"Definitely not."

"His name is Luke Logan."

The name struck an unharmonious cord in his mind. He looked up and gave Lori a look that a murderer might give his victim. "How many different ways can I tell you I am not speaking to whoever's up front?"

"Charming as ever," came loud and edgy from behind Lori. As Luke Logan entered Mike's doorway, the reporter continued, "You know, you should be in politics. Or you could just sell your soul to the devil now and eliminate the middleman."

Immediately, Mike noticed Luke was dressed in the same clothes he was wearing the night before. He watched as Luke eased around the embarrassed volunteer, who took that moment to disappear without notice. Luke stood in the space as if he owned the small but adequate office before pulling up a sturdy metal folding chair on the opposite side of Mike's desk. The disheveled man sat and smiled.

Mike leaned back in his chair and said, "I'm a very busy man, Mr. Logan. Please tell me what I can do for you, quickly, so I can expedite your departure."

Luke just stared and continued smiling. Mike thought it was supposed to make him nervous. It worked. Mike leaned forward and grabbed his pen, twirled it once, then again, then set it back down. Seeing this, Luke's smile grew and somehow he became even more silent.

Mike sighed. "Mr. Logan …"

"Look, I'm a reporter. You don't like me because it's my job to tell the people all the wonderful ways in which you fuck up their lives. I get it."

"Actually, I don't like you because you're an asshole. I try not to be bigoted against people based on race, religion or occupation. But please, continue."

"We both know there's no such thing as 'off the record,' right? But here's the deal. I need to know a few things, for personal reasons, things which under normal circumstances you would never tell me."

"And you think that by telling me we're off the record, I'm going to tell you what you want to know?"

Luke Logan's face contorted beyond facial features into a massive ball of furry hate. He leaned over the desk and whispered, "No. I think I'm going to get what I want to know from you by threatening to beat you until you're an unrecognizable mass of human tissue. And when I get tired or my fists begin to hurt, whichever comes first, I'm going to strangle you until your hateful eyes bulge out of that condescending face of yours and you draw your last breath, your body twitching in my cold, steely grasp. Then, once you're dead, I'm going to douse you with kerosene, set you on fire, and throw you out that fucking window behind you with such a pretty view of downtown. And finally, once I make my way outside, I'll piss on your broken and battered corpse until my bladder runs dry. That's how I'm going to get you to tell me what I want."

Mike Hart actually felt his pupils dilate. He consciously subdued the urge to pee his pants. He sat, motionless, wondering why he never asked out that sweet girl from Flagstaff who sat next to him in his sophomore International Business Law class. Then, he watched Luke Logan reach back, pull his All-COM from his hip and set it down on his desk. Luke pushed a button and Mike heard again the dark, menacing diatribe of the man sitting before him.

...I'll piss on your broken and battered corpse until my bladder runs dry. That's how I'm going to get you to tell me what I want.

"Here," Luke said, his face ungnarled, beaming a pleasant, pearly grin. "You keep it. And if anything we discuss here today gets published, you can take that to the District Attorney's office and have me arrested. I suggest you try A.D.A. Vazquez. For some reason she doesn't like me. I'm sure she'd be more than happy to prosecute me to the full extent of the law. Six years for threatening a public official, I think. But, then again, yours is not an elected position, so maybe I'd get off with less. Still, I like being out of jail." His grin became uncomfortable and relaxed into a stoic expression of apathy. "So there it is: leverage. Your leverage over me."

Mike Hart looked through the furry man in the parka, his mind churning, processing the myriad angles, traps and pitfalls, for himself and the party, for the man opposite him, trying to determine his next move. Clarity left him, as if it were doused, burned and thrown out the window.

"Do you know who Vincent Clay is?" Luke asked.

Mike grabbed the All-COM from his desk to make sure it was not recording. He pulled open the desk drawer to his left, threw the device in, shut the drawer and locked it. "I'm sorry, who?"

"Vincent Clay."

"No, I don't." Mike would have said *no* even if the name had meant something to him. The fact that it meant nothing relieved him.

"He was the man you met last night at Heaven's Gate."

Relief is often short lived. "Heaven's Gate?"

"Seriously?" Luke said sarcastically, his face slowly hardening. "You're gonna play games with me?"

Mike thought a moment. "Ah, yes. He told me his name was Clay. I assumed it was his first name." He felt particularly proud of his quick comeback.

"You guys talked a while. What about?"

151

Mike opened his mouth, paused, then stopped. He smiled and spoke carefully. "After you interrupted our dinner, my boss, the executive director—"

"Lilith Samuel. Yeah, she was in an accident. You said you were busy. Let's move this along."

"I got a call from Mr. Clay saying he had information about the accident."

"Lone wolf activities?"

"I don't know what a lone wolf is let alone what kinds of activities such a thing would do."

"The fuck you don't," Luke mumbled under his breath.

Mike shifted in his chair. "We had a discussion about heaven and hell. He told me some ...," he refrained from using the term *lone wolf*, "crazy man thought my boss was the devil, so he rammed the car she was in from behind."

"Did he say anything else?"

He thought about the threats. "He said the crazy man was going to kill Lilith. And then spouted some gibberish."

"Have you warned your boss? Told her about these threats?"

"She's AWOL. She went out to Goodyear with Father Joe and your Mexican friend but I can't reach her. And her All-COM's GPS chip is in her office."

"That gibberish, could you make heads or tails of it?"

"I haven't given it a second thought. Why?"

"Figures you'd ignore it. Well, if it'll make you feel any better, your boss isn't the devil."

"I don't need a newspaper reporter to tell me that."

"If my sources are correct, and they usually are, she's not the devil ... she's a demon, one of the devil's minions. A Mesopotamian storm demon, to be exact, a temptress and bearer of ill will. And the man out to kill her? Get this. He's an angel. Michael the Archangel, to be exact." Then Luke's visage became disturbingly upbeat. "He's gonna smite the living shit out of her."

Mike sat in astonishment. "You're just as whacked as Clay."

"Maybe so. But you know, the funny thing about sanity is it's so hard to be completely objective about it."

152

Luke sat and smiled. Mike found his smile more disturbing than his sneer. "Do you want to hear more?" Luke asked.

"There's more?"

"Oh yeah. Lots," Luke said enthusiastically.

Mike shrugged his shoulders.

"Well, with you being so busy and all, I thought ..."

"Yeah, yeah. Whaddaya got?"

Luke opened his notepad and unfolded a piece of paper. Then he said, as much with his hands as with his mouth, "All right, that gibberish I assume you're referring to, was it 4-Q-5-1-0-dash-5-1-1?"

"Probably. It was something like that, anyway. What about it?"

"Go ahead, type it into your All-COM," Luke instructed.

Mike pulled his All-COM and asked, "What was it, again?"

Luke repeated it.

Mike Hart entered the data and hit search. As he read through the listing of hits, Luke continued.

"It refers to a passage from the *Dead Sea Scrolls*. Apparently, it's like a prayer to exorcise her from your mind."

"Her? Her who?"

Luke looked up from his notepad. "Your boss." Then, unfolding a piece of paper, he read aloud what Mike pulled up on his All-COM. *"'And I, the Instructor, proclaim His glorious splendor so as to frighten and to terrify all the spirits of the destroying angels, spirits of the bastards, demons, Lilith ...'"* Luke stopped reciting and commented, "Notice that the author actually calls her by name." Turning back to the paper, *"'... bastards, demons, Lilith, howlers, and those which fall upon men without warning to lead them astray from the spirit of understanding and to make their heart and their soul desolate during the present dominion of wickedness and predetermined time of humiliations for the sons of light, by the guilt of the ages of those smitten by iniquity—not for eternal destruction, but for an era of humiliation for transgression.'"*

"The Dead Sea Scrolls?" Mike said. "That's outstanding!"

What little interest Mike had in what Luke Logan was telling him disappeared as quickly as Lori had from the doorway. "Let me ask you something. Where do the homeless go during the day when it's cold outside?"

Luke looked indifferent and gave no indication of offering an answer.

"To the library. A warm public space with plenty of ideas to capture your imagination. This Clay fellow probably made the whole thing up?"

"You're a lazy man with a small mind and no capacity to believe in anything beyond your five senses. You're an idiot."

"And you're wasting my time."

"How'd Clay know about the accident?"

Mike thought a moment. "You said something about a lone wolf earlier?"

"They work alone. Hence the name."

"Okay, so he's a lone wolf. Or he's not a lone wolf, he's part of a dynamic duo or something," Mike replied, annoyed at the ridiculousness of his statement. "Someone else actually rammed Lilith from behind. And now the two of them are sharing the same delusion that she's this demon and spoon feeding it to you, a reporter, for crying out loud."

"That's all very possible. It's plausible, logical and easy enough for others to believe. But it lacks balls, you know. Chutzpah! Do you know what Chutzpah means?"

"We have a fair-sized population of retired Jews here. We try to keep up."

"Your version lacks chutzpah, Mr. Hart. But mine, angels, demons, divinity, it's got bestseller written all over it."

Luke sat and waited for Mike to comment. No comment came.

"I tried to get in to see the governor and explain all this to him, but he's gone for the day. Any chance you could get to see him?"

Mike held up his hand, made an "o" with his fingers, looked through it and said, "Zero!"

"You can call him, though."

"And why would I do that?"

"To tell him what's going down."

"You can't be serious."

Luke said nothing.

"Look, if anything, I'm calling the police. My boss is being threatened by a couple of psychotic homeless men. Besides, even if I believed you, which I don't, you're as crazy as these two nut jobs if you think I can dictate policy. I make recommendations."

154

"Dictate policy? Who said anything about dictating policy?"

"You're not about to tell me to call the governor and ask him to grant this Rodriguez woman clemency because … what … she's crazy? Or she actually is the Daughter of God?"

"Did I tell you you were an idiot? Well you are. I was going to ask you to recommend to the governor that he stay as far away from Lilith Samuel as possible."

"She's the party leader; my *boss*! They work in tandem. I can't—"

"Just until after the execution. Tell him she's, I don't know, a carrier for some flu epidemic or something. Lie. I know you can do that."

Mike looked at Luke Logan and wondered. "You don't strike me as the kind of man who believes in demons and angels, Mr. Logan. What's your angle?"

"My angle? I told you. Bestseller."

"If you're any good as a novelist, you should be able to turn two crazy men trying to kill a major political figure because they think she's a demon into a best seller just as easily as this supernatural crap you're feeding me."

"True. But where's the chutzpah? And then there's C-Y-A. I assume you know what that means, too."

"I'm in politics, Mr. Logan."

"Of course, you spend half your time covering your ass. Or someone else's. Me, I'm just making sure that, if she is who she says she is, I cover my ass. Anyway, can you contact the governor and tell him to stay away from Lilith Samuel?"

"And what do I get in return?"

"The warm fuzzy feeling you get from doing your fucking job. Now, give me back my All-COM."

A wry smile crept across Mike's face. "I don't think so."

"No? Why not? I did all the talking. You didn't say anything I didn't already know. You effectively avoided incriminating yourself on the whole lone wolf issue. Gimme back my All-COM."

"You never really know when something like that might come in handy, Mr. Logan. No, I think I'll keep that for when I need something from you."

"It's blank, you idiot. I wiped it clean."

"I don't think so. It's been locked in my drawer. Remember?"

"With the world as paranoid as it is these days, you'd be amazed at the kinds of applications you can download onto you All-COM. Hell, you're in politics, the whole fucking lot of you should be the Beta-testers for all the damn spyware and anti-spyware that's out there. Now give me my All-COM before I follow through with what you think you have in that drawer. I've had a lot of coffee this morning and my bladder's aching for some relief."

Mike unlocked the drawer and pulled out the device. He pulled up the History menu and read the last action taken: *Delete Most Recent Recording*. He fiddled with the device a while longer before realizing there was no trace of the previously recorded message. He handed it back to Luke Logan.

"You know," Mike said, "nothing is ever truly deleted. You can always retrieve something from the hard drive."

"Man, you are technologically retarded. There are programs available that'll let me shove this thing up your ass, tickle your uvula and pull it back out and *still* have it smell like roses."

They both laughed.

Luke Logan stopped laughing suddenly. "I'm serious."

Mike knew he wasn't, but the look on Luke's face was more than enough to stop his laughter.

Luke stood to leave and on his way out, he turned around and said, "You tell the governor to steer clear of your boss."

"I'll do that," Mike said. Then, once he saw Luke clear his sightlines, he whispered to himself, "When hell freezes over, you giant hairy asshole!"

CHAPTER 27

The small group of protestors remained outside, bundled up against the relative cold as Governor Driver, Bishop DeMarco and Lilith Samuel walked into the State Prison Complex at Perryville, followed closely by the governor's driver. The governor walked up to the counter that jutted out from the thick plexi-glass barrier. He couldn't decide if the woman behind it was a dark skinned Latino, a light-skinned AfAm or a mixture of the two. After the thought passed, he stooped down to speak into the small holes bore into barrier. The woman of curious decent beat him to it.

"Who are you here for?"

"Estephania Rodriguez," the governor answered. AfAm, he thought. Definitely African American, but you can't rule out some Chicana blood in there somewhere.

"Not today," the woman sang. "She's scheduled for execution. No visits are allowed except for family and friends." She looked up. "And ain't none of you look like family." She reached across her desk, grabbed a clipboard and flipped back the top few sheets.

"I'm sorry, but I'm the—"

"I don't care who you are," she snapped, staring at him through the glass. "Unless she wrote your name on her visitor's list, you ain't goin' nowhere." Then, looking over the governor's shoulder, she said, "Except the padre, here."

Chicana blood, the governor concluded.

"Bishop Manuel DeMarco, correct?" the woman continued.

Stunned, the bishop stepped up to the holes in the plexi-glass. "Yes. I'm Bishop DeMarco."

"All right, but that's it for clergy." She held up two fingers. "Two's the limit." Then, "Now, is your name Felipe Martinez?"

"No, I'm—"

"Don't care," she said, her eyes still focused on the clipboard.

"Is the warden available?"

"She's overseeing an execution in about," she looked up at the clock on the wall, "a little over an hour. I think she's busy."

"I'd very much like—"

"Look, I don't care what you would like or who you are. Unless you're Damien Driver or Lilith Samuel, there ain't nothing more to talk about."

Stunned, the governor answered, "Actually, I am Damien Driver."

She looked at the man suspiciously. Then, shifting her attention to the woman with him, she asked, "And are you Lilith Samuel?"

"Yes," Lilith answered.

"All right," the receiving clerk went on, shuffling various papers on her desk. "Now, you see what happens when we listen instead of talk, talk, talking all the time. Things get done. I tell my kids that and they still talk all day. Talk so much my ears're nearly fallin' off. Anyway, that's all she's got on the list, so unless that big fellow's Felipe Martinez, he's gotta stay out there," she said swatting her hand in the general direction of the lobby. "I need the rest of y'all to listen up. You need to press your thumb on the access panel, wait for it to clear, and then press your index finger. Once the system okays you, the door'll buzz, and you step through, one at a time. The metal detector and bio-filter'll do the rest. Got it?"

The governor told Lilith and the bishop to go ahead while he coordinated with his driver when and where to rendezvous later. Once on the other side of the metal detector and bio-filter, the governor asked the receiving clerk, "When did she write down those names?"

"I don't know. Probably Saturday. The condemned's list is due 36 hours before the scheduled execution, to run background checks on everyone on the list and load up their fingerprints into the system. Why?"

"Just curious."

The receiving clerk passed them on to a corrections officer who led them away from the front lobby and down a very long, very wide hallway that amplified the echo of their footsteps to almost deafening levels. The governor whispered to the bishop, just loud enough for the bishop to hear him over the din. "How'd she know we were coming?"

"How should I know?" the bishop said loudly.

"It seems to lend a bit more credibility to her claims of divinity, wouldn't you say?"

"Putting down the name of the only man who can keep you alive seems more like self-preservation than transcendental enlightenment."

158

Damien smiled and shook his head. He thought about continuing the argument by noting Lilith's addition to the list but, because of what he perceived as the bishop's highly flawed reasoning of his dream and the penny, he thought better of it.

They continued through a labyrinthine network of passages. At the end of each hallway were two sets of plexi-glass doors with a metal detector and bio-filter sandwiched in between them, segregating one passageway from the next. A corrections officer monitored the access panels that controlled the doors and made sure the doorway sandwich was entered one person at a time. While waiting in line, the governor looked around. All the walls and ceilings were painted the same neutral beige as the stained concrete floor, making the hall seem more like a tunnel. He also took notice of the damp mustiness that hung in the air, making the tunnel seem more like a brightly lit cave.

"So governor," Lilith said, "any thoughts on staying the execution? Last night you seemed awfully keen on the idea."

The governor peered down at her. "I had this same conversation with the bishop on the way here. There just doesn't seem to be any legal foundation for such a decision."

"No legal foundation? Are you kidding me?"

"I've been over this a hundred times and—"

Lilith interrupted. "And after all the arguments, the fact still remains that a woman who threatened the masses with peace and tolerance was unjustly convicted of being a hydro-terrorist. The Judge was ambivalent, the jury biased, and the defense incompetent. You could use any one of those as a basis for your decision."

"Judges are supposed to be ambivalent, jury bias is an unavoidable byproduct of an imperfect system and the defense wasn't incompetent, merely unable to overcome the jury bias. And if I did decide to stay the execution on the basis of any one of those, it would provide every criminal in the system, regardless of whether or not they're on death row, with another round of appeals, resulting in more time and money wasted by the state to keep the guilty locked up."

Then he turned to her with an inquisitive look. "And why are you so interested in staying the execution? I thought the GOP embraced capital punishment like a security blanket?"

"This case is unique," she said. "But all legalities aside, I know you have an opinion as to whether or not she's a nut job, another case for staying the execution, mind you. Or if she is in fact the Daughter of God."

"As I told the bishop, I can't base my gubernatorial decisions on my beliefs. They can influence, guide and sway, perhaps."

"What if you're wrong? Are you willing to let an innocent woman die on your watch?"

"She was tried and convicted under the previous administration."

"Do you think anyone's going to care? If she's innocent, like you seem to believe she is, or crazy, which is what I believe, and you're wrong about her being the Daughter of God, then you are a murderer, governor. An innocent woman will die because you didn't stop it. Her life rests in your hands. Her blood stains your soul."

Damien Driver walked the rest of the way thinking about that one thing.

* * *

The Death Watch Cells were not dissimilar from the other cells in P-Ville. They each had a bed tucked into the corner of the small space: 11 feet, 10 inches long by 7 feet, 4 inches wide. A stainless steel toilet and sink were mounted firmly to the wall and a few personal belongings were scattered about. The smell of ammonia was subtle, yet immutable. The three cells' doors opened to a large Anteroom. The doors themselves were sheets of thick plexi-glass, like at the front desk, with a tall, rectangular patch of small holes drilled out for effective communication. A large slot was notched out of the bottom of them. Inside the first of the three cell doors, on the floor in front of the notch, was a cafeteria tray covered with dirty plates, utensils and napkins. The tray provided those who saw it with instant understanding for the door's lower notch.

Two gun metal desks were pushed together against the back wall of the Anteroom. One female corrections officer sat at each desk taking turns writing the meticulous notes required by the state, logging in great detail the events of the day in 15-minute intervals. In the middle of the room was a square, stainless steel table bolted to the floor with a bench on either side. They, too, were bolted to the floor. At the opposite end of the Anteroom, running along the same wall as the cell doors, and therefore completely out of their occupants' sightlines, was the entrance to the Execution Chamber. More specifically, it was the entrance to the Viewing Room attached to the Execution Chamber.

A stainless steel chair sat next to the cell door and on it sat Father Joe, his Spanish Bible opened to one of the later books of the Old Testament. He read aloud, in Spanish, until the footsteps and hushed whispers of an approaching entourage filtered into the Anteroom. Father Joe closed his Bible and stood, smiling, awaiting the bishop's entrance.

"Governor Driver," he said, confusion flexing every muscle of his face as the small group entered the room.

"Father Joe," the governor said, walking across the Anteroom to shake his hand. Once their hands met, the governor's eyes left the priest and surveyed the cell in front of which sat the now vacated chair.

She was petite, much smaller than the governor had expected. She sat on the edge of the bed, upright, shoulders back, head cocked just a bit to embrace the eyes that now fell upon her. Her hair and eyes were as black as pitch, her skin a smooth, creamy mocha. She wore a bright and cheery floral-print summer dress and sandals given to her as part of the official procedures. The governor thought the dress was entirely inappropriate for the situation.

"*Hola*," she whispered, her voice supple and soothing.

From behind, the bishop made his way around the governor to the cell door, almost pushing Father Joe aside. He looked upon her, expressionless.

"This is the Daughter of God?" came loud and scornful from the other side of the governor. All heads turned to Lilith. "This is God made flesh?" she scoffed. "You're fuckin' kidding me, right?"

"While I agree entirely with the sentiment, Ms. Samuel," the bishop said, all eyes shifting to him, "could you please refrain from using such coarse language?"

The governor turned his attention back to the small woman in the cell. "Are you okay?"

"Sí," she answered.

"Does anyone else think that dress is inappropriate?"

Her eyes glazed and she looked to Father Joe. "¿Que?"

161

The priest translated the governor's question, she replied and Father Joe spoke. "She doesn't care what she wears."

The governor pulled Father Joe aside. The bishop followed them as they moved away from everyone else.

"She doesn't speak English?" the governor asked.

"A little. Common phrases, mostly. What's it matter?"

The governor thought. "I suppose it doesn't. It's just I've spent the last few months studying and reviewing documents and it never occurred to me that she didn't speak English."

"I'm an okay translator."

"I'm sure you are, Father. It's not a problem. I guess I'm just … I don't know. Call me narrow-minded, that's all."

* * *

While the others talked in hushed whispers on the other side of the Anteroom, Lilith walked over to the cell's plexi-glass door and took the chair in which Father Joe had been sitting. The crafty politician spoke in fluent Spanish. *"You poor, dear thing. Imprisoned for doing Your Father's work. And now, You only have an hour left to live."*

Estephania sat up straight on her bed, politely listening.

"You know, I could end all of this. You just say the word and I can get the governor to let You live. Continue your mission. I mean, this really is one big misunderstanding, right? Who would have thought a simple analogy could have led to this. What was it You said? Oh yes, Your own little Sermon on the Mount: 'All those who thirst, of this nation and all the nations, need but ask Me and they will drink their fill. I will provide you with the waters of this land and all the land.'

"You see, it really was the combination of 'all nations' and that last little bit about 'this land and all the land' that got You into all this trouble. With the world grappling with a water crisis, and everyone wanting what we've got, phrases like that tend to sound un-American. Treasonous. Blasphemous. It's a shame, too. What a truly Christian sentiment: 'the last shall be first and the first shall be last.' And then it was taken completely out of context and blasted across every All-COM in the world. And when the finger-pointing finally ended, You were their scapegoat.

162

"But now, here I am, a devout Christian of sorts, doing my good deed, loving my neighbor, so to speak, offering You Your life back. And all You have to do is say it's all a lie. The whole thing. Tell the governor You're just a poor mixed up Mexican woman who heard voices in her head. He's got the bishop, the party's largest supporter, telling him to stay the execution. He's so confused right now he doesn't know what to do. You tell him it's all a lie, I convince him that the rest of the party will back him if he stays the execution and You're back with the general population by 1:00. Hell, give me a couple months and I'll get You a full pardon."

Estephania sat motionless, maintaining her statuesque posture, her eyes wide and her face dispassionate.

They continued in Spanish.

"Do You understand?" Lilith asked.

"Yes."

"So what are You going to tell the governor?"

"I am the one Who is, the one Who came to speak the truth; and all who come to hear My words hear the truth."

"The truth?" Lilith scoffed. *"What do You know about truth? You're a* pinche puta loco, *for Christ's sake."*

Hearing the slanderous remark, Father Joe quickly ran over to the two women. He, too, spoke in Spanish. *"Excuse me, Ms. Samuel, but the Bishop would like the opportunity to pray with Ms. Rodriguez for awhile."*

Lilith stood and glared at the small woman wearing a flowery sundress and sitting on her bunk. *"The offer still stands if you change your mine."*

"What offer," Father Joe asked.

Ignoring the question, Lilith looked down at her All-COM and spoke in Spanish. *"Tick, tock, sweetheart. You don't have much time."*

"I have all the time in the world," she replied.

In English, Lilith said, "She's all yours, Padre. Perhaps you and I could put our differences aside and tag team the Governor, talk some sense into him, get him to let this woman continue her ministry."

The priest's eyes squinted, "I thought the GOP would be hell bent on seeing Her put to death."

"I'm not working for the GOP today. The fact is I've got my own reasons for having the governor grant her clemency. Or better yet, commute her sentence. You want Her around to continue Her ministry. I think it's in everyone's best interest if we work together on this."

"What could you possibly gain from that?" Father Joe asked.

"Not all of my responsibilities have to do with the State, Father. I have global issues to contend with. Universal issues, actually. You'd be surprised who I know and what they ask me to do."

CHAPTER 28

"You know she's a fraud, don't you?" Lilith said.

"What are you talking about?" Damien replied.

They were sitting on the stainless steel benches on either side of the stainless steel table bolted to the floor. Lilith had her back to the cells providing the governor full view of Bishop DeMarco, Father Joe and Estephania Rodriquez as they quietly prayed in Spanish.

"She's nuts. She all but said so."

"What? When?"

"Just a few minutes ago when I was talking to Her. She said She heard voices, not God. She says She's scared to die, too. Not the brave face you'd expect from someone looking to save the world."

"It doesn't matter. There's nothing I can do."

Lilith whispered, "The fuck there isn't. You and I both know She got a bum rap at trial. There was blood in the water, the sharks swarmed and She was torn to shreds. But the feeding frenzy is over, Governor. Look at the pathetic attempt at a protest outside. Nobody gives a shit what happens, now. You have the power to set things right."

A foreign voice was added to the conversation. "She's right, you know."

Damien looked up and saw that the bishop had moved to stand beside the table.

"You have the power to set things right," the bishop said.

"'Blessed are those who have not seen and yet believe,'" Damien replied.

"Excuse me?" asked the bishop.

"John 20:29."

"Yes, yes, I'm well aware of the passage. What does that have to do with the price of water in Turkmenistan?"

The governor simply stared at the table top, looking at the mutated reflections in the shiny surface.

The bishop furrowed his brow in contemplation. Then he looked at the governor in horror. "Jesus, Mary and Joseph! You believe in her divinity?"

The governor shrugged his shoulders and nodded.

"You believe this woman is the Daughter of God? You *are* crazy!"

Father Joe overheard the discussion and joined in. "Governor. I'm sorry but did I hear the bishop correctly. You believe She is la Hermana de Jesus?"

"I do."

"And yet," Father Joe went on, "you plan to allow the execution to go on as scheduled. How can you do that? This world needs Her now more than ever. How can you … If … I'm, I'm, I'm at a loss."

"Of all people, Father," the governor answered, "I thought you'd get it."

"Get what?"

The governor sat, looking at nothing at all. "I must do what I must. What's been prophesized." The governor looked at the priest waiting for the light to go on, but it never came. He continued. "'And he began to teach them that the Son of man must suffer many things and be rejected by the elders and the chief priests and the scribes and be killed and after three days rise again.' Mark 8:31"

Bishop DeMarco, bewildered, muttered, "I can't believe what I'm hearing."

"She's suffered many things," the governor mumbled. "She's been rejected by our judicial system, by you, Your Eminence. And, She's been vilified by the media."

"So fucking what!" Lilith whispered loudly. "I mean, come on! There are hundreds, no, thousands of people who fit that profile. Hell, you, Governor, fit the profile. Rejected by the party elders because of your social liberalism. Rejected by the Bishop, here, because of your lesbian daughter. And the media have had a field day with you since the moment you took office. Are *you* now all of a sudden going to claim sovereignty of the downtrodden?"

Understanding came to the bishop's face. "It's rubbish! Pure rubbish! I knew it in the car coming over here. You're just as crazy as she is." Then, looking at Father Joe, "You're both as crazy as she is."

The governor persisted. "My beliefs are my own, Bishop, crazy or otherwise. 'We don't receive wisdom; we must discover it for ourselves after a journey that no one can take for us or spare us.'"

"John, Mark, and now Proust. That's impressive for an insane, washed up politician." Then, an expression came to the bishop's face as if something had caught in his mind. "But you said earlier that you couldn't let your beliefs dictate your actions."

"That's true. But like I said, I've gone at this from every angle and my hands are tied. Regardless of what I believe, I can't stop this thing from happening."

"And I'm here to tell you that you can," Lilith offered. "She's nuts. The Bishop knows it. I know it. The entire Mexican population knows it. Everyone knows it but you, this very nice, very simple-minded priest and the ego-maniacal psychiatrists who want to use Her as the basis for their next published article in the medical journals. Stay the execution for a couple months while a panel of impartial doctors fully examines Her."

The bishop seized the momentum. "Yes, yes, of course. Just put it off for a few months. You don't have to grant her a full pardon or anything monumental. Just stay the execution and order a full evaluation. That's an excellent solution. You can even meet with her yourself and resolve whatever issues you have, one way or the other."

"Eleven thirty!" one of the female corrections officers shouted. "Showtime, people! The priests can stay, but you two," she said waving her pen at the Damien and Lilith sitting at the table in the middle of the room, "y'all need to leave. We gotta prepare the prisoner."

"Think about it, Governor," Bishop DeMarco pleaded. "A temporary stay makes abundant sense."

"No!" echoed loudly throughout the day room. Everyone turned to Father Joe. He stood resolute, an air of defiance about him. With his Bible in one hand, he bent over and rested the knuckles of both of his hands on the steel surface. "All this time I've been selfishly trying to get you to stay the execution so that She could continue Her ministry. But you're right, Governor. Your hands *are* tied. God has bound them. She must die so that She may rise again."

"Don't listen to him," Lilith said. "He's a raving zealot. She's crazy. And if anyone believes She's the Daughter of God, then that person's crazy, too."

The corrections officers were now standing between them and the Execution Room, physically moving them with their mere presence toward the exit. "Let's go, you two," one of them said. "The clergy can stay, but you gotta get up outta here."

As they stood, Damien looked Lilith in the eyes and whispered, "Call me crazy."

CHAPTER 29

Damien and Lilith went out the same way they had entered less than an hour before, their footsteps echoing off the beige walls as they made their way down the long corridor connecting the Death Watch Facility from the rest of the prison. On the left, halfway between the two checkpoints at either end of the hallway, was a beige door. There was no knob, just a keyhole inside a lockset sitting flush with the door. Damien wondered if he had even noticed it before when he walked past it.

The corrections office jingled her keys and opened it. "This'll spit you out into the Staging Room. Just tell 'em you're on the guest list and they'll find a place for you."

The door slammed behind them, keys jingling on the other side, as they walked forward. The corridor elbowed left, presumably to another corridor, leaving no real exit visible. It was narrower and much darker than the main hallway they'd just left and Damien felt his heart beat faster with an approaching uneasiness.

"You're not claustrophobic, are you?" Lilith asked.

"I wasn't," Damien quipped. "You?"

"You'd be surprised at the tight spots I've found myself over the years."

They walked on and turned at the elbow. To Damien's relief, a door stood only a few feet away. As he reached for the knob, the door swung open. Damien jumped back in surprise.

"My apologies, Governor," came from a husky female voice, thick with a Mexican accent and weathered by time. On the other side of the door stood a slight woman, very dark-complexioned. At one time she may have been an imposing figure to the convicted felons that made her job necessary, but standing before him in that room, she looked more like a nurturer than an enforcer. "Didn't mean to scare you, sir."

The room they entered was not at all large, about the same size and shape of the Anteroom adjoining the Death Watch Cells, windowless, but far better lit than the corridor from which they escaped. The beige from the previous hallway continued, but only as far up the wall as the fifth row of cement blocks. All the rows above that were painted a gloss white in an attempt to make the room appear somewhat homey and less industrial. Damien was pleased with its calming effect on him.

"Juanita Sanchez," the old woman said, sticking out her hand. She said it as if the governor was supposed to know who she was. "Director of the Department of Corrections. We've been in the same room a couple times for various meetings, although no real introductions have been made."

He took her hand, shook it and nodded in recognition. "Yes, Juanita Sanchez. You were in the State of the State briefing at the Capitol."

She smiled and shook his hand vigorously. "Yes, sir, I was." Then, she turned to the very large man next to her in a glossy, custom-fit suit. "And you already know the Attorney General, Miguel Torres."

"Yes, of course. Miguel, how are you?"

As the two men shook hands, Juanita turned to Lilith. "Lilith," she said evenly.

"Juanita."

The two glared at each other only long enough for the governor to notice.

"Sir," Juanita said, "Welcome to our Staging Room. I wish I'd have known you were coming."

"I hadn't made up my mind until this morning, though I'm surprised you didn't know."

Juanita gave him a questioning look.

"I was on Her guest list. I thought for sure you'd—"

"Ah!" She smiled. "Once a defendant runs through family, the governor's name is usually the next one they write down. Wishful thinking."

"Wishful thinking," he repeated.

"Quick question, sir," Attorney General Torres said, his English devoid of any accent. "Are you staying the execution?"

Surprise rushed Damien's words. "Why is everyone asking me that?"

The expression on Juanita's face indicated the answer was obvious. "Why else would you be here? No governor as long as I've been here has ever come in person to see an execution. And I've been here a while."

He nodded in understanding. "There had been so much made of this particular case, in the media, the general public, within the party." He shot a look at Lilith who seemed ambivalent to the conversation and its participants. "Plus, since it's the first execution under my administration, I felt somewhat obligated."

Everyone contemplated his last statement and the Staging Room fell silent.

"I hope you've been treated well here," Juanita inquired.

"Well enough," Damien said, remembering the terse and impolite manner in which he was greeted at the reception desk. "I was told there are spots available in the Witness Room."

"Many. Usually there's a list a mile long of people wanting to witness an execution. But this time I had to offer time-and-a-half to the staff just to get all twelve spots filled. But, sir, if you want, you can stand in the room with the defendant. There should be plenty of room."

Lilith perked up, "Sir, you really should keep some distance. For appearance's sake, if nothing else."

General Attorney Torres added, "You could watch on the All-COM feed in the Media Room. I think there's only one reporter in there and I suspect that's all we'll have."

"Just one?" Damien asked.

"Yes, sir," Juanita said softly.

"Honestly sir," Lilith said, "you should probably steer clear of the media, too."

"Where's the Media Room?" Damien asked.

Juanita Sanchez walked a few steps and pointed to a painted steel door with a small, square, tempered-glass window. Damien peeked through the glass.

He turned around. "Him? He's the lone representative of the media?"

"Yes, sir," Juanita said softly again.

Damien ran his fingers through his hair and then placed his hands on his hips.

"Sir?" Juanita asked, wondering what to do next.

He reached for the doorknob, but before he could grasp it, Lilith shouted out, "Sir!"

Damien froze. Then he turned his head.

"You really don't want to do that," Lilith said.

He ignored her. "You stay out here," he said. "I'll only be a minute."

Entering the room, he said, "Mr. Logan. You seem to have the scoop on everyone else in the state. It's still called a scoop, isn't it?"

"Yes and yes," Luke Logan answered, not taking his eyes of the All-COM monitor. He was dressed just as he was in Mike Hart's office, just as he was the previous night, which, Damien thought, explained the reporter's musky odor.

"I see your general disposition hasn't changed much since last night."

"Not true. I've come across a few tidbits of information that help me see things in a whole new light."

"Anything worth sharing?"

"Lilith Samuel is one of Satan's minions," he said flatly.

"Really? That might explain her ruddy completion."

Luke glanced at the governor, offered him a quick smirk and reaffixed his crazy eyes onto the monitor. "According to my sources, she's going to be terminated later today."

Damien moved next to Luke and stared at the monitor, too. "That would be a shame. She's quite an effective fund raiser."

"That's not what I mean."

They exchanged curious glances.

In a mocking tone, Damien said, "You're not the only one with sources, Mr. Logan."

The two stood silent for a few moments staring at the monitor. In the Execution Room, Estephania Rodriguez stood in shackles by the door as the two corrections officers that shooed Damien and Lilith out of the Anteroom busied themselves around the specially designed recliner that was to be her death bed.

"She's a lot shorter than I thought She'd be," the governor finally said.

"Two thousand years ago, the average Middle eastern male would have been about five feet and a couple inches. How tall did you think Jesus' sister would be?"

"I didn't know you were an anthropologist in your spare time."

"You'd be surprised what kinds of interesting things crop up while you're researching a story."

172

Damien moved from where he stood to in front of Luke, facing him, with his back to the door. "Look, Mr. Logan, let's cut through the fun and games. Why are you here?"

"I'm the third estate, Governor. I have the right—"

"Yes, yes, you have the right to be here. And I have the right to vacation in Antarctica, yet I choose not to. Why have you chosen to be here for this? No one else sees any newsworthiness in all of this, as evidenced by your being alone in here."

Luke said nothing.

"I'm looking for some trust, here, Mr. Logan. And no offense to you personally, but I'm not all that trusting of the media. So I'll ask you again, why have you chosen to be here for this?"

"Trust, huh?" He tried to put his thoughts together quickly. "I'm here on the off chance that this execution will in fact be 'newsworthy'. Get the scoop, so to speak."

"Good," Damien said immediately, placing his hands on Luke's shoulders. "So am I. But don't quote me on that."

He smiled and moved toward the door.

"I just wanted to make sure you weren't writing a slam piece."

"Not today, Gov. I'm taking today off and exploring a personal curiosity. Besides, I'm pretty sure I'm going to be arrested for assaulting my editor before I can get any of this written and uploaded to the feed site."

"Assault, huh? Then I was right."

"How so?"

"Your general disposition hasn't changed much since last night."

They shared a unique moment of silent intimacy. Then, the governor said, "In an effort to shed some light on this personal curiosity of yours, I'm going to stand with Her when they administer the cocktail. Is there anything you'd like me to ask Her?"

Luke just shook his head and stared up at the monitor.

"One day," Damien opined, "the historians are going to look back on all of this and say, 'Damien Driver did the right thing.'"

"'The right thing?'" Luke said, his attention firmly affixed on the small woman in shackles. "Are you fucking kidding me? Think this through for a second. If things turn out the way you think they will, if

173

She is who you think She is, the historians aren't going to say you were a hero. They're going to say you were a Christ killer,"

Damien grabbed the knob and pulled open the door.

"God, I hope so!"

* * *

On the other side of the door, Lilith and Juanita were arguing vehemently in Spanish while General Attorney Torres stood by looking at his watch.

"Whoa, whoa, whoa, ladies," Damien yelled out. "Can we have a little civility, here?"

He physically pressed himself into the small gap between the two women who each instinctively took one step back.

"I don't care what this is about—"

Juanita cut him off. "But she—"

To which Damien cut her off. "I said I don't care. You, Lilith, you go into the Witness Room," he said pointing to the door on the opposite side of the Staging Room from where he had just exited.

"Where are you going?" Lilith asked.

"I'm going with them. With Her."

"Sir, you can't leave me here alone."

"You won't be alone. Luke Logan is in there," he said pointing to the Media Room door, "and there are twelve corrections officers in there," pointing to the Witness Room door. "I'm sure you'll be just fine in either one."

To the two others in the Staging Room, he said, "Let's go."

* * *

Damien, Juanita Sanchez and Attorney General Torres walked back through the doorway to the narrow tunnel as Lilith shouted to them from where she stood, "She can't die, sir. Not today! You have to stay the execution. You have to!"

The door made a soft yet solid sound when it shut. Lilith turned and walked toward the Witness Room, dejected and concerned. She failed to sway Estephania Rodriguez. She failed to sway Damien Driver or Father Joe earlier that morning or Felipe the night before. Her constituency would certainly voice its disapproval. All she could think to do was watch the prophesized inevitability.

She cringed at the thought of Estephania Rodriguez gasping her last breath. She had failed.

CHAPTER 30

They hadn't walked more than two or three steps down the narrow corridor when Juanita Sanchez said, "I'm sorry, Governor."

"About what?"

"The shouting at Ms. Samuel. She ..." the warden paused, processing the Spanish-to-English dictionary in her mind, "she irritates me."

"Forget it," Damien simply dismissed. "She irritates me, too, sometimes, and today in particular." Then, catching a fleeting moment of clarity, he said, "Oh, and before I forget, I'm pretty sure somewhere in this facility is a Felipe Martinez. Would it be possible for you to somehow find him and have him delivered to either the Witness Room or the Media Room, wherever Ms. Samuel is *not*."

Juanita immediately got on her All-COM, made a call regarding Felipe Martinez, spoke just a few sentences in Spanish and hung up.

"Anything else?" she asked.

Surprised, the governor said there was nothing else. Then, he reconsidered. "Actually, could you please tell me how this whole thing works?"

Juanita Sanchez described, in basic terms, the process to which Damien Driver was to be a witness. "The convict is on the table, the prison nurse puts in an IV, the doctor slowly pushes the three syringes and then the convict is declared dead."

It wasn't the slightest bit different from Damien's understanding of the entire procedure. He had hoped the warden would offer some unknown fact that could only be divined through first-hand experience or some poignant or ironic detail that romanticized the ordeal, but she didn't. Even if she had, he thought, her use of simple English and her heavy accent would have hidden any anecdotal qualities. Understanding the entirety of it all made him sad and the concept of death crept into his thoughts. Her death. His death. His parents' death. The ceasing of all human existence. The immortality of the soul, eternal salvation and eternal damnation, purgatory, heaven and hell, and the alternative: eternal nothingness. Worm food and nothing more.

Within moments, Damien was again back in the Anteroom. Walking past the bolted benches and table toward the doorway on the end, Damien glanced back at her cell. The sheets were stripped and the mattress was semi-rolled at the head of the cot. Gone were all the personal items she had strewn about. Presumably they were in the banker's box that sat curiously by the open cell door.

As he moved closer to the Execution Room, his stomach tightened and his eyes grew bleary. Father Joe and Bishop DeMarco were in an animated discussion and blocking his view of the room's interior. He had seen it on the All-COM monitor, the camera tucked high in the corner, but he wanted to see it for himself, he needed to see more.

The two clergymen broke from one another and approached him, both speaking in oddly hushed yet loud tones. Both spoke of God's will and the need for the governor to act accordingly, but the actions each suggested he take were entirely different. He couldn't quite comprehend their words as he passed by them, intent on seeing the Execution Room. And even though their discussion escalated in intensity, their voices trailed off behind him as he walked on, ignoring them.

The door from the Anteroom, which the governor thought led directly to the Execution Room, actually led to another, larger room. On the right was a large, expansive window and a door much like the clear plexi-glass doors that sealed the Death Watch Cells, except this door had no holes for communication bore into them, nor a slot at the bottom for a food tray. As he walked into the large Viewing Room, as the warden called it, the other door, immediately to the right, opened into the Execution Room. The space was small, much smaller than Damien ever thought possible: about eight feet square. The warden and the Attorney General could not have possibly expected the three of them to stand in the Execution Room and watch, the governor thought. The invitation must have been to watch from the Viewing Room in which he now stood, peering in. Another door without a doorknob, only a keypad, sat perpendicular to the large window. It was solid and painted in an unsuccessful attempt to help it blend in with the walls. The door was closed and presumably locked.

Through the window Damien saw what looked like a modified leather recliner sitting in the middle of the room. Her thin, brown ankles were strapped down with a black poly-webbing that looked strong enough to secure a rabid elephant. Her wrists were also strapped down with the same webbing, only not directly to the recliner but to the padded armrests that jutted out from the sides of the chair. Another thick strap ran across her chest, under her arms and around the back of the chair. He imagined the view Luke Logan had of her from the Media Room: the international symbol for the Ladies room, complete with the hem of her dress reaching across the width of the recliner.

In the crux of each of her arms was an IV feed and from under the neckline of her dress two wires ran up and over her shoulder. All of these tubes and wires passed through one of the walls below an enormous mirror on the far left side of the Execution Chamber. It was the same wall that the knobless door in the Viewing Room breached, the room Damien now understood to be where the doctor sat, watching the cardiac monitor and where he would inject and flush each of the three elements of the lethal cocktail. Damien looked up at the encirclement of green fabric covering what he could only assume was another wall-sized, two-way mirror, the other side of which would sit the various witnesses of the state.

Something behind him rustled. It startled him and he turned quickly in a fit of panic. A Latino couple stood quietly in the corner staring back at him, their faces curiously blank.

"Are you Her parents?" Damien asked. "¿Madre y padre?"

"Sí," they answered in unison.

"Maria and Jose Rodriguez?"

"Sí," they answered again.

"Lo siento," he apologized as best he could.

"No incumbe a usted," the woman said softly.

"Incumbe? What's that mean? Can someone tell me what she said?"

The warden complied. "She said, 'It's not your fault.'"

The governor simply nodded in understanding. Then, out in the Anteroom, the governor heard something that caught his attention. It was the word "martyr." His curiosity of the Execution Room satisfied, he walked back out into the Anteroom to see Bishop DeMarco and Father Joe vehemently arguing.

The bishop looked sharply at the young priest. "I beg your pardon?"

178

"You heard me! If She dies at the hands of the State, She goes down as a martyr and neither you nor the Church can have that, can you?"

"Now who's being delusional?"

"No, it makes sense," Father Joe shot back, becoming more and more agitated as he spoke. "You let Her die in jail at the end of a life sentence and She becomes a statistic, with Her ministry and all Her teachings dying with Her. But if She dies, like Christ, at the hands of the very people She's trying to save from damnation, then everything She's done takes on added importance. People write gospels and suddenly She becomes more than a martyr, She becomes the new risen Christ."

"Please, Father Joe. I can indulge a questioning of one's faith, but this … *this*? I don't know where all of this is coming from, but I assure you my motives are not based on fear of this woman or her following. I will grant you, it makes for a nice fairy tale, but …."

"Like Saul on the road to Damascus," Father Joe muttered.

"What are you talking about?" Bishop DeMarco asked, his face flush. Damien couldn't decide if it was from anger, embarrassment or fatigue.

"I finally see the light," Father Joe said standing up. "She's bad business. That's what you're afraid of, a new competitor for the weekly coffers. The Catholic Church is finally running in the black again after rebounding from all the diocesan bankruptcy problems. And now that it's back, you're eliminating the competition."

"I'll say it again, Joseph, you're delusional. And so is she. She's a crazy little creature with as much claim to divinity as, as, as a bubble gum wrapper."

Father Joe's face scrunched into a balled up sock of muscles and eyebrows. He lunged at Bishop DeMarco and, due to a reflexive jerk by the bishop, a move Damien considered exceedingly spry for man his age, only grazed the side of the bishop's head with a clenched fist. Both clergymen, thrown off-balance by their respective actions, staggered a few feet away from one another, just far enough for the governor to place himself between them.

"Gentlemen?" Damien said. "That's quite enough. You're Her spiritual advisors, not the under card to the main event. Now, get a hold of yourselves."

Father Joe and Bishop DeMarco squared off facing each other, each breathing hard from the multiple verbal volleys they had exchanged prior to Father Joe's physical attack. Bishop DeMarco rubbed the spot on his head where Father Joe's knuckles made contact. Damien thought it was more out of shock than of pain.

Father Joe's face instantly ran white as he dropped to his knees. "Oh my God," he said. "My most sincere apologies, Your Eminence. I don't know what came over me. I have never been more embarrassed in all my life. Please forgive me."

"Get up, Joseph," the bishop commanded. "Get up and remember who you are. You are an ordained priest. You act on behalf of the Church through Word, Sacrament, and leadership."

Father Joe stood up. "Yes, Your Eminence."

"It's Bishop DeMarco," he said.

Seeing a lull, Damien spoke. "Have you gentlemen fully attended to the condemned's spiritual needs?"

The question caught them off guard and they failed to answer intelligibly.

"We have less than ten minutes. If you two are finished, as governor of this state, I'd like to have a moment alone with the young lady." He looked at the warden and continued, "Does anyone object?"

The room fell silent with everyone shaking their heads. But the only gesture that Damien felt mattered was that of the weathered warden. He looked at her alone awaiting her response.

"If she says it's okay," Juanita said softly, "then go ahead."

Damien walked into the Viewing Room, past Maria and Jose Rodriguez, and into the Execution Room.

Her head lulled to the side and tilted up to see who had entered. "Hola."

"Hola," Damien said laughing at the awkwardness of the scenario. He walked toward the other end of the recliner so they could face one another and she would not have to strain her neck. "Are you comfortable?"

"Yes," she replied. Even with such a simple and common word, Damien felt her accent weight it down.

"I want to tell you something."

Damien hadn't had much time to prepare properly for the moment in which he hoped he would find himself, so when the exact moment was upon him he had no idea what to say. He bent down on a single knee, reached up and held her hand in both of his, ensuring her skin didn't get pinched by the restraints. He looked at their hands, entwined, embarrassed to look into her eyes. Tears began to make his vision blurry. He looked down and blinked, allowing a tear from each eye to land on the floor rather than free his hands from hers and wipe the tears away.

"What do you have to say?" she whispered, almost inaudibly.

"Lots of things," Damien started. He gathered his courage and blurted out the two thoughts that were crowding his mind. "But right now, all I want to say is, I love you and I'm sorry."

She smiled. "Le perdonan."

Damien bent over and rubbed his face on her opened hands. Then, he stood, their fingers still entwined, and wiped his eyes with his sleeves. He couldn't see the row of on-lookers peering at him through the large two-way mirror but he knew they were there: the warden, the attorney general, the bishop and prison chaplain, her parents. He turned around and was relieved to see the curtain on the window behind him, the one he assumed was to the Witness Room, was still drawn.

He looked down at her and said, "There are so many things I wish I could have said and done. So many questions I would have asked."

"Esté en la paz," she said softly.

Looking deeply into her eyes, Damien patted her hand and smiled. He left her in the chamber strapped to the table with IVs and monitoring wires adhered to various parts of her body. The scene that was to follow was going to be too much for him to bear. He felt the tightness in his stomach return as soon as he left her presence. He felt her, now more than ever, and knowing what he had to do, he felt as though he might vomit. The need to leave, to run away, was nearly overwhelming, but he consciously relaxed and walked with a purposeful but unhurried stride. He had almost reached the door of the Anteroom when Warden Juanita Sanchez grabbed his sleeve. He turned.

"What was that all about?" she asked.

"What was what all about?"

"Holding hands. The tears. She's a convicted felon, Governor, sentenced to death for treasonous acts against the State."

"She's more than that, warden."

He said the word 'warden' harshly, as if it was a racial epithet or slur. The hurt the warden felt was obvious and Damien was ashamed of himself.

"That came out wrong," he said.

Juanita stood and stared, her faded eyes holding his. "Just answer me one question and then I'll let you get back to all your important business at the Capitol Building, Governor. Are you going to stay the execution? Should I be awaiting your call?"

Damien smiled. "Esté en la paz. That means 'be at peace,' right?"

"Yes."

"Then, esté en la paz, warden. Be at peace. You can proceed with the execution, follow procedures and know you're doing your job. Just like me. There will be no call."

He turned and stood at the Anteroom's exit waiting for the guard to unlock the door. He knew the warden stood behind him, staring at him, judging him, but his capacity to care was gone. When the buzz and click released the lock, Damien didn't look back or say good-bye. He simply walked through the door and, after a few controlled steps, broke into a full sprint down the beige corridor, the smell of ammonia engulfing his mind as he ran.

CHAPTER 31

Father Joe stood and watched the vein in her left arm pulse. The tubes that ran from her arms were covered with gauze at the points there the needles pierced her skin, but just above and below the gauze the blue lines of her veins throbbed ever so slightly. He found it mesmerizing. In his trance he thought about the time he had spent with her, about these past nine months of her incarceration, the last hour or so with the bishop, these last few glimpses through the window. His trance was broken by a loud voice.

"Where's he going?" Bishop DeMarco shouted to everyone in general, but to Warden Sanchez in particular. She was just joining the small group in the Viewing Room.

"He didn't say," the warden replied. She stood by the door with her hands behind her back, her attention focused on the small Mexican woman strapped down to the padded recliner.

"What *did* he say?" the bishop insisted.

Still looking through the window, the small, elderly woman said softly, "He told me to be at peace and to follow procedures."

The bishop's voice rose in volume and in intensity. "That's it?"

He received no response. Instead, the room fell into a deep pall, visceral, palpable, spiritual. Even the bishop, after looking around and seeing that he was the only person in the room not watching the static inactivity unfold on the other side of the window, followed suit and focused on the petite woman in the ridiculous flowery dress and strapped to the chair.

"I'm sorry, Your Eminence," Father Joe offered.

The bishop waved his hand and shook his head as if to indicate there was no harm done during their skirmish in the Anteroom. But it wasn't his attack that he was apologizing for.

Father Joe was sorry for his inability to enlighten the bishop, to make him understand that what was happening inside the Execution Chamber was not a senseless death but prophecy. That she was not being put to death but rather allowing herself to be placed in a position to resurrect.

He leaned in and whispered into the bishop's ear. "Quadrumvirate. That's got such a pretty rhythm to it. You did have to look it up, didn't you?"

The bishop's head tipped only slightly, his eyes rolling fully into their corners to see the man next to him. "The governor needed to know I understood the situation."

"Now that you've met Her, talked to Her, hasn't your understanding—"

"Joseph, stop," The bishop turned further to face his young charge. "She's a criminal, tried and sentenced to death. And, tragic as it may be, death is what she will receive. There is nothing more I can do for her. We've lost the battle, but the war rages on and we must persevere, lick our wounds and prepare for the next battle. Whatever you believe is going on here can be discussed at a later date. Not now."

They both turned and watched her.

Father Joe smiled widely, wryly. "History is written by the victors, Your Eminence."

"For the millionth, time, will you please stop calling me Your Eminence," the bishop replied.

"I'll try."

From where Father Joe stood behind the window, along with rest of those gathered, Estephania Rodriguez faced the opposite direction. He had a three-quarter's view of the crown of her head and her left shoulder as the rest of her extended away from them toward the curtained wall on the other side. The perspective flattened her face and made it appear distorted and grotesque to Father Joe's eyes. It was not the image by which he wanted to remember her, so he moved to his left, closer to her parents, closer to the camouflaged door, beyond which he imagined the doctor sat awaiting instructions.

Father Joe looked down at the All-COM affixed to his belt: 11:58. Two minutes until the blessed Estephania Rodriguez was to be executed by the state in accordance with its civil justice system. One hundred and twenty seconds until God's only begotten daughter was to die so that all of humankind could live forever. Millions of ideas ran around inside his head, but the only ones that stuck were centered on the singular thought of what could be done in two minutes time. How far could a ray of light travel? Could someone get through a decade of rosary beads? Could a basket of French fries be cooked that quickly?

"¿Está todo listo?" Juanita Sanchez said into an All-COM box affixed to the wall next to the doorway. *Is everything ready?* Father Joe hadn't noticed the oversized box until it was in use and was curious how something so obtrusive could have escaped his notice.

"Sí," the All-COM squawked back.

Father Joe looked at his All-COM again: 11:59. The seconds passed unregistered and he longed for his father's analog watch, with its sweeping second hand. It sat, unwound, in the top drawer of his desk at the Christ King rectory. It's dead, he thought of the watch, just like she'll be. It was an uncomfortable thought, to have something so useful and sentimental lying dormant in the darkest recesses of his memory. He vowed to dig it out from its resting place and wear it for the rest of his life as a reminder that every second he was alive could be spent doing something to validate the time he had spent with her. He would carry on her messages of love and peace.

Warden Sanchez walked around the recliner on which Estephania Rodriguez laid to the opposite side of the room. She drew back the curtain that hung on the far wall, moving from right to left, revealing a large mirror. In the mirror was a series of reflections of the small room with the small woman lying on a padded recliner. The reflections went on infinitum, getting dimmer and darker the deeper the reflection went, and it was then that Father Joe realized he wasn't standing behind a large window but a two-way mirror.

The priest paused in wonderment at her image reflected onward forever, infinitely. He was fascinated by the new perspective, a frontal view of her in the initial image in the mirror. He looked at her face, soft and glowing, peaceful, her eyes closed and her mouth shut with only the slightest smile, like that of the Mona Lisa. His heart warmed. Having drawn back the curtain, the warden exited the chamber through the plexi-glass door and joined the others in the Viewing Room. Father Joe instantly felt the utter emptiness of the chamber, how completely alone she was. The only other person she could even see was the warden, reflected in the mirror standing somewhat in the doorway, but she could only see the warden if she chose to, which she didn't. Instead, she kept her eyes closed. He thought it appropriate that someone, *something* so unique should be wholly solitary and he began to cry, never even trying to hold back his tears.

The warden spoke into the All-COM box. "Proceda, por favor."

It echoed around the room and rang in Father Joe's ears for even longer as he looked around. The words had little impact on her parents. They watched expectantly, not angry or upset, but calm and content, as if they were watching their child dutifully brush her teeth. Bishop DeMarco seemed displeased but resolute. The two corrections officers standing in the Anteroom, just beyond the warden and the doorway, appeared ambivalent—another day at the office. The warden appeared noble and regal to Father Joe and he imagined her as a Roman centurion, with a flowing red cape and glowing silver helmet, giving the order to a soldier from his cohort to hammer the spikes through the feet of Jesus, an unfortunate yet important cog in the mechanism of the resurrected Christ.

He turned his attention again to the frail little woman in the recliner. In the two-way mirror opposite him, he could see her face was unchanged. *Everything* remained unchanged. Not a single item inside the chamber or the room in which he stood moved. A collective gasp of breath was held for seconds, minutes, millennia. He focused in on her lips. They were moving, faintly, as if she were saying something in her head and her lips involuntarily formed the words. The faint movement of her lips slowly ceased and the daVincian smile returned.

Father Joe stared at her in the mirror, salty streaks lining his cheeks. He watched her chest rise and fall less and less with each breath. He looked at her mouth once more and, though not a single muscle on her face had changed, he no longer saw the smile. Instead, he saw emptiness. And in an instant he knew she was gone. He looked again at her chest and confirmed his suspicions. It rose no more.

"Su corazón ha parado," squawked from the All-COM. *Her heart has stopped.*

Warden Sanchez walked back into the chamber, somber and respectful. She gently skirted around the recliner, grabbed the curtain and drew it closed. She studied the form in the recliner for a moment then walked through the doorway into the Viewing Room and went immediately out into the Anteroom. The bishop followed her out and stood off to the side near the metal desks, waiting. For what, Father Joe couldn't even guess. Maria and Jose Rodriguez finally exited the room and approached the warden who was discussing something with the two idle corrections officers.

Father Joe wiped his tears and watched it all, unable to think of anything else to do. He took a few short steps toward the Anteroom and stopped. He looked through the plexi-glass door to his left. From where he was standing, the top of her head and her shoulders were all he could see, her torso and legs eclipsed. For no reason he could articulate, Father Joe pushed open the door to the Execution Chamber, walked over to the side of the recliner and stood over her, looking at her face. He bent down and tenderly kissed her forehead. As he stood up, he noticed a stray hair had clung to his lips. He grabbed it with his thumb and forefinger and held it just in front of his eyes. It was jet black and straight as a desert highway. He opened his Spanish Bible, turned to Luke 21 and read silently of what Jesus said to his apostles:

12 *"...and they will seize and persecute you, they will hand you over to the synagogues and to prisons, and they will have you led before kings and governors because of my name.*

13 *It will lead to your giving testimony.*

14 *Remember, you are not to prepare your defense beforehand,*

15 *for I myself shall give you a wisdom in speaking that all your adversaries will be powerless to resist or refute.*

16 *You will even be handed over by parents, brothers, relatives, and friends, and they will put some of you to death.*

17 *You will be hated by all because of my name,*

18 *but not a hair on your head will be destroyed.*

19 *By your perseverance you will secure your lives.*

Father Joe rubbed his fingers together, rolling the long, black strand of hair into a small ball. He placed the hair between the pages of his Bible and shut it. Then, he placed his hand on her shoulder where the image of a bright orange daisy bloomed on her soft cotton dress and walked out of the chamber.

Warden Sanchez was speaking to her parents. Father Joe was able to catch only a few words but pieced together their conversation. They were making arrangements for the release of her body. He wanted to ask them about the funeral, perhaps even ask to preside over the Mass of Christian Burial, but he decided to wait. Instead, he walked over to the bishop and leaned against the wall next to him.

"Once again, Your Emin … Bishop DeMarco, I do apologize for my unacceptable behavior."

"And once again, I accept. Let's please not have this be the opener to every discussion we have."

"Of course. It won't be. I promise. Thank you."

"You're a passionate man, Joseph. There's nothing wrong with passion as long as it's properly directed. Perhaps, now that this distraction has been removed, we can once again focus on more pressing issues."

The peace and calm Father Joe experienced watching Estephania's lips utter their unheard message, watching her chest rise and fall, her veins gently pulse, was swept away by a tidal wave of adoring rage. He thought of nothing else but his desperate desire to throw another punch, this one landing squarely on the bishop's nose. However, unlike before, he restrained the impulse and instead of throttling the arrogant, ignorant imbecile that leaned against the wall beside him, he merely nodded his head in agreement.

"Your work here is extremely important. Here and at Christ King parish."

Again, Father Joe nodded his head.

"And speaking of Christ King," the bishop continued, "How are you getting back there? With the governor gone, I seem to have lost my ride back."

Seeing an eminent break in the Rodriguez's conversation with the warden, Father Joe curtly said, "God will provide, Bishop DeMarco. Please excuse me."

He hurried over to the couple as they made their way to the secured exit.

He spoke to them in Spanish. *"Excuse me. My name is Father Joe. I've been your daughter's spiritual advisor during Her,"* he paused, *"Her incarceration here. I was wondering what arrangements you've made regarding a funeral."*

CHAPTER 32

"I can't believe She's gone," Felipe whimpered.

Luke Logan turned his head and focused his crazy eyes on Felipe in unabashed irritation but said nothing. He glanced back up at the All-COM monitor and watched the small, frail, lifeless body lay dormant. It was not the first time he'd watched a woman die. However, it was the first time he'd witnessed one die so peaceably.

Felipe offered another whimper. "What are we supposed to do now?"

Luke's irritation was no longer contained in his eyes, it now occupied his entire face. "Who's 'we?'" he said bitterly.

"The world," Felipe insisted. "You. Me. Her other followers."

"What other followers?"

"They call themselves the Adherentes. *We* call *our*selves Adherentes. Tom Jones is one. There's a bunch of us."

Luke stared at the monitor.

"What about you?" Felipe asked.

"What about me?"

"Are you a follower?"

"Hell no!" he snapped. "I don't know this lady from Eve. I'm an interested third-party who just so happened to do an extensive topical non-fiction piece on the injustices of our judicial system."

"Just so happened, huh?" Felipe said, trying to goad his companion. It worked.

"What?" Luke asked.

"Nothing, I guess. I just think you're naïve if you think everything you've done up to this point was all coincidental, that's all."

"Free will, man. I choose my own destiny." He said it forcefully in an effort to make himself believe it, too.

"Really?" Felipe said with a touch of sarcasm. "Then what are you doing here?"

Luke's irritation instantly turned to anger and then, just as immediate, it turned to confusion. He stared out the little window of the door. What am I doing here? he thought. "Like I told Governor Driver," he stammered, "gut instinct. I'm here on the off chance that something big's gonna happen. With everything that's been going on with Her for the last couple years, what kind of journalist would I be if I didn't listen to my gut instinct?"

"Your gut instinct? Are you sure that's not God you're listening to?"

Luke playfully mumbled the word "asshole" under his breath.

Though there were rows of stackable chairs, they both stood watching the medical personnel detach the various wires and tubes from the lifeless body.

"You ever wonder why they swab the arm with alcohol and iodine before inserting the needle?"

"That's to prevent infection."

Luke gave Felipe a sideways glance. "She's gonna be dead. Who cares about infection?"

"Oh," Felipe stammered. "I guess they have to just in case the governor calls."

"I know. I'm just trying to lighten things up a bit. Make some small talk."

They watched as a gurney with a body bag rolled into the chamber. The corpse was gently lifted and placed inside it.

"So, how'd you get here?" Luke asked.

"It's funny you should ask. After we kind of barged in on the governor and Bishop DeMarco, I was riding back to Goodyear with—"

"Not Goodyear," Luke said abruptly. "I meant how'd you get into the Media Room?"

"Oh. Well that's a funny story, too," Felipe began.

Luke grunted in frustration.

"Me and Father Joe, you remember him from last night, the priest who just kissed Her on the forehead?"

Luke grunted again, this time it's tone was one of agreement.

"He had an employee pass, but it only lets in one person, so I was detained by these two mean guards. I thought for sure they were going to beat me. They all but told me they were going to. They joked about the training they receive, the many ways they were taught to subdue a prisoner and how those same tactics could be used to teach an intruder the error of his ways. But then I heard Her voice in my mind, and Her teachings filled my heart, and I found the strength to accept their torment and hatred and love them nonetheless."

Luke let out another small grunt, this one of disbelief.

"They were walking toward me and then the All-COM in the room chimed. The tough one, the one who was talking the most, he answered it and talked to whoever was on the other end just a couple minutes. The two guards huddled together, uncuffed me and told me to stay in the room and stay quite. Then they left. A few minutes later, a woman came into the room and told me to follow her. She led me here, to the Media Room."

Luke grunted his frustration again. "That's all so very fascinating, but why are you *here*? In the Media Room? Are you press?"

"Oh, that. I still have my media credentials from KPHE-TV. I was the station manager there a few years back."

"You see. Was that so hard? Now that's what we call small talk. Short bits of information that the listener can absorb and to which the listener can respond. Now it's your turn. You ask a simple question that I answer briefly."

"Have you always been this obnoxious and abrasive?"

Luke beamed with delight. "My mom always said I was a sweet child. It wasn't until college that I really found my stride. You?"

"I don't consider myself obnoxious or abrasive."

"No?" Luke said, drawing it out purposefully, "I guess you wouldn't."

They found another stolen moment to watch the monitor, the gurney now being rolled out of the Execution Chamber. They stared at the empty room as they turned off the lights. When the room went dark, the lights from the Anteroom cast a soft glow onto the recliner. Its clean, glossy padding reflected what little light reached it, showing the undulating indentations where not ten minutes earlier Estephania Rodriguez had expired.

"Kind of a modern day Shroud of Turin, huh?" Luke said. "Only of Her ass."

"Do you have to be so crude?"

192

Luke ignored the comment and looked out the window of the door again, hoping to see something that wasn't there. "That governor is a pretty smart cookie, you know that?"

"You think so? He just killed the Daughter of God."

"What is it with you true believers? You can't see a fucking thing beyond your own noses." Then, in a mocking, high pitched squeak, he said "What are we supposed to do now?' 'I'm lost without Her." Then, reverting back to his true, gruff voice, he said, "You just don't get it, do you?"

"Get what?"

"Man, how'd you get this far in life? You might as well go back to your buddy Tom and the rest of the gang and shut yourselves off from the world for the next few days for fear of persecution."

"What are you talking about?"

"The risen Christ, you idiot! If She is the 'I am,' and you give every indication that you believe She is, then, come Thursday, She's walkin' and talkin', drinking sangria and eating tacos back at the hacienda."

Understanding slowly erupted on Felipe's face.

"Hell, the governor never even met Her and he knew what to do. All this time he looked like he was trying to find a loophole to stop the execution. But all along he's been making sure that from a political and legal standpoint there was no way he *could* stop it."

"I have to go," Felipe said excitedly. "I have to tell the others."

He ran to the door and stopped abruptly. "Dammit!" He turned around. "Tom has my car. I need a ride back to the city."

Luke stared at the dark and empty room on the monitor.

"Did you hear me? I need a ride."

"I heard you," Luke said, still looking up.

"Well?"

"Well what?"

"Can I get a ride?"

Luke brought his eyes down to meet Felipe's. "This *Savior* of yours, la Hermana de Jesus, did She preach anything other than love thy neighbor? You know, like manners?"

Felipe, looking exhausted, took a deep breath. "Could I please get a ride back into the city with you if it's not too much trouble?"

"Absolutely. As soon as I'm done here."

"What do you have left to do?"

"Nothing, really. Just waiting. But since I'm doing you a favor, you need to work around my schedule."

Luke glanced through the window in the door once more and excitedly said, "Okay, we can go now."

***

As they exited, on the opposite side of the Staging Room, they saw Lilith Samuel walking through the door of the Witness Room toward them. Flanking her were two corrections officers. They were laughing out loud and carrying on about something that had obviously taken place in the Witness Room. Felipe found their behavior abhorrent. Laughing and carrying-on after the lethal injection of an unjustly convicted woman, his personal savior, seemed crass.

"Do you think you could show some respect?"

The two officers walked over to Felipe. Their bodies were thick, muscular. Felipe thought to himself that their heads could be similarly described. They stood imposingly in front and in back of him, attempting to intimidate him. The one in front of him spoke first. "Why don't you mind your own business?"

"Yeah," the other one echoed.

"Leave him alone," he heard spoken from behind the daunting officer before him. Surprisingly, he recognized it as Lilith Samuel's voice. All three of them turned as she stepped out from behind the officer.

"He ain't worth the paperwork," she said and motioned for them to follow her. "Hey, is either one of you heading towards the city? I lost my ride."

Felipe's eyes and stance seethed with a passionate hatred searching for an escape.

Luke placed his hand on Felipe's shoulder and whispered, "Easy, there, big fella. Let's just be on our way and let things work themselves out."

"That woman makes my skin crawl," Felipe said.

"What do you expect?" Luke replied. "She's a Republican."

Both Felipe and Luke listened to the loud trio's obnoxious ramblings as they followed a few paces behind them through the various corridors that eventually funneled them into the front reception area. As one of the corrections officers split off and disappeared into another corridor, Lilith and her new-found friend continued out the front doors and past the few remaining protesters scattered about the front courtyard. As the courtyard narrowed into a sidewalk, a row of enormous Mexicans stood, fencelike, behind the protesters.

As Lilith and the security officer squeezed their way past the burly mountain range of men, Luke and Felipe watched one of the protesters break from the tiny throng. He was tall and thick, like the Mexicans he passed between, but dressed all in white. His hair was long, curly, dark, and it bounced with every exaggerated step he took. He held a sign that read *The Child of God Will Rise Again.* He followed in step behind Lilith and the man who was presumably giving her a ride.

Then, as if he knew Felipe and Luke were watching him, the man in white turned and whispered mischievously, "Hold this for me, please," and handed Felipe his protest sign. Felipe recognized him as the man from the previous night, the one who stopped to chat in front of Father Joe's parish.

The man in white hurried to catch up with the corrections officer walking beside Lilith and tapped him on the shoulder. Before the officer had fully turned around to see who had tapped him, the man in white had already landed his stony fist squarely on the corrections officer's chiseled jaw. The man fell to the ground hard, his head making an unpleasant thud as it hit the cement.

Lilith turned around and stared at the man in white. "What the fuck did you do that for?"

"Intimidation," the man in white said. "You failed and now your time has come."

And with that, the man in white pounced on Lilith, knocking her to the ground. He knelt on his right knee and pummeled her with his right fist. In the midday sun, his clenched hands appeared as large and as solid as a small boulder attached to his arms, rising and falling again and again and making horrifying crunching sounds. Felipe heard several of the

195

protesters gasp, but all of them were helpless to help, trapped behind the line of massive men.

"Oh, dear Lord have mercy," Felipe said, appalled by the viciousness of the attack.

"Not today," Luke added, his eyes glued to the action.

Her face instantly ballooned and turned a deeper reddish-purple as each massive strike was delivered. Flesh was ripped from her bones. The man in white continued his attack until, after landing a dozen or so blows, he suddenly stopped and stood up. Felipe stared at Lilith's body, unmarred, as it lay on the ground, her arms and legs spread only slightly. In stark contrast to her untouched body, every feature of her face, darkened slightly by the shadow cast by the man in white standing over her, was crushed, unrecognizable, as if a very small child had tried to create a sculpture of a woman's face with a thick pile of crimson mud.

The man in white, immaculate and unstained, stood and looked back at Felipe. "You know what?" he said. "Maybe you should keep that sign." He smiled and winked and walked away from the body that had once been Lilith Samuel.

Felipe dropped the sign, ran to a planted tree in the courtyard, bent over and wretched.

* * *

Luke watched the man in white walk deliberately through the parking lot, pull his keys from his pocket and climb into the cab of an enormous garbage truck. The unmistakable roar of an antiquated combustion engine broke through the white-noise-murmur of those surrounding Lilith's lifeless body on the sidewalk as they frantically shared their eye witness accounts with one another, corrections officers from the prison and those they called on their All-COMs. The men who had stood as boundaries to the violence walked past the body and calmly made their way to the parking lot exit.

The sound of grinding gears chewed at the air and the truck lunged forward, slowly making its way through the parking lot and toward the stop sign adjacent to the exit. The large men who had previously lined the crowd of protestors scattered to all sides of the truck and jumped onto its sideboards, clutching the protruding metal handles, and leaving behind no trace that they were ever there. As the weight of each man jumping on shook the truck, a glint of shiny metal on the rear of the truck caught Luke's attention. There, in stark contrast to the dull rust and faded, chipping paint, beneath the bumper sticker that read *No God, No Peace. Know God, Know Peace*, were two, Christian fish emblems facing one another, like the eyes of a blind woman with crow's feet captured in chrome.

Luke saw them and understood.

CHAPTER 33

His ride home was a restless one. He fidgeted in his seat. He tried finding something to watch or listen to on his All-COM and the thought to abandon what he was doing came as quick and as necessary as the original thought to initiate it. He wrung his hands when they weren't being used and when they were being used he fumbled everything he touched. As they drove away from the prison she was further and further away from him, yet, with each passing second, she became ever more present in his mind and he felt more and more uneasy. He tried watching the bright and barren landscape pass by only to feel the hollow in his stomach, an internal echo of her, vibrate through his entire being, growing blacker and colder with every mile.

By the time they reached the city limits, he was all but drained of energy. His mind swept ever back to the tubes and wires crossing the room, floating, connecting her to the brutality and bureaucracy of humankind, connecting her to him for all eternity.

She was no treasonous felon, no saboteur, no *pinche puta loco*. She was a gift from God, a gift for all people and for all times. Her life rested in his hands and he snuffed it out. He allowed her to die. And now he felt as if he were dying. His breathing was short and patchy, his mouth dry, his skin icy and his eyelids heavy and unable to open. He rolled down the window. The cool air on his skin made him shiver violently and he rolled the window up again.

The car pulled off the highway and a single salient thought pierced his descent, So this is how a junkie feels. The knowledge that he had to let go of his addiction was overwhelmed by the need for more and more and when none came, the need grew stronger and manifested physically into utter discomfort. He wanted to vomit. He thought he would wet himself. He mentally searched his medicine cabinet for something that would settle his nerves knowing full well that nothing of this earth could.

Pulling up to the governor's residence Damien didn't even wait for the car to come to a complete stop. He jumped out of the car, stumbling momentarily, and sprinted to the mansion's door, his mind unable to focus on any one thing but millions of intangible things that at one time made sense to him but now were only thoughts without meaning.

He burst open the door without a thought to shut it behind him, throwing his coat and suit jacket on the floor. His hands clumsily pawed the handrail as he staggered his way up the stairs, down the hall and into his bedroom. Damien released his belt and undid the various fasteners that kept his pants secure, stepping out of his shoes and socks and pants as he walked. His shirt he didn't even unbutton, pulling it, his tie and his undershirt off in a single motion and leaving them in a pile outside the bathroom door.

He turned on the shower and sat down on the toilet seat waiting for the water to warm. He could no longer hold his emotions at bay. His face folded in upon itself and he wept violently, his body shaking, nearly convulsing, as his pain and anguish were released in flooding torrents of tears. Precious water ran down the drain unused as steam escaped the seams edging the shower doorway. He slowly slipped from the toilet to the floor, wrapping his weak and weary arms around his knees and balling up on the bath mat.

"Honey? What's going on in there?" came Sophia's voice from beyond the door.

He said nothing. Instead, he coughed forth the uncontrollable, weighty sobs that had taken hold of him.

"Are you okay?" she asked opening the door.

Her face paled at the sight of her husband curled up on the floor. Grabbing a towel, she quickly joined him on the floor and laid the terrycloth over him like a blanket. "Oh, God. Are you hurt? Do you need an ambulance?"

Embedded in his wrenching sobs she heard the words, "I killed her," repeated over and over and she understood. For several minutes thereafter she lay across his shoulder and stroked his hair, softly breathing soothing tones into his ear. "Shhhh." His tears and wracking sobs eased as his thoughts of her were washed away by the cascading water in the background.

She felt his body move beneath her and subconsciously knew to move away. He sat up, readjusted his towel and rested his back against the wall opposite the heavy glass shower door. He pulled his knees to his chest and again wrapped his arms around them, the fetal position in vertical. He rested his head sideways on his knees and looked at his wife sitting on the floor next to him.

Steam engulfed her as she stood and turned off the water. "Rough day at the office?" Sophia joked.

A weak smile crept across his face.

"Are you all right?" she asked.

He closed his eyes and nodded laterally without lifting his head from his knees. "I will be."

"Do you want some tea? Have you had any lunch?"

"I'm not hungry," he said.

Sophia playfully ran her fingers through his hair and said, "I'll fix something easy and light. You need to eat."

He watched her take a step toward the door and said, "I'm going to resign."

She stopped and turned. With just a single word, she told him she didn't approve. "Really?"

"I think so, yeah."

"You're almost 60 years old. What are you going to do?"

"I don't know. I still have some friends in the business community. After all, I haven't been in office long enough to make too many enemies."

His wife looked longingly at him. "Why? And why now?"

Damien took a deep breath and lifted his head from his knees. "I spent so much time gearing up for the nomination, going to all the right events. Gallery openings, fund raisers, school lunches. I cozied up to the affluent and the well-connected … and the party mafia. Mike Hart and Lilith Samuel and the God-damned lobbyists."

His wife listened intently.

"And the whole time, you know what I thought about? Me. About how this was going to be my moment in the sun. Sure, I wanted to do good, you know, make the state a little bit better, improve the schools, reduce crime, level the playing field so everyone got a fair shake. All that crap. But I made promises I had no intention of keeping. I let the GOP set policy that was absolutely contrary to what I believed. And lo and behold, I won. I won the nomination and then the special election and, boom, I was governor. You and me in this beautiful house.

"You stood with me as I placed my hand of the Bible and lied through my teeth and I took office knowing I was a fraud. And I was scared shitless. Scared shitless, Sophia. I had no idea what I was supposed to do. And I let the party mechanisms do their thing. I just sat back, collected a paycheck and let the inertia of the political machine chug along."

He broke off and stared at the hand towels next to the sink.

"But not today. Today, I made a decision. My decision." He laughed. "It took me nine months, but I did it. Today, I let an innocent woman be put to death. Why? Because I believe She is God's only begotten daughter."

He laughed again and rocked side-to-side where he sat. "It's the only thing *I've* done since taking office. How can I govern this state with that as my legacy?"

Sophia stood just outside the doorway, where she had been standing the whole time he talked. She, too, was smiling. "You're a good man, Damien."

He scoffed at her.

"You are! You're a good man. And when the dust settles, you're going to realize that there isn't a better man out there more capable of leading this state, more able to make the state a little bit better. No one more committed to improving the schools, reducing crime or leveling the playing field."

His self-degrading smile blossomed into one of genuine joyfulness.

"You're a good man, Damien Driver. And, damn it, I voted for you because I thought that you were the right man for the job. And I still think that. As for resigning, well, that's not a decision you have to make today."

"True," Damien agreed. "But I did."

"You resigned?" she shouted. She covered her lips with her fingers apologetically.

"No. I just made the decision today. I think I'll tell everyone in the office tomorrow and hold a press conference on Thursday. It'll keep the media occupied while the Good News goes on without them."

A confused frown broke on Sophia's brow for only a moment. Then she said, "We can talk all about that later. You take a shower and clear your head."

She turned and walked away.

Damien sat on the floor, his head now resting against the wall along with his shoulders, and watched the faint reflection of his wife escape into the vastness of the governor's residence. He rolled to one side and pushed himself to his feet, letting the towel drop to the floor. He turned the water back on, stepped into the shower, adjusted the temperature and stood for a very long time in the streams from the high-efficiency showerhead. The water pounded his skin. It was oddly soothing and comforting.

"Yup," he softly spoke aloud. "Press conference Thursday morning."

CHAPTER 34

The governor stood at the podium. The pause in his speech was for effect and he was subsequently greeted by a short burst of applause. Then the governor continued.

"I have tried, since taking office nine months ago, to be a beacon. A beacon of hope for the hopeless. A beacon of strength for the weak. A beacon of conscientiousness for the corrupt. And I have done my best in the days since my inauguration to be that beacon.

"I give many thanks to the citizens of this great state for their confidence in me. It is a great honor to have served you, though only briefly. At one time I shared your confidence and if that had continued I might very well be sitting in that great office in the Capitol Building attending to matters of the state. However, the confidence I have in myself has been shaken so fully that I no longer believe I can effectively carry out my gubernatorial duties.

"The tragic loss of a my very close friend just a few days ago, a victim of the senseless killing I wish to forever eradicate, was devastating to me personally and professionally and its impact will be felt for years to come. Her death was the catalyst for my decision to step down and Her death will be the catalyst for all that I do in the future."

Bishop DeMarco watched impatiently, rubbing the remote control, wondering how much longer the governor was going to continue, oblivious to the hidden meanings to the governor's words. Even if he had paid attention to the hidden meanings sprinkled throughout the governor's resignation speech, he would have thought them ridiculous. He'd already said as much. However, understanding is a funny thing. To some it comes quick and easy, like a bolt of lightning. To others, it requires years of continual exposure. And still others, it never comes. Bishop DeMarco understood, but not until the governor ended his speech.

"But know that as I leave, I leave you in more capable hands. However you view this day, do not look upon it as a day of sadness. Today is a day of rejoicing. Much rejoicing. For today is a day of new-birth.

"Today, my friend and ally, my political sister if you will, Lieutenant Governor Mariposa Calderon will carry on where I left off. She will be the beacon you elected, the beacon you deserve, the beacon I can no longer be. She will be a rampart against the status quo that stands between you and your dreams, between what is and what can be. Knowing her as I do, I believe she will stand for all things worthy and noble and I will feel safe and secure knowing she is watching over us.

"And finally …"

"Thank heaven," Bishop DeMarco said aloud to the empty room.

"…please know that I will keep you all in my heart as I pray that God's love and the true grace of all His children are with you today, tomorrow and forever more.

"Thank you."

He was sitting in the only recliner in the rectory's lounge area. It faced the big-screen TV donated just a few months earlier by a parishioner who had purchased an even bigger unit for himself. The recliner's leather was worn on the over-stuffed arms as well as the footrest that only accordioned out in support if properly coaxed. It, too, was a hand-me-down from a parishioner. That morning, the bishop had spent the time to coax the footrest, yet it still only extended half as far as he knew it could.

On the tray table beside him sat a once-white plastic plate that had aged a light beige. His lunch, a bologna and cheese sandwich cut in half diagonally, julienne slices of prickly pear cactus and a large, square brownie from the fresh-baked batch Father Enrique had made after saying that morning's mass, sat on the plate, untouched. Next to his lunch, also untouched, sat a small, blue plastic cup with a worn silkscreen print of Spider-Man swinging into action. It was filled with milk.

The bishop grabbed a strip of cactus and popped it into his mouth. He watched as Damien hastily stepped down from the podium. He was surprised that the governor slipped away and vanished behind the background screening instead of staying to witness his Lieutenant Governor taking her oath flanked by Mike Hart and Johara Melendez. Fed up with the whole affair, he pointed the remote at the TV and clicked it off. Then, he set the remote down on the side tray table and picked up his glass of milk. He took it in both hands and looked at the fading print.

He smiled and thought, With great power comes great responsibility. Then he said aloud, "Nicely done, Mr. Driver. William Wrede would be proud."

CHAPTER 35

Since the Order of Christian Funeral had been administered at Christ King parish in Goodyear earlier in the morning, now all that remained was the graveside Committal Service. The uneventful half-hour drive from Goodyear to Surprise was made by only a small convoy. Felipe had counted ten cars including the hearse.

A gentle, autumnal breeze blew past the mourners as they sat, held captive by the stone walls surrounding the Calvary Meadows Catholic Cemetery. The audience listened intently as Father Joe offered his second, briefer and more succinct eulogy to the woman whom they'd come to love with all their hearts. They were seated to one side of a precisely cut rectangle in the earth. The silver casket appeared to hover above the hole, weightlessly, as the black poly-webbing straps of the hydraulic mechanism awaited the push of a button to start lowering its load down to its final earthly destination. A mound of dirt, covered by green outdoor carpet, was positioned opposite the mourners.

"In committing the body to its resting place," Father Joe said, "the community expresses the hope that, with all those who have gone before marked with the sign of faith, the deceased awaits the glory of the Resurrection. The rite of committal is an expression of the communion that exists between the Church on earth and the Church in heaven—the deceased passes with the farewell prayers of the community of believers into the welcoming company of those who need faith no longer, but see God face-to-face."

He stopped and waited, forcing a moment of quiet reflection upon those gathered.

"And now, if you'd like, you can offer your personal intentions."

Since her death, Father Joe had become fast friends with Felipe and, subsequently, the other Adherentes. He offered them comfort in their time of mourning and they reciprocated. Father Joe watched as the Adherentes and the scant few others in attendance passed the casket and paid their respects. None cried. However, many ran off, disappearing into their various cars and then again disappearing through the cemetery entrance as quickly as possible. Father Joe thought that many of them saved their tears for the privacy of the car ride home.

Two destitute men, each reminding Father Joe an awful lot of Luke Logan, were the last to pay respects. The first, Nate the Great, stood at the foot of the coffin and said nothing. The second, mumbled low and inaudibly. The only words Father Joe could make out were "the man in white" and "I did it for you." When the last man had finished mumbling, unlike everyone else who had escaped from the cemetery walls in their cars, the two vagrants penetrated deeper into it, disappearing behind a hedge row some ways off in the distance.

Father Joe finally paid his respects to the death of the body and said a quick prayer for her and to her. By the time he had finished leaving instructions with the cemetery manager to proceed with the burial, only Tom, Felipe and Luke remained. They stood around the two remaining cars with their hands in their pockets fretfully kicking at small pebbles on the road.

Father Joe approached them, unsure of their mood. "Does anyone want to get a cup of coffee?" he asked.

"Sure" they all eagerly replied.

There was a Jittery Joe's coffee shop just a few blocks from the entrance of the cemetery. They each had their own personal favorite Jittery Joe's concoction and happily ordered it as their turn came. Luke, the last one to order, paid for all of them and joined the other three as they sat huddled in a booth. They stared at their cups, sipping them and fiddling with them in equal measure. For almost thirty minutes the four of them sat and sipped their coffees, unable or unwilling to engage in anything other than shallow, meaningless ramblings. They chattered on about the simple elegance of the service, both at the church and at the grave site, about how thankful they were that it hadn't rained, about the rich, full-flavor of their coffees.

Then, completely out of nowhere, Felipe asked, "Father, did you check the coffin?"

"What do you mean did I check it?"

"Did you see if, um, it was ... empty?"

A quizzical look cross Father Joe's face. "No. It never occurred to me."

207

"I mean," Felipe said sheepishly, "today is the third day, right? The two Mary's and Salome, and then Peter and John, they all found the tomb empty. So, who's going to find the tomb empty?"

The others mimicked Father Joe's expression.

"Should we go back?" Tom asked.

"We can't exhume the grave!" Luke replied.

"But if the grave isn't back-filled yet ..." Tom began.

Father Joe said, "She was in the casket before the service at the church."

"But what if she rose from the dead since then?" Felipe asked.

Like cats on ice, they all scrambled out of the booth and out the door. While Felipe and Luke ran into the back parking lot of Jittery Joe's to retrieve their cars, Tom and Father Joe ran across the street and into the cemetery. In front of them they could see the excavating machine rolling into place immediately in front of where they had gathered no more than 30 minutes earlier. Tom ran up onto the lawn as the two cars drove past. Father Joe lagged behind. By the time Father Joe reached the grave, the two drivers had parked and walked to the grave and Tom had already convinced the excavating machine operator to exit the cab.

The five of them peered over the edge of the grave at the silver casket which had already been lowered into the grave. The hydraulic mechanisms, poly-webbing, and the green ploy-turf were nowhere in sight.

"So what's this all about," the grave digger asked.

The four men looked at one another waiting for someone else to answer.

Luke pulled out a hundred dollar bill. He held it out to the grave digger and said, "Could you go away for a while?"

"You gonna have sex with a dead woman?" the grave digger exclaimed, the horror visible on his face.

Father Joe jumped in. "Sir, it's nothing like that." The priest clapped his hand on the grave digger's shoulder and led him away from the grave. "My name's Father Joseph Romano and my friend, here, Felipe, wanted one last chance to say goodbye."

"He could have done that at the service, for Christ's sake!"

While Father Joe further distracted the grave digger, Luke and Tom helped Felipe scurry down into the grave. He stood on the foot of the coffin furthest from the small, unassuming headstone and turned, nervous.

"What if she's still in there?" Felipe asked, staring down at the coffin.

"What if she isn't?" Tom countered.

Felipe stood still, paralyzed.

After a few lingering moments, Luke said, "Shit or get off the pot, Gunga Din."

"Shut up," Felipe yelled back.

Felipe bent down on his knees, slid one leg further down to touch the very bottom of the grave and then slid the other. He gripped the edge of the coffin, braced himself and lifted the upper portion of the lid. It slowly rose up and the three of them peered inside. Estephania Rodriquez's body, her face serene and hands crossed over her chest, rested peaceably in the coffin.

Felipe, disheartened, said, "What's it mean?"

"I think it means we were duped," Tom said.

Felipe closed the lid and slowly crawled out of the grave. "No," he said softly, more to himself than those around him.

The grave digger and Father Joe joined the others grave-side.

"Her body was still in there?" Father Joe asked.

Felipe nodded his head.

"Well, where else would it be?" the grave digger asked climbing back into the cab of the excavator. "Can I bury the box now?"

"Go ahead," Father Joe told him, smiling weakly.

The four men shuffled back to the two cars in silence. The loud, fossil fuel engine of the excavator roared to life. Its back-hoe efficiently weaved back and forth to replace the dirt, large clumps making dull thuds as they fell onto the coffin's lid.

"You know," Father Joe started, "the earthy vessel is immaterial now." He chuckled to himself at the double meaning of his phrasing. When no one else appeared to get it, he explained further. "Jesus rose from the dead and His body was gone from the tomb, right? So let me ask you, when He ascended into heaven 40 days later, did His body magically levitate into the sky? Is there going to be a physical Jesus sitting at the right hand of the spiritual Father?"

The three faces looking back at him were blank.

"There is no physical place called heaven. During Jesus' ascension, He shed His material body of the physical world and took a different form, a kind of spiritual mirror image of your corporal body. It's called the Glorified Body. Basically, it doesn't matter whether or not Her physical body is in the coffin. Her resurrection is no more or less valid. I mean, how is She going to sit at the left hand of the Father unless She, too, sheds Her physical body and takes the form of the Glorified Body?"

"But Jesus broke the bands of physical death," Tom said. "That was the whole point. The miracle of rising from the dead."

"Yes," Father Joe explained. "And who's to say she hasn't risen? As the second Messiah, the band's been broken already. This is simply the culmination of God's gift."

"Her dead body was lying in the coffin," Tom shouted. "How can it be said that She's risen when She's still dead?"

Father Joe said only, "Believe."

A gust of wind passed by and caused each of them to hunch over, adjust his clothing and wrap himself with his arms to stave off the cold.

"Gentlemen," Luke said. "As entertaining as this is, I have to get back to the city. Who needs a ride?"

Tom casually raised his hand and said, "I do."

"So do I," added Father Joe. "My car's still in the shop."

"Tell you what," Luke said, "I'll take Tom, here, and Felipe …"

"Actually," Felipe said, "I don't feel much like driving." With that he threw Tom his keys. "Here, you take Father Joe back to Goodyear and I'll ride with Luke. I'll meet you back at the Fischer's restaurant."

"That way," Luke added, "you two can continue your debate as to whether or not a tree falling in the woods without anyone around to hear it actually makes noise." Then, as they were all getting into their cars, he whispered to Felipe, "I need to take a leak and get another coffee."

"That's fine," the somewhat despondent man replied.

"I wasn't asking," Luke said, low and gravelly, his eyes burning with the same crazy intensity as the first time they met.

"Well, this ought to be a fun trip."

Business at the Jittery Joe's across the street from the cemetery had picked up since they left. Few tables were open and a short line formed in front of the register. Luke ducked into the bathroom while Felipe walked over to the store's front window and stared out of it and into the cemetery. He walked as far as he could, his thighs pressed against the small table which in turn was pushed up against the wall under the window.

"¿Puedo ayudarle?" the woman sitting at the table said. *Can I help you?*

Felipe, startled, looked down at her, and in Spanish he answered. *"I'm sorry, I was distracted. I didn't see you sitting here."*

"No problema," the woman answered, smiling.

Felipe backed away a few steps, just enough to retreat out of her personal space. He continued to stare out the window.

"What are you looking for?" the woman asked.

Felipe thought a moment before answering. *"Hope."*

He smiled at her.

She smiled back. *"Maybe I can help you find it."*

"I doubt it," Felipe said quietly without looking at her.

She said to him, *"Put your hope in God, who richly provides us with everything for our enjoyment."*

Felipe was not paying attention to the stranger, his focus elsewhere, out the window and across the cemetery. She grabbed his sleeve and tugged at it.

"I need a ride into the city. Are you heading that way?"

"Yeah, sure," he said, still distracted.

"Would you mind giving me a lift?"

Just then, Luke joined them.

"Ready?" he said gruffly to Felipe.

"Yeah," Felipe said, his eyes transfixed on the open spaces of the cemetery. Then, pointing to the woman at the table, "And she's looking for a ride into the city, too."

"What am I, a taxi service?" Luke growled. He looked at her as she rose out of her seat. It was a long look, more like a leer, his eyes taking in far more information than just the features of her face or the style of her clothes. "Do I know you?" Luke asked.

"I don't know," the woman replied in her heavy accent. "Do you know me?"

"You look familiar," Luke said. He looked at her once more and, as if giving his approval, nodded his head. "Yeah, fine. Let's go."

As they made their way through the surface roads toward the highway, the woman in the back seat asked, "What have you been doing the last couple of days?"

Felipe replied, "Have you been living under a rock for the last three years? Don't you know about the things that have been happening?"

And she replied to them, "What sort of things?"

They told her of the things that happened to Estephania Rodriguez, who was a prophet mighty in deed and word before God and all the people.

About the Author

Patrick S. Lafferty is currently the creative director and senior copywriter for a small marketing communications firm just outside of Milwaukee, Wis. For the last twenty years he has spent his days creating persuasive ad copy and informative brochure copy, writing trade publication feature articles and press releases, and otherwise developing myriad other marketing materials. For the last twenty years he has spent his nights writing fiction, typically mainstream fiction with a genre bending twist.

Before becoming a copywriter, he spent 18 years sitting through the lesson plans of the nuns, priests, brothers and laypersons employed by the various Catholic schools he attended, the final six years resulting in a BFA in Commercial Design from the University of Dayton and an MA in Advertising Copywriting from Marquette University. It was from these institutions that the foundation for *Anno Domina* was laid ... and subsequently cracked.

Patrick is a member of the Milwaukee Writer's Circle and the Milwaukee Writer's Workshop (MWW). He, his beautiful, supportive wife, and his two exhausting boys graciously share their home in the Milwaukee suburbs with their oddball dog, Macie.

ALL THINGS THAT MATTER PRESS ™

FOR MORE INFORMATION ON TITLES AVAILABLE FROM
ALL THINGS THAT MATTER PRESS, GO TO
http://allthingsthatmatterpress.com
or contact us at
allthingsthatmatterpress@gmail.com